DOW

Please return / renew by date shown.
You can renew it at:
norlink.norfolk.gov.uk
or by telephone: 0344 800 8006
Please have your library card & PIN ready

Withdrawn from stock

NORFOLK LIBRARY
AND INFORMATION SERVICE

Published by Accent Press Ltd – 2014

ISBN: 9781783754298

To the memory of my parents,
Avis Poulson (1926-2008) and George Poulson
(1926-1962)

Acknowledgments

I want to thank:

Sue Hepworth for reading many drafts and for her endless encouragement and support.

Amanda Rainger for being my very own personal plot doctor.

Jonathan Waller for kindly commenting on drafts of the novel.

Jo Burn, Linda Chainey, Maria Clark, and Sheila Miles for help and support of various kinds.

David Poulson, who introduced me to Matt Harrison at Portland College.

Matt Harrison and the students at Portland who shared with me their experience of living with disability. They are an inspiration.

Jay Dixon, my thoughtful and efficient editor at Accent Press.

Madeleine Parkyn and Martin Haggarty for lending me their house and their cat.

Charlotte Dingle for letting me borrow her name and piercings.

And last but not least, my husband, Peter Blundell Jones, without whom …

.

PROLOGUE

His memories of that last day were fragmentary, but some things stood out with a strange clarity, in particular the arrival at the house on the outskirts of Leicester.

He could see Mia in the kitchen, dumping the bag of stuff they'd grabbed from the fridge at home. She straightened up and ran a hand through her hair. The roots were greasy. In the rush of events she hadn't washed her hair for days. He watched her look around, taking in the details of their new home. The house was spotlessly clean and not much smaller than their house in Chiswick, but it was drab and characterless. It was as if someone had gone into a shop with a list and simply picked out items that were both cheap and inoffensive.

Joe came in carrying a cardboard box full of odds and ends that they had hastily packed. Benji, the black Labrador, trotted after him with his tail between his legs, infected by the sombre mood of his humans. Last of all came Sam, staggering under the weight of his own box of videos, books, and toys. It had been hard to persuade him to leave anything at all behind.

Sam's eyes went to Mia's face to see what he ought to think about the house. Jay saw the effort with which she dredged up a smile for him.

'What are we having for dinner?' Sam asked.

'I'll cook,' Jay said at the same moment as Joe said, 'Tell you what – I'll go out for pizzas.'

'Yeah!' Sam punched the air. At ten he was still young enough for this to be a big adventure if it was handled in the right way.

Joe said, 'Hey, did you know that the National Space

Centre's only a few miles away?'

'Cool! Can we go, Dad?'

Jay hesitated. His eyes met Joe's and asked the question. Would that be wise? Joe gave a tiny shake of the head.

'Tell you what,' Joe said to Sam, 'I'll take you.'

The child's face lit up.

Mia went to bed when Sam did. Jay and Joe ran over the arrangements for the trial, and then fell to chatting about this and that. They had a Scotch from the bottle that Joe had thought to bring. It occurred to Jay that Joe was an old hand at this. How many times had he done it before? Jay didn't feel like asking. 'I won't stay the night,' Joe had told them earlier. 'There's a motel down the road. I'll give you a bit of privacy.'

Jay walked him to the door. It was late August and the evening had darkened. It was a clear night with stars appearing. Seeing the unfamiliar street outside, Jay was struck all over again by the strangeness of it all. How far away they were from everything and everyone they knew. Now that the moment had come, he didn't want to let Joe go.

Joe must have seen that in his face. He asked him what the matter was.

'I hope to God I'm doing the right thing.'

'Never doubt it.' He clapped Jay around the shoulders in a manly half-hug. 'Any worries – anything at all, even if you just want to talk – you ring me straightaway – doesn't matter what time. OK?'

Jay looked in on Sam. He was lying on his back, arms flung out in total abandon. His hair, like Mia's, was as pale as thistledown, bleached from the summer sun. Jay leaned over, rearranged the duvet with its pattern of planets and spaceships. At the last moment, when the police car was drawing away from the house in Chiswick, Mia had shouted for it to stop. She had run back into the house and had come staggering out with bedding spilling out of her arms. That was so like her – to know what a difference it would make to Sam to climb into a bed that smelt of home.

Benji was asleep at the foot of the bed. That wasn't normally allowed, but Jay hadn't the heart to boot him out.

Jay cleaned his teeth and undressed in the bathroom. He thought that Mia might be asleep, but when he opened the bedroom door, he saw her eyes glistening in the light from the landing. She was lying on her back staring at the ceiling. He slipped into bed beside her. He leaned over and through long habit put his mouth directly on hers. He tasted salt and ran a finger down her cheek. It came away wet. She had been crying.

'I'm sorry,' he said.

'We're together. That's all that matters.'

'We'll be back home before we know it.'

They lay curled together like spoons. Her breathing settled into an even rhythm and he knew she was asleep.

He rolled over onto his back, too wired to relax. Would they really be back home soon? Would they be safe even after he had testified? He simply didn't know.

After a while he fell into a restless sleep.

Something tugged at him. He tried to pull back into the refuge of sleep, but it was no good. He groaned and opened his eyes. Benji was whining. A pale colourless light was seeping round the edge of the curtains. Benji scrabbled at the door, claws clicking. Jay got up to let him in. But when he opened the door, the dog shot off down the stairs. Jay went into the bathroom, pulled on jeans and a T-shirt. Yawning, he made his way downstairs and unbolted the back door. The dog pushed past him and Jay followed him out onto the lawn.

The day had that newly washed feel. Jay gazed around.

Everything was absolutely still and silent. Too still and silent? The shrubs and the pond, the clouds in the sky were freighted with expectation as if something were about to happen and they knew what it was.

Benji whimpered. Instead of relieving himself he went back to the door. He stood with one fore paw on the threshold and the other held up, like an heraldic beast. He cast an imploring look at Jay, showing the whites of his eyes.

At last Jay understood what the dog was trying to tell him.

But it was too late.

The leaking gas reached the cooker and was ignited by the pilot light and as Jay hurled himself towards the back door, something met him coming the other way, a blast of air –

It lifted him off his feet and threw him across the garden.

When he came round in hospital, Joe was by his bed-side.

Joe's hands were bandaged and he looked ten years older. The explosion had woken him in his bed at the motel. He had rushed to the house. The fire brigade had arrived to find Jay unconscious in the garden and Joe scrabbling with his bare hands at the smoking rubble.

The two people Jay loved most in the world had been blown to kingdom come. The faithful dog had gone with them and for a long time Jay wished that he had, too.

FIVE YEARS LATER

Chapter One

'This is my last day.'

Jay didn't take in what the cab-driver said. He was too busy looking through the back window, trying to decide if he had seen that car before.

The traffic was slowing down, grinding to a halt.

'Yes,' the cab-driver said, 'my last day on the job. Demob happy, that's me. I'm retiring. Well, I say retiring, me and the missus are opening a bar in Spain. This time next week, I'll be playing golf in the sun.'

Yes, it was the same car, Jay was sure of it. Oh God. But surely he was safe enough for the moment. They were hardly going to pull him out of a cab going round Piccadilly Circus in broad daylight, unless ...

What if the cab-driver was in on it, too? His eyes went to the man's licence. Darren Clarke was the name – and this was a properly licensed black cab. He looked at the man's solid meaty shoulders and the straw-coloured hair fringing a shiny dome. That ratty jumper – grey-and-white lozenges with pulled threads – he couldn't be anything but a cab driver. Could he? And surely it was pure chance that Jay had stepped into this particular cab. He didn't see how they could have planned it.

'What's up, chum?' Darren asked. His eyes met Jay's in the rear-view mirror. 'You've been like a cat on hot bricks ever since I picked you up.'

Maybe it was the rosary dangling from the mirror that decided Jay.

'I think someone's following me,' he said.

'Oh ho,' Darren said, 'so that's it. Your girlfriend's hubby? Some geezer you owe money to?'

They had reached the north end of Haymarket. The traffic was inching forward.

Darren laughed. 'Nah, let me guess, if you tell me, you'll have to kill me!'

He wasn't so far off the mark.

'So which one is it?' Darren tilted his head to look into the rear-view mirror.

'The dark blue Citroen.'

'That!' he said scornfully. 'A mini-cab –'

'Do you think you can –'

'Lose it? Wouldn't be much of a cab-driver if I couldn't! Fasten your seat-belt, you're in for a bumpy ride!' Darren spun the steering wheel. The cab swerved and shot down the bus-lane, flinging Jay back against his seat with a jolt that took his breath away. The cab swung left into a narrow canyon of a street. Jay gripped the handrail and braced his feet on the floor. They emerged into a little square where people sitting at tables outside a restaurant looked up startled. Ahead the road narrowed to one lane. On one side was the back entrance of the National Gallery, on the other Westminster Reference Library, and in the middle a van was parked, blocking the road. Darren didn't even brake. The cab tilted as it mounted the pavement. The rosary swung wildly from side to side. Jay wanted to offer up a prayer himself. He resisted the temptation to cover his eyes. They slid past the van and a line of bollards with a hairsbreadth to spare.

They shot round a corner. A queue of taxis was waiting to turn into St Martin's Lane. The lane for in-coming traffic was empty. Darren swerved into it. The traffic was solid, but Darren nudged his way in. The driver of another black cab budged over just enough to let Darren through. Darren acknowledged the courtesy with an airy gesture. He muscled his way through the second lane, eliciting a V sign from a bus driver, and shot off down William IV Street and into Maiden Lane.

'Have we lost the Citroen?' Darren asked.

Jay craned his neck. 'Yes – oh, no, no, oh fuck! He's just come into view!'

'OK!'

Darren took a right turn. The traffic lights were green and in moments they were heading south across the Strand. They took another right and doubled back along John Adam Street.

Darren turned left. To his horror Jay saw that they were heading for a dead end. In that terrible moment he knew that he had been wrong about Darren. Darren was not his saviour, but his abductor. A trap was closing around him. The ground dropped steeply away to an underground car park. They plunged into the darkness like a rabbit going down a hole. This time Jay did close his eyes, expecting the cab to screech to a halt. But it didn't so much as slacken speed. He opened his eyes to see rows of parked cars sliding past on either side. The cab shot out into daylight. Jay caught a glimpse of grey choppy water. They were on the Embankment. Darren laughed. 'Not many people know about that. I bet that's foxed the bugger.' The traffic was running freely here and the cab sped along towards Blackfriars. Jay braced himself against the back seat and looked out of the window. The Citroen was nowhere in sight. As the cab went into the underpass beneath Blackfriars Jay allowed himself a sigh of relief.

'It was Waterloo you wanted?' Darren said.

'Doesn't really matter. I just need to get out of London.'

'Liverpool Street do you?'

'Fine.' Jay leaned back. Now that the tension had relaxed, he had to clasp his hands together to stop them trembling. As the cab headed north-east at a more sedate pace, he concentrated on slowing his breathing and planning his next step.

The cab drew up outside Liverpool Street and Jay reached for his wallet.

Darren turned. 'Not on your life – it's all on the house today.'

Jay saw him full on for the first time. He had a slab of a face and little piggy eyes, but at that moment Jay loved him like a brother.

Darren said, 'And if you ever find yourself in Malaga, there'll be a drink on the house.' He fumbled in his jacket pocket and brought out a card.

Jay reached for it, his fingers grasped it, but Darren didn't release it. He looked expectantly at Jay. Something hopeful and wistful shone out of his face, something even a lifetime of ferrying arrogant city types and drunken hen parties hadn't quenched.

For a moment Jay was puzzled, and then it dawned on him.

Of course. Darren wanted to know what it was all about. The least he could do for this fine man was to give him a story to take into his new life, something to tell his customers. Jay could see him with his elbows propped on the bar: 'Last day on the job, and who do you think he turned out to be – no, honest, straight up –'

He cast around, uncertain what to say. Then it came to him. He leaned forward, catching a whiff of a pungent cologne. He put his face close to Darren's and told Darren what he wanted to hear.

A MONTH LATER

Chapter Two

Something was badly wrong. Lisa was way behind schedule with her commission: an anthology of the poets of the T'Ang dynasty. It ought to have been easy to capture their elegiac tone. God knows, she felt miserable enough. But the deadline for the first part was looming and she had done drafts of only twenty-four out of a hundred and eighty poems. They weren't any good, but her editor was asking to see them.

Can translators have writer's block? Normally she was scarcely aware of the individual characters. They were a window onto a familiar world. But today they lay inert on the page. She found herself examining them as if she had never seen them before, struck by their strangeness and complexity, just as when she'd first studied Mandarin. The character for woman, for example, she used to see it as a seated figure leaning forward to embrace a pregnant belly. Now the figure seemed to be hugging herself in grief.

She gazed around her study. It was immaculate. But surely there must be something she could tidy up. On her desk was a mug stuffed full of leaking biros. She tipped them out and began testing them on a piece of scrap paper, chucking the dead ones in the bin as she went. Some had come through the post from charities that she supported, like the Red Cross and the British Heart Foundation, and some from charities that she didn't. This one advertising a car dealership must have come from her friend, Stella ; a pen with a liquid compartment in which a gondola went up and down, that was a memento of a holiday in Venice; and this one from some hotel in Sweden, that would be one of Lawrence's from one of his work trips. He used to say that the place was like a rest home for old biros, but he was as bad as anyone at throwing things out ... and Ricky positively sought them out, the more recherché the advert, the better. The Swedish pen was a cut above the others, rather elegant in fact. She liked the way it felt in her hand. She began doodling with it. She came to herself with a start. Time was getting on.

She went out onto the gallery that ran along the back of the long, double-storey living room. The house was on a plateau overlooking the Bristol Channel. On clear days the Welsh coast was visible and the constantly changing seascape was like a living picture that filled an entire wall. Today it was hard to tell where the sea stopped and the land began. The coombes on either side of the house were filled with water vapour like a landscape in a Chinese watercolour. She sighed. A dull, flat day. That was how she felt too, as if her head was full of fog.

Ricky's room was immediately below her study. Normally he would have been at school, but this was the autumn half-term. She went down the spiral staircase, knocked on his door, and went in. There was an image of a rocky landscape with figures on the computer screen, then Ricky clicked on his mouse and it disappeared. The screen was filled by a photo of a surfer racing ahead of a breaking wave as big as a house.

Ricky spun his wheelchair towards her.

'Here's looking at you, kid,' said a dark-brown voice.

Ricky was mad about old movies and Lisa never knew if she was going be greeted by Humphrey Bogart or Marilyn Monroe. He'd only had this state-of-the-art software for a few weeks, but he'd quickly learnt to manipulate it. It's default setting was a young male voice like the one Ricky might have had if cerebral palsy hadn't slurred his speech.

'Play it, Sam,' Lisa murmured, putting plenty of huskiness into her voice.

Ricky grinned his crooked grin.

'Are you about ready to be off, Ma?' he said in his own voice. Should she ask him what he had been looking at on the computer? She decided to let it go for now.

'I'll be leaving in about an hour,' she said. 'What are you up to this weekend?'

'Charlotte's coming round so that we can do our photography project together.'

'Again?' Lisa asked and wished she hadn't. She'd always welcomed his friends to the house. Wasn't this why she had worked so hard to get Ricky into mainstream education, so that he would meet a mixture of people, not just other children with disabilities? And yet …

Ricky frowned. 'Why don't you like her? It's because she's a Goth, isn't it? I thought you didn't believe in judging people by their appearance.'

She didn't. And God knows, she herself had looked strange enough as a teenager, but it wasn't just that. Charlotte smoked for one thing, and maybe not just tobacco. But it would just make Ricky keener if she made a fuss –

'What was on your computer screen when I came in?' she heard herself say.

A look of open-eyed innocence came over Ricky's face. 'That? Oh, that was just my website. I was updating my blog. Look, I've been wondering – what do you want for your birthday?'

It was a transparent attempt to change the subject, but she let it pass.

'Oh, I don't know, when you get to my age, you'd rather not think too much about it.'

'Yeah, forty-five. That is pretty ancient,' he said seriously, 'but you don't look too bad. No grey hairs,

11

anyway.'

'Oh thanks. Look, I'm just going to take Piki out before Peony gets here. I won't be long.'

'But your birthday?'

'Surprise me!'

Piki was lying in her usual place by the back door. Her eyes swivelled in Lisa's direction, but she didn't lift her head from her paws. It wasn't Lawrence, that was all that mattered. It never would be Lawrence, but she didn't know that and was still waiting for him.

And Lisa wasn't so very different.

She would find herself wandering from room to room and realise that she was searching for him. The place was still saturated with his presence. She was forever thinking that she saw him out of the corner of her eye, but it always turned out to be something hanging on the back of a door or a shadow cast by the birches that crowded up close behind the house.

The death of a parent was a bit like having a baby. Nothing could really prepare you for it – and after it nothing was ever the same again.

Lisa took Lawrence's overcoat off the peg by the back door. It was old and woolly and a dark bottle-green. She always wore it when she walked the dog. For a surprisingly long time it had smelt of Lawrence, especially around the collar. He had always used a particular citrus aftershave.

Piki clambered to her feet. She was a funny little animal with stumpy legs and a chocolate brown coat as woolly as a teddy-bear, the result of a liaison between a poodle and a Jack Russell terrier. Lawrence used to say that she had the cleverness of the first and the strength and determination of the second.

Lisa locked the door and set off down the footpath towards the headland with Piki at her heels.

12

At first she fretted about Ricky. He never used to be secretive and she couldn't quite think when it had begun. In the past the connection between them had almost amounted to telepathy. Now there were times when she had no idea what he was thinking and those times were getting more frequent. It was natural, of course it was, he was sixteen for God's sake, but still …

She concentrated on the rhythm of her footsteps and let the stillness seep into her. The path brought her out near the tree-house on the headland.

The tree-house had always been Lisa's special place. Lawrence had built it at the same time that he had built the house. It had been a simple structure in those days, just a platform, four walls and a roof, reached by a rope ladder. Later Lawrence had decided to turn it into something more elaborate, a place for Lisa to work. He ran an electric cable out from the house and replaced the rope ladder with a spiral staircase. There was a desk and an electric heater and a place for Lisa to plug in her laptop.

It was out here that Lisa had found Lawrence's body eight months ago. Piki had returned alone from a walk and had led Lisa to him. Lawrence had had angina for a while. Most mornings he was in some discomfort, but exercise was part of his regime and he was usually fine by the time he got back from his early morning walk. But not that day. He was lying on his back, still grasping his walking-stick and Lisa had known right away that he had gone.

Today, like every day, Piki stretched herself out near the spot where Lawrence had lain. She whimpered softly. Lisa squatted down beside her and put one hand on the dog's wiry coat. Lawrence had only been sixty-nine, no age at all. Why do people have to die? It's not fair. She would give almost anything to go back to the days before they knew that Lawrence had heart disease. She hadn't understood how precious that time had been. If she could only go back, she would know now how to appreciate it.

There was a boom so stunning that it filled her head. Piki let off a volley of barks. For an instant Lisa caught sight of the military airplanes low overhead, huge, dark, cruel shapes, like something from a sci-fi film. They were moving so fast that she saw no movement. They were there and then they were gone, leaving the air vibrating. Lisa put her arms round the trembling dog. Her own heart was racing and it was a minute or two before she stood up. These practice flights occurred at least once a week, but they weren't something you could ever get used to and they always took a second pass twenty minutes later.

She glanced at her watch and was surprised to see how late it was. She'd better be getting back. She had a long drive ahead.

Chapter Three

Lisa was only ten miles from the cottage when it happened. There was a jolt, the car swerved and veered to the left. She steered it over to the verge. She knew what it was even before she got out to look. A flat tyre. This would have to happen when she was already late. She'd forgotten what a long and tedious drive it was from Exmoor to Norfolk and she had been held up on the M5 by a bad accident. Edging past on the other side of the carriageway she had caught an unnerving glimpse of ambulances and people sitting by the roadside covered in blood. Her shoulders ached with tension and fatigue. And now this. What to do? She weighed the options. Should she ring Jay or ring the breakdown service? Jay would be at the cottage by now. Probably best to ring him and get him to come for her. They could sort out the car tomorrow.

She hunted in her bag for her phone. It wasn't in the compartment where she usually kept it. She tipped everything out onto the passenger seat and sorted through it, but no ... She turned the bag upside down and shook it, patted the compartments, unable to believe that it really wasn't there. When had she last used it? In her mind's eye she saw the phone sitting on the table in the café at the service station where she'd stopped a couple of hours ago. She had got it out to check for texts. Surely, surely she had put it back in her bag? Had it fallen out in the car? She got a torch out of the glove compartment and shone the beam around the footwell. Nothing.

OK. A public phone, then, or maybe she could knock on someone's door.

She got out of the car and looked up and down the long

narrow road. The sun was setting, leaving stripes of indigo and lemon in the sky and darkness was rising like smoke from the fields. On one side was a grove of pine trees and on the other a vast ploughed field stretched into the distance. There were no houses or lights in sight.

At least she'd had the foresight to pack the local ordnance survey map. She got it out and located her position. She could hardly have picked a worse place to break down: no village, or phone, or pub within five miles. And in the ten minutes she had been here, not a single car had come along the road. Tears welled up. They were never far from the surface these days. She took a deep breath and got a grip. She did – in theory – know how to change a tyre. Lawrence had made sure she was up to speed on practical things. She got the jack and the wheel brace out of the boot and put on an old raincoat over her good red cardigan, the one that Jay had given her as a Christmas present. She propped up the torch on a stone. As she set about removing the hub cap, she felt flecks of rain on her face and with them came a sudden drop in temperature. She attached the wheel brace to a hub nut and leaned on it. It didn't budge. She tried another one, that didn't move either. Her fingers were growing numb, but she was sweating. Panic was rising in her. She was going to be stuck out here ... How could she loosen the nuts? WD40? Was there a canister in the boot?

There was. She sprayed it on the hub nuts and waited for it to take effect, hugging herself against the cold. Light had drained from the sky now and the landscape lay dark and silent around her. She tried again with the wheel brace. Nothing. She took a deep breath, gritted her teeth and put all her weight on the brace. There was a creak and it started to move. She heaved a sigh of relief.

After that things went smoothly. She got the jack under the car alright and removed the tyre. The treads were almost worn down. When had she last checked? She

16

couldn't remember *ever* checking. Lawrence had always done that. She went round and shone the torch on the others. They seemed OK, but she'd better have the car serviced when she got home.

She got the spare tyre on and tightened up the nuts. She had just straightened up and was massaging her aching lower back, when there was the sound of a car and she saw headlights approaching. Just when she'd almost finished! No point in waving it down now. But the car stopped anyway and a figure got out. He was just a shape in the darkness. The headlights on full beam made her squint and it wasn't until he spoke that she even knew it was a man.

'Can I help?' It was a pleasant voice, low-pitched and cultured, but she was suddenly uneasy.

'I'm fine, thanks – almost done –'

'Oh surely –'

'No, really, I'm fine.' Her voice came out high-pitched, anxious.

He stepped forward and she instinctively stepped back. The car headlights shone on the wheel brace in her hand.

He hesitated. Then he threw up his hands. 'Suit yourself, you ungrateful cow.'

He got in his car, slammed the door and revved the engine savagely. He shot off down the road. She watched until he was out of sight, then bent to remove the jack. Her fingers trembled and she kept looking up to check that he wasn't coming back. Once she was safely back in the car with the doors locked, she felt better. As she drove on towards the cottage she tried to arrange what had happened into an amusing story for Jay, but it didn't work. She really had been frightened and still felt shaky. Never mind, she would soon be in Jay's arms and then nothing else would matter.

She drove on through the night, her anticipation mounting. That first kiss, after a month apart ... she'd thought of little else throughout the whole long drive. She ached to feel Jay's lips on hers.

When at last she turned off onto the grassy track and pulled up outside the little Gothic cottage, it took her a few moments to realise that the place was in darkness.

The key was where she remembered from the previous time they'd been here: under the mat. When she opened the door clammy air came out to meet her and a smell of furniture polish with something musty underlying it. The fire should have been lit. There should be the smell of cooking. Surely Jay hadn't broken down, too? Oh, if only she hadn't lost her phone! She cursed her carelessness. She would have to go out and find a phone box. No one passed her as she drove along the narrow road, flanked by conifers on either side. At last she reached a junction with a few houses grouped around it and a red phone box.

Someone had pissed in the phone box and not that long ago. She wrinkled her nose as she fumbled for change and fed it into the slot. She dialled the number of Jay's mobile. Nothing happened. She tried again. Still nothing. Why wasn't she even getting his voice-mail? Would it be worth ringing home to see if he had left a message? He never rang her there, but if it was an emergency …

It was a long time before the phone was picked up and she was growing afraid that something was wrong there, too, when she heard Peony's voice.

'Is everything alright?' she asked.

'Sorry.' Peony sounded out of breath. 'Didn't hear the phone.'

'But what about Ricky?'

'In the garden.'

'In the *garden*? But it's dark!'

'That friend of his? Charlotte? She's out there with him. Something to do with that school project: the photography one. Ricky asked if she could stay over. I was in the spare room making up the bed, but I wasn't sure. It's

OK, isn't it?

'I suppose.'

'It's good, isn't it, that they get on so well?' Peony had picked up on the doubt in her voice.

'Of course it is. No, really, it's fine. Look, has anyone rung for me?'

'No.'

Lisa explained that she'd lost her mobile. 'I'll go back and look for it tomorrow. Or I'll buy a new one. I don't like being out of touch.'

She didn't tell Peony about Jay not being there, because Peony didn't know about Jay. And neither did anyone else.

After she had hung up, she tried Jay's mobile again, but still nothing. Jay travelled so much that he didn't bother with a land-line. She was at a loss as to what to do next.

She drove back to the cottage, hoping against hope that Jay would have arrived, and their weekend could at last begin.

But the place was just as she had left it.

She lit the fire that lay ready in the hearth and put the kettle on. While it was boiling, she drew back one of the curtains and looked out. The darkness was absolute. The cottage was one of the few remnants of a grand Norfolk estate, set back from a little-used country road, and surrounded by woodland. The big house had been demolished long ago. She stood there for a while, looking out, hoping to see the lights of a car.

Memories came flooding in. They had last been here three years ago, soon after they had first met. They had still been shy with each other. They'd gone out for a stroll before supper and they had been walking in single file on a path through a dense conifer forest. She had been walking ahead. Jay had fallen silent. She had turned round to look at him. Without a word he had taken her in his arms. She had yielded to his embrace, their knees had buckled, and

19

they had sunk to the ground. The scent of crushed pine needles, ferns scratching her thighs, the sky deepening to violet above them: the memory gave her a sharp pang of longing. She closed her eyes and gave herself up to it.

She came to herself with a start. Was that a car? But the sound faded and the road remained dark.

She drank some tea and ate some of the cheese and biscuits and fruit that she'd brought with her. She willed herself not to look at her watch too often. She flicked over the pages of a thriller that someone had left in the cottage, but soon tossed it aside. What if something really bad had happened – a car crash, or maybe he'd been taken ill?

At eleven o'clock she made a cup of camomile tea and took it to bed. At home there was always the sound of running water, the wind in the trees, the murmur of the sea. Here the silence pressed in. And it was years and years – she couldn't remember how long – since she had slept in a house alone. Without her mobile phone, she felt cut-off, vulnerable.

She switched on her little portable radio and fell asleep to the shipping forecast.

She was woken by a dazzling light. She hadn't closed the curtains and it must have been the light of a passing car scanning the bedroom wall. The sound of a car engine faded into the distance. A taxi? She sat up in bed, hoping to hear a knock on the door. But there was nothing except a murmuring from the radio.

When she woke up again sunlight was streaming through the window. She sat up, blinking.

She got out of bed and, still in her nightdress, she went into the sitting room and opened the front door. The rain had cleared overnight. It was one of those crisp, invigorating autumn days. The bracing scent of pine-needles filled her nostrils. Light filtered down through the trees. The sun was warm on her face and birds were singing. Her spirits lifted. Jay could still turn up – if his car

20

had broken down, there was always the train ...

A phone began to ring. The sound was faint and so unexpected that she thought at first that it was a bird. But no – it *was* a phone and it was her phone! That was her ring-tone. She couldn't tell where it was coming from. She turned back into the house, but it seemed fainter in there. She ran outside, the grass cold and wet beneath her bare feet and, yes, it was coming from her car. Where the fuck had she put her keys? She ran back into the house, snatched them up from the mantelpiece. She sprinted to the car, stepping on something that crunched underfoot, and then she was fumbling to get the key in the door, all the time willing the phone not to stop ringing.

'I'm coming, I'm coming!'

She wrenched the door open. The phone was lying in the passenger foot-well – how on earth had she missed it the night before? – and at the very moment that she scooped it up, it stopped ringing. But there was bound to be a message from Jay – several messages – and she scrutinised it eagerly.

There was one text and it was from Ricky, saying goodnight and sending her a funny little message. Nothing else – and no indication of who had just tried to ring her. So Jay had not tried to contact her. And that meant she had heard nothing from him since they had last met, a month ago. Anything could have happened in that time. More: something *must* have happened for him to let her down like this. He could have been killed in a car crash on his way home from their last meeting and she wouldn't know.

As she stood there, shivering in her nightdress, cold fingers closed around her heart.

Chapter Four

Dead again!

Ricky had thought that he had it all sussed out, but as soon as he edged round the corner of the building, he saw his mistake. His hand went for his gun, but he wasn't quick enough. The other dude got there first and Ricky took the blast full in the chest.

Not that it really mattered. In Second Life, no-one dies. They are merely teleported back to their home base, which in his case was no hardship. His mansion was on an island in an azure sea, lapped by waves that he had installed himself. The house was absolutely bloody enormous and it had taken him hours and hours to construct and furnish.

When he had arrived in the sitting room, Mao, his Persian cat, was lying on the hearth. She sat up and said, 'Welcome home, honey.' That was all she *could* say at the moment. When he had some free time, he'd programme in some more speech. He looked around, appraising what he saw. The black marble floor, which he had thought was so cool a few weeks ago – was it the kind of thing some God-awful celebrity might choose? No problem: with a few clicks of his mouse it became slate grey.

He clicked onto his inventory and browsed through his wardrobe. It was all conventional stuff. Some people went in for pretty wild clothes – and more than clothes, extra arms, a tail, an animal head even. But all Ricky wanted was a strong, young body and in Second Life he had that. He took off his T-shirt and he liked what he saw: muscular, but not too muscular, and lightly tanned. Bodies like this were two a penny here and Ricky didn't stand out from the crowd. Except for the wings. And even they weren't what you'd call unusual. Everyone could fly in Second Life, wings or no, but Ricky had elected to have actual wings, or rather virtual ones.

So: what to wear? Well, that depended on what he was going to do. He wondered about going north where he'd heard that there were the remains of a moth-worshipping civilisation. Word had it that the ruined temple was sometimes visited by the moth god. That would be way cool, but it would be more fun with one of his friends and none of them were online yet.

There was somewhere he'd been meaning to go to alone. He'd been working up the courage for it. But was he likely to be interrupted? He didn't think so. Peony was out walking Piki and was good for another half-hour. Charlotte was still in bed and you couldn't call her an early riser ...

Might as well look his best. His right hand moved rapidly across the keyboard. His left hand was weak and clawed, of limited use, but he was the fastest one-handed typist in the West, the west of England, that is. He chose a white T-shirt, a pair of designer jeans, and a new pair of trainers and he was ready to go. No need for a coat. In Second Life it's never cold and it never rains. And none of the tedious business of being hoisted out of his wheelchair into a car. All he had to do was type in the coordinates and he was teleported to his destination ...

'Hello? Hello? Planet Earth to Ricky!' Oh, Christ, it was Charlotte. Ricky spun his wheelchair, blocking her view of the screen.

'What *was* that?' Charlotte said. Ricky slapped his hand on the mouse. The picture on the screen disappeared.

'Nothing.'

'I saw someone without any clothes on!'

'It's nothing.'

'It's pornography!'

'No, it's not. Not really. It's Second Life ... '

24

'What *was* it?'

'A pole-dancing club,' he muttered, deliberately slurring his speech more than usual. But he didn't fool Charlotte. She was the only one of his friends who understood everything he said. He didn't need to use his voice aid and that was great. On the other hand it was hard to slip anything past her.

'Oh, gross! You can do that in teen Second Life?'

He didn't reply.

Charlotte scrutinised him. 'You weren't in teen Second Life, were you?'

Ricky shrugged.

'You lied about your age?'

'Oh, lighten up, Char. Why don't you join? Plenty of people have Goth avatars. You can be as weird as you like.'

Charlotte raised a quizzical eye-brow, inviting him to consider her appearance. She was dressed completely in black: black T-shirt emblazoned with 'Sisters of Mercy' in Gothic letters, black trousers adorned with a lot of zips, clomping great Doc Martens. Her face was a pale matt with pink cheeks like a doll. There was a ring in one of her nostrils and another in her lower lip. Her hair, dead straight with a fringe like a blade, was a dull black enlivened by the occasional blue panel.

'Yeah, well ...' He grinned. 'Hey, tell you what – you could disguise yourself as someone *ordinary*.'

The mist was thicker than Peony had expected. It was like descending into a cold steam bath. Beads of moisture clung to her face and hair.

The dog ran ahead, disappearing for a few moments in the mist and then reappearing.

Peony's thoughts returned to the question that had been nagging away at her for weeks. When was she going to tell Lisa that she planned to leave the agency? And that she wouldn't be looking after Ricky any more.

She was nearing the beach and could hear the muffled booming of the waves. Mist was rolling off the sea like steam from boiling water. The beach was just a narrow strip of shingle, a jumble of smooth stones, grey, pink, mottled, hard to walk on. The stakes of a ragged groyne, twisted, weathered, stuck up like underwater plants. Something loomed up on the edge of her vision making her start: a large bleached piece of driftwood, twisted and sinuous like a sea serpent.

Peony picked up a stick and threw it. Piki dashed after it, slithering and bouncing over the shingle. The stick disappeared into the mist and Piki plunged after it. Peony picked her way cautiously around the headland.

For a long time the job here had suited her down to the ground. Goodness knows they'd needed the money. And Gavin was quite capable of looking after the kids once a month. In fact she'd told Lisa – only half jokingly – that it ought to be the other way round: *she* ought to be paying Lisa. When you've got three young children, the chance of an uninterrupted night's sleep is a luxury. And that was the thing – these days it *was* uninterrupted – Ricky was getting more independent, preferred to manage for himself. She had a yen to get back to a proper nursing job, and Josh was seven now. It really was time …

Funny that Piki hadn't returned with the stick. The steps that led up through the coomb appeared out of the mist. Peony paused at the bottom and called Piki. An answering bark came from above.

She clambered up uneven steps cut into the earth. The drifting mist gave her a feeling of vertigo, as if it were the trees that were moving and she was standing still. Piki was yelping, a conversational sound that she usually made in greeting. Peony quickened her pace, pushing against the clammy air, coughing as she inhaled it. She emerged onto the headland, near the tree-house. At the foot of the ladder

26

that led up to it, the grass was pressed down and crushed. Her eye was caught by something white nestling between the roots of the tree: a packet of Marlborough cigarettes. She bent down and picked it up. It was clean and there were still half-a-dozen cigarettes in it. Someone must have dropped it recently. She didn't like the idea of someone wandering around here. The main route for walkers was the South West Devon Coast Path which ran several hundred feet above the house.

She slipped the packet into the pocket of her coat. Piki had fallen silent. Peony called her name, but there was no answering bark.

Peony made her way up the path towards the house, certain she would find the dog waiting at the back door. But when she got back to the house, Piki was nowhere to be seen.

Chapter Five

The clock exerted a terrible attraction. So did the telephone. Twice Jay's hand reached out as if it was acting of its own volition. Once he even began dialling Lisa's mobile number, but he slammed the phone down before he got to the last digit. He pulled the phone out of its socket. Even better, why didn't he remove himself from temptation altogether?

He shrugged on a coat, thrust the house keys into his pocket and shut the front door behind him. He turned left and headed down the steep narrow alley, turned left again, right past the church, and emerged onto the promenade. The beach curved away in an elegant sickle towards a line of blue headlands that grew paler as they receded.

It was late October, but it might have been June if it hadn't been for a certain opaque quality to the light. The tide had recently turned, leaving behind wet sand and sea-weed. It was half-term and the warm weather had drawn families to the beach, but now in the late afternoon they had departed, leaving elaborate sand castles with moats full of water. He tried to focus on his surroundings: grey plovers skittering across the sand, a dog racing in circles around its owner, and at the far end of the beach, past the Spa, a single surfboarder, who kept falling off his board and climbing doggedly back on. Male or female? Hard to tell at this distance.

It was four weeks exactly since he had spotted Sandra at King's Cross. It had been a mere glimpse – she'd turned away immediately, and lowered her head, pretending to rummage in her handbag. She was older, far more smartly dressed, but he would have known her anywhere. He, too, looked very different these days, and it was years since they had last met, but he knew that she had recognised him. He had been on his way home from Sussex, where he had spent the weekend with Lisa in a cottage near Lewes. If he hadn't seen Sandra, and if it hadn't been for good old Darren and his cab, it would have been all up with him.

Lisa ... oh God, oh God, why had he ever let himself get involved with her? When he thought of her waiting for him right now in Norfolk, he groaned out loud. What a selfish bastard he had been ... Since that time there hadn't been a waking hour when he hadn't wondered if there was a way that he could safely contact Lisa, but always he came back to the same thing: when all this had begun with Lisa, he had made himself a solemn promise. If it ever became necessary he would walk away. No explanations, no goodbyes, no looking back. He had to stick to that.

Would Lisa have left the cottage or was she hanging on, hoping to hear from him? He kept wanting to look at his watch. He unbuckled it and thrust it deep into the pocket of his jeans. He walked as fast as he could along the beach and climbed the steps to the Spa. He never came this way without thinking of his parents. He had come on holiday here with them once when he was a child. Right here where he was walking now, he'd played a thrilling game, waiting for the waves to crash over the sea-wall and running out of reach just in time. It was lucky that he was an only child, and that Mum and Dad were dead.

He could see now that the surfer was male, probably a teenager. He stopped to watch but that was a mistake. If he didn't keep moving, thoughts of Lisa crowded in. He climbed the steps up to the chequerboard floor of the Spa and followed the winding path to the Italian gardens. In the summer this was a good place to sit and read. It is surprising how much time you have when you don't have a wife or children or even a proper job. In this second life of his, he read a lot. Today the reeds and the water lilies

30

were yellowing and dying.

He continued up to the Esplanade. Lights were coming on in grand Victorian houses. They had mostly been turned into hotels and flats, rather grand ones, illuminated by standard lamps with tasselled shades and furnished with Persian rugs and solid, respectable furniture. Usually he was comforted by glimpses of people doing ordinary things, watching TV, drinking tea, and felt a not unpleasant melancholy, hugging to himself the knowledge that Lisa was waiting for him at the end of the month. It wasn't just the sex, it was the talking and the sharing of meals and the knowing that for two nights there would be the comforting animal warmth of another body beside him. Over the last three years he had come to feel – not happy exactly, but not unhappy either. Only now did he understand how much he had grown to love her. All the old loneliness came flooding back and he hurried past the lighted windows without glancing in.

The seaward side of the esplanade was lined with benches. He chose one with a view of the harbour and the funfair and sat down. Surely by now Lisa would be on her way home. He hoped to God she wouldn't try to look for him. 'It's alright,' he murmured to himself. There was no way that she could find him. He had been careful, so careful. He had never relaxed his guard for a moment. She'd be angry and perplexed, but there was nothing she could do. She would grieve for a while, and then one day she would understand that their life together was over. She would begin to forget him.

But he wouldn't forget her. All he had now were his memories.

He let his thoughts drift back to the day they had met.

He used to go about once a month to the Percival David Museum of Chinese Art to build up his knowledge of Chinese porcelain. That was before the collection was moved to the British Museum, when it was still in a house in Bloomsbury. On that cold, wet November day he had the place to himself – or so he thought. He gazed at pots that were becoming as familiar as the crockery in his kitchen and were infinitely more beautiful: Qing dynasty bowls with delicate designs of peach and cherry blossom and chrysanthemums; Ming plates with brilliant green dragons chasing their tails on a lemon-yellow ground.

It was when he turned to look at the Ru ware that he realised he was not alone.

There was a woman, wearing a belted raincoat, raindrops glistening on dark hair. She stood before the case transfixed. He didn't wonder. The pots were perfect: so simple, so plain and undecorated and such a wonderful colour, hard to define – a greyish, greenish blue. As he drew closer, he saw that she was staring at a little bowl.

'That's one of my favourite pieces,' he heard himself say and she gave a little jump. The carpet must have muffled his footsteps. 'Sorry, I didn't mean to startle you.'

She looked round.

He could see her now and felt a pang of longing. She wasn't young: when she smiled, little sheaves of lines appeared at her eyes, but something about her direct intelligent gaze had attracted him straightaway.

She gestured towards the pot. 'I was just wondering how they did this. It looks so modern somehow. It's hard to believe that it's 800 years old.'

'They were the first ceramics made exclusively for the imperial court.' Only afterwards had it occurred to him that they had spoken as naturally as if they had known each other for years.

He explained how the pot had been made, that the colour was the product of a particular glaze.

'Are you an expert?' she asked.

'Just an enthusiastic amateur.'

That was how it had all begun. Later she told him that she had only come in to get out of the rain. Sheer good luck, he had told himself at the time. Now he wasn't so sure.

He shivered and buttoned up his jacket. The light had gone out of the day and so had the warmth. He stood up and looked down at the beach to see if the surfer was still there. He was disappointed – he hardly knew why – to see that the young man had emerged from the sea and a woman was handing him a towel.

He turned up his collar against the chill and headed home. There were things he had to do, while there was still time.

What is it they say in Spain? 'Revenge is a dish best eaten cold.' Revenge: an old-fashioned word and an old-fashioned idea, redolent of Jacobean drama or the Mafia. Vengeance was an even better word. He rolled it around in his mouth. There was something heavy and blood-laden about it.

'Vengeance is mine,' sayeth the Lord, but Jay had no intention of leaving it to Him.

He let himself into his little house.

The front door opened straight on to the living room from the street. There was only one room downstairs with a kitchen and dining area at one end. This was the perfect house for him and the perfect area: lots of rented accommodation, people coming and going all the time, little businesses springing up and just as quickly closing down. His only close neighbour was an elderly lady who was grateful when he swept snow off the pavement. Jay went upstairs. At the end of the little corridor there was a full-length mirror. He knelt down, curled his fingers under the frame, and pressed the concealed latch. The mirror swung back to reveal a bank of narrow shelves. His eyes travelled over the pots arranged there: a pair of palace bowls decorated with five-clawed dragon medallions from the Kangxi period, a Yongzheng doucai bowl decorated with lotus flowers, and, loveliest of all, a Qianlong bowl, perfectly plain with a yellow glaze.

These were not the only treasures. On a shelf at eye-level was a small battered Dinky toy, a bread van in miniature. Propped up against it was a photograph, torn on one side and with a wavy black edge on the other, as if it had been thrown into a fire and snatched out just in time. It showed a younger Jay, seated on a jetty of broken-up stones, his arm around the woman sitting beside him. Her fair hair had been bleached almost white by the sun, and so had the fluffy hair of the little boy who stood between her legs, squinting into the camera. Behind them the sun struck flashes of light off the surface of a lake. He put out a finger, touched the faces of the woman and the boy.

Beside the photo was a little velvet envelope about an inch in diameter. He reached for it and shook out onto his palm a little winged horse, made of gold. He looked at it for a while, then slipped it back in its sheath and put it back on the shelf.

He reached up to one of the higher shelves and brought down something heavy, wrapped in cloth. He let the gun slide out into his hand. It was smooth and heavy, the metal cool against his skin. He had discovered the Browning pistol and ammunition in the attic while he was clearing out his parents' house after his father's death only weeks before he and Mia and Sam had gone into witness protection. He'd guessed that it was a souvenir from his father's National Service in Malaysia in the fifties. He'd known that he ought to hand it into the police, but some instinct had told him to hang onto it. He wrapped it up again, replaced it, and took one of several mobile phones off the shelf below.

Time to see if the bait had been taken. There was a game he used to play with his son: if you were a fish, what kind of fish would you be? Well, if Lars were a fish, what kind of fish would he be? A shark? Maybe ... No, not a

34

shark, not a fish at all, but something just as powerful and primitive, a crocodile, lying concealed beneath the surface of the water.

Very well, then, Jay had staked out the goat. Time to see if anything was stirring in the water. He took a few deep breaths before he dialled the number. He had moved so slowly, playing a long game, to establish himself in Lars's mind as a dealer in ceramics. He had in fact become that dealer and his connection with Lars had been built up over the last couple of years through the occasional sale conducted through e-mail. All the same the first time they had spoken on the phone a couple of weeks ago had been tricky. But Lars had seemed to suspect nothing and he was interested, very interested, in what Jay had to propose.

There was no exchange of preliminaries. The telephone was picked up at the other end and the familiar voice with its barely discernible accent said, 'Yes?'

It still gave Jay a jolt to hear that voice and his mouth went dry. He reminded himself that the man at the other end of the line couldn't see him – had no way of knowing who he was. On the other hand, after the encounter at King's Cross, Jay would be very much on his mind – if he made the connection –

'Yes?' The voice said again with a hint of impatience.

'Have you thought it over?' Jay asked.

'You are confident you can do what you say?'

'Yes.'

'And the price.'

'Twenty-five million.'

'Dollars?'

'Pounds.'

'A trifle steep.'

'For the pair? I don't think so. You'll never get another chance like this.' There was silence. Jay took this as consent. There was one more thing, the most important thing. Could he pull it off?

35

'You have to be there in person for the hand-over,' he said.

'That won't be possible,' Lars said immediately.

'I can't deal with an associate. Not for this.'

Again, a silence.

'No show, no deal.' Jay said. 'With the risk I'm taking .

'OK.' The voice was laconic. 'How will I know when you've done it?'

'Watch the newspapers.'

Jay hung up. He leaned back against the wall and took a deep breath. He was drenched in sweat and his heart was racing. But he was grinning, a big, idiotic grin. He punched the air. 'Yes!'

It had begun.

Chapter Six

Fog was drifting across the Somerset Levels as Lisa headed west from Bristol. The sun was a pale disc low in the sky. Now and then the fog shifted and she was squinting into a dazzling sunset.

She had hung around at the cottage for the rest of the weekend, constantly checking her phone and thinking that every car that came down the road might be Jay's. She'd even wondered briefly if she'd come on the wrong weekend. But really there was no possibility of a mistake. At last, reluctantly, around lunch-time on Sunday, she set off for home. That was the time she would normally have left and she didn't know what else to do.

Her head was throbbing and her eyes felt as if they were full of grit. For the hundredth time she ran through the possibilities: an accident, he was lying in some hospital with concussion. In a few days he'd be better, he would ring her. But what if it had been a *serious* accident, or a heart-attack ... no, she told herself, don't go there. Not yet. Give it time, a few days at least. If she didn't hear anything, she could always drive up to where he lived in Derbyshire. She'd have to do *something*.

At Bridgwater she turned onto the A39. At one point the winding road ran close to the sea. It was disorientating, the way mist and water and sky merged together and she slowed down to a crawl. But then as she drove up out of Porlock she left the fog behind. The light of the setting sun ignited a moorland landscape already tawny with the colours of autumn. A few miles further on she turned right onto a narrow unmarked road. It wound down half a mile through a tunnel of trees to Falling Water. She could almost have driven down it blindfold.

The drive home was like an emotional decompression chamber. It marked the transition between the two compartments of her life. But today Lisa wasn't ready to go home. About half-way down the track she pulled up at the point where a public footpath crossed it and ran down to the sea. It was still just light enough to see the path. She grabbed her coat and set off slowly downhill, scuffing up leaves. Her thoughts returned to her mobile phone. She'd been so sure, so absolutely sure, that it wasn't on the floor of the car. It was silver: surely the beam from the torch would have picked it up if it had been there. But it must have been there, because it was there the next morning. But it hadn't been there. But it must have been there. The thoughts chased each other round her mind. There was an uneasy feeling in the pit of her stomach. Was she losing her grip? She couldn't afford to let that happen now that it was just her and Ricky. The phone must have slipped under the seat and then slipped back out when she braked. It was the only explanation.

A flicker of light from the house showed through the trees. She left the path and picked her way through rocks and ferns to a little piece of open ground. This was one of the best views of the house. Built of timber and glass and brick it merged into the landscape and was at home there. Her father had been an architect – a distinguished one – and the house combined his love of Scandinavian modernism with his admiration of Frank Lloyd Wright. It was called Falling Water in homage to the great architect. To Lisa as a teenager it had simply been the family home and an inconvenient one at that: too far away from the shops in Barnstaple or Minehead. Even to reach the bus stop meant a walk of over a mile up a steep track. Later the house had been a haven for herself and her son when her marriage had broken up.

The long narrow pond that stretched the length of the

house was dark and still, a few dead leaves lying on the surface. The sitting room was empty now, like a stage set waiting for the actors to make their entrance. As if on cue a door opened and Ricky came through in his wheelchair, turning his head to speak to someone out of sight. Peony came into view. She leaned forward to catch what Ricky was saying. They started to laugh.

There was a sound somewhere behind her. Lisa turned her head to listen. A badger probably – twilight was the time to see them – or even a red deer. There was silence now, but the sound had brought her to herself. What was she doing here, staring into her own house? She turned to set off up the path. There was a rustling and something sprang out of the undergrowth. Lisa gasped and her hand went to her breast.

There was a volley of barking. Piki! The dog rushed up to her, squirming in delight.

Lisa bent to stroke her. 'You bad girl! What do you think you're doing, giving me a shock like that?"

The kitchen was steamy and there was a delicious smell: onions and bacon and oregano.

Peony was chopping mushrooms. Lisa still felt a sense of surprise every time she saw Peony. She was beautiful. There was no other word for it. She was like a black Madonna, the symmetry of her face so perfect that it seemed almost artificial.

Her expression relaxed into one of relief when she saw Piki. 'She's been missing all day. Ran off when I was walking her this morning. I was worried. Thought she might have fallen over a cliff or something.'

They contemplated the dog. She was looking from one to other, wagging her tail tentatively, aware that she was the object of unfavourable comment.

'Stella rang,' Peony said.

Lisa shook her head and lifted a hand. 'I know what

that's about. How's Ricky been?'

Peony pursed her lips. 'Oh, fine.'

Lisa's maternal antennae shot up.

'But?' she asked.

Peony wasn't meeting her eye. At last she said, 'He does seem to spend an awful lot of time on that computer.'

Lisa had a feeling that it wasn't what she had originally intended to say.

Peony went on. 'I got up to go to the loo last night and he was still at it. It was half past two! Another thing, a couple of times when I've gone in, he's switched it to the screen-saver right away.'

'You think …?'

'Well, a boy of his age ... there's some pretty strange stuff out there … '

'You mean ... pornography ... !' The headache Lisa been aware of earlier was coming back with a vengeance.

'He *is* nearly seventeen …' Peony went on.

Lisa rubbed a hand across her forehead. 'That chat room for other kids with disabilities? He's probably busy with that.'

Peony didn't look convinced. She turned back to the chopping board and the mushrooms.

'It isn't good for him to be spending too much time on-line,' Lisa conceded. 'I'll have a word with him.'

Peony nodded.

'There's something else, isn't there?' Lisa said.

Peony put down the knife and turned round.

'I've been wanting to say it for a while …'

'Yes?'

'I'm not sure that Ricky really wants me here any more.'

Lisa stared at her. 'But you've always got on so well!'

'Of course we have. I don't mean that – just, there are times when he doesn't want *anyone* around. Anyone adult that is. That's just the way kids are at his age.'

40

'But Ricky's not just any kid.'

Peony was silent.

'It's not Ricky, is it? It's you! You don't want to come any more!' Lisa couldn't keep a note of accusation out of her voice. She saw the look on Peony's face and reached out to touch her arm. 'I'm sorry, I know that's not fair.'

Peony put her hand over Lisa's and squeezed it.

In her basket by the door, Piki sat up and whimpered. She regarded the two women with anxious eyes.

'Sometimes I feel I'm not much more than a glorified baby-sitter,' Peony said. Piki came up and thrust her nose into her hand, 'or dog-sitter,' she added with a smile.

'Piki would certainly miss you. But not as much as I would.'

'I've got to be honest. I need a change, too. Now that all the kids are at school ...'

'You want a proper job.' Lisa spoke without heat.

'You know, Ricky could manage more than he does now. He can heat things up in the microwave. He can use the hoist in the bathroom. He could be on his own a bit more.'

'You think I'm over-protective, don't you?'

'The truth? A bit. But it's natural. Look, I'll wait until after Christmas before I start looking around. In the meantime, why don't you have a day out and let Ricky have a friend over? See how they get on. Someone sensible. Someone like Charlotte.'

After supper Peony insisted on washing up and Lisa was too tired to protest. She went upstairs to unpack her bag.

Wrapped in the underwear that she hadn't worn was a copy of Tove Janssen's shimmering little novel, *Fair Play*. Her heart lurched. She had packed that for Jay. Every time they met they exchanged presents. He had such good taste. This cardigan she was wearing, red cashmere, not many men would have had the confidence to choose this. She wouldn't even have chosen it for herself, but she loved it. Here in her bedroom, she was surrounded by things Jay had given her: silk scarves, one with a black-and-white dog's tooth check, another with a Marimekko label; a bottle of scent – *Sublime* by Patou; a pile of CDs with Johnny Cash on top.

'I don't like country and western,' she had protested.

'You'll like this.'

And she had. Willie Nelson, too. And Schubert's String Quintet in C Major. Not to mention Shostakovich and Frank Sinatra. Jay had extended her musical horizons. The things they had done to feel close when they were far apart: listening to the same music, watching the same DVDs, reading the same books. Ah, the books he had given her ... She scanned the shelf where she kept them: classics, crime novels, contemporary fiction, quirky books that she would never have thought of buying for herself. One weekend she'd handed him a book she had bought him and he had burst out laughing. He'd brought the same book for her. And it wasn't even as if it were a recent best-seller. It was Willa Cather's *Death Comes for the Archbishop*, the story of two missionary priests in nineteenth-century New Mexico. Solemnly they had exchanged copies.

'Lisa?' Peony called up the stairs. 'I'm off now.'

Lisa went down to say goodbye.

Peony gestured towards Piki, who was whining and scrabbling at the back door. 'She's desperate to go out again.'

'Probably needs a pee,' Lisa said. 'I'll take her out.' She reached for the leash and bent to attach it to Piki's collar. 'We don't want you making a break for it again,' she told the dog.

But when they went outside Piki didn't want a pee. She whimpered and strained on the leash. Lisa had to brace herself to hold her. Then all of a sudden she gave up and flopped down, face on paws.

Lisa watched Peony's headlights disappear up the track. When the sound of the car died away, it was very quiet. Lisa lingered by the back door, listening to the small sounds of the forest, the constant murmur of the stream that fed the pond. All at once her scalp was prickling and her mouth had gone dry. She didn't know what had spooked her. Piki gave a low growl and got slowly to her feet. Had she seen something – or was she reacting to Lisa's fear?

She stepped back into the kitchen, dragging the reluctant dog with her, and locked and bolted the door.

She went through into the sitting room and switched on all the lights, illuminating the area in front of the house, the pond and the lawn. Of course no-one was there. She saw only her own reflection in the glass. She was tired and anxious; the weekend had been a terrible strain, that was all it was. If they were to go on living here without Lawrence, she couldn't let her imagination get the better of her like this. The first winter without him ... people said it got better after the first year.

Her head was throbbing. She put her hand up to her forehead and the figure outside did the same.

The big windows were fitted with blinds, but they were rarely used except in very cold weather. The house was overlooked only by distant vessels out in the Bristol Channel. She had never minded before, but today she felt like a fish in an aquarium. She flicked a switch, there was a whirr-whirr-whirr and two motorised blinds began to descend.

She knocked gently on Ricky's door. Always, last thing, she looked in on him. These days he was often still awake, watching DVDs or reading – thank God his sight hadn't been affected. She couldn't imagine a life without the printed word. Taped books just weren't the same. Tonight though, there was no answer when she tapped on the door and when she opened it a crack, the room was in darkness. She slipped in and stood by the side of her son's bed. In the sliver of light from the sitting room she saw that he was fast asleep. He looked even younger than he really was. She put out a hand and smoothed back the hair that flopped over his forehead.

Whatever had happened to Jay – and she was full of foreboding – there was still Ricky. Nothing mattered more.

Chapter Seven

'And so Little Red Riding Hood set off through the wood. And although her mother had told her to go straight to her grandma's, she couldn't resist straying off the path to pick flowers.'

Lars was sitting on the sofa with his little girl, Brigitta, snuggled up beside him. When Sandra came in, he looked up briefly, nodded and went on reading from the book open on his lap. 'Little by little the light began to die from the sky … '

Sandra needed a gin, God, how she needed a gin. She went over to the drinks cabinet. She opened the ice bucket, used the tongs to pick out a couple of cubes, and dropped them in a glass. Listening to Lars with half an ear – Little Red Riding Hood had reached her grandmother's cottage – she took a small, sharp knife and cut a slice off a lemon. She reached for the bottle of Plymouth gin, poured out a good measure and filled the glass with tonic.

She took a sip. Ah, that was good.

She went over to one of the window seats and sat down. Lars happened to look up as she eased her shoes off with a sigh of relief. They were black suede with pointed toes and kitten heels. They had been absurdly expensive. He gave her an ironic glance and she made a face at him.

She put the disappointment of the weekend to one side – she'd thought enough about it on the way back from Norfolk – and let herself be soothed by the warmth and comfort of her surroundings. The long, first-floor room was often filled with light from the river, and even with twilight coming on there was a sense of airy space. The carpet with its rich colours and intricate pattern could have

45

been Persian but was actually nineteenth-century Arts and Crafts. Lars had bought it at auction for a stupendous price. The cabinets were full of Chinese porcelain, the walls were hung with English watercolours. The best of everything: Lars didn't settle for anything less.

Behind her the story continued and she admired the expression Lars put into it.

' "Why, what big eyes you've got, Grandma." "All the better to see you with, my dear."'

She gazed out at the broad expanse of the Thames. There was a single sculler on the river. A plane, looking improbably large, passed overhead on its way to Heathrow.

When she had first got to know Lars she hadn't been able to understand why he was still living in Chiswick. OK, the house was large, it was Georgian, it fronted onto the river, had its own mooring, but he could have afforded something so much grander. But in time Sandra had come to see the point of it. This little slice of Chiswick, with the river on one side and the Great West Road on the other, was a community all of its own and Lars's part in it – chair of this community group, honorary member of that rowing club – gave him a standing and respectability that money alone couldn't buy. It said he wasn't flash, he wasn't a fly-by-night. Five or six years ago, when he had come under suspicion of murdering his wife he had been able to muster a lot of local support. People simply didn't believe he could have done it.

Lars was reaching the end of the story now. Sandra turned and gave it her full attention.

'"And what big teeth you have, Grandma." "All the better –"' he paused. Brigitta knew what was coming – her mouth was open and her eyes were like saucers. '"TO EAT YOU!"' And ...' He let the moments stretch out. 'Quick as a flash the wood-cutter jumped in through the open window and cut off the wolf's head with his axe.

46

And they all lived happily ever after.' He clapped the book shut.

'Come on, now, time for bath and bed.'

'Oh, Daddy, Daddy –'

'Yes, my darling.' He stroked her hair with a tenderness that he rarely showed Sandra – though in truth tenderness was not exactly what she looked for from Lars.

'Did Little Red Riding Hood marry the wood-cutter?'

Lars considered this. He shrugged. 'Oh, well, maybe '

The child thought this over. 'I prefer the wolf.' Sandra smiled to herself. Brigitta was a chip off the old block alright. But what woman wouldn't in her heart of hearts prefer the wolf? Wasn't he the best character in the story: resourceful, ruthless, sexy? She remembered reading somewhere that in the original story the wolf ate Little Red Riding and got away free. Yes, the wolf's my kind of guy, she decided.

She'd always had an affinity with law-breakers. It was why she had joined the police. Of course most criminals were hopeless lowlifes, bungling incompetents, addicted to drugs or booze, randomly violent. She had had to rise a good way through the ranks before she met Lars, but she had always known there would be a Lars.

At first it had been about money: a hefty sum up front and after a suitable interval, strings pulled, and a job that gave her the income she deserved, without having to work so hard that she couldn't enjoy it. But over the years it had become more than that, much more. They were two of a kind, a team.

Lars returned from delivering Brigitta to her nanny. He went to the drinks cupboard and opened the small built-in freezer. He took out a bottle of Absolut Blue Vodka. To anyone else he would have seemed impassive. There was something almost blank about his square, pale face. When Sandra had first met him she'd had the strange thought that it was as if some of his personality had been worn away.

He was still opaque to her in many ways, but she knew him well enough to read the signs that others would miss: he was worried.

'I expected you earlier,' he remarked. 'How long did it take? Two hours, two and a half?'

'More like three. No motorways in Norfolk. Bloody awful drive. And all for nothing.'

'No, no, don't say that. You had no trouble getting hold of her mobile?'

'None at all. She had no idea I'd lifted it.'

'So we do at least have a trace on her now.'

She watched as he measured out the vodka. She liked to see him doing practical things. His hands were well cared for, his movements deft, economical.

'If only I hadn't let him lose me in London.' She clicked her tongue in frustration.

He shook his head to indicate that it wasn't worth discussing. 'It's going to be harder than we hoped, that's all.'

She sighed and swilled the gin around her glass. The ice cubes clinked.

She had been on her way back from a weekend visiting her sister in Brighton. Her sister had dropped her off at the station and she got the shock of her life when she saw Jay get out of the car in front. Luckily he'd only had eyes for the woman in the car and she had recovered in time to get the registration number and to follow him onto the train. She'd tracked him across London and it was bloody bad luck that he had spotted her at King's Cross.

It was a blow, no point in pretending it wasn't. When the months had passed and then the years, she had allowed herself to believe that Jay was dead. But Lars, she knew, had never relaxed his vigilance. The security here – ostensibly to protect his collection of Chinese porcelain – was second to none. In fact it was impossible for anyone to get close to him at any point in his day.

Lars was standing near her now, a glass of vodka on the rocks in his hand.

'Lars … '

'Yes, my dear?'

'Just how much of a threat do you think he is?'

'Hard to say.' He sat down next to her, put an arm round her shoulder. 'But in any case we have to follow through. No loose ends. We are agreed on that, are we not?'

'Oh, yes.'

'This woman. This Lisa. She's still our best chance. We wait for him to make contact. I think we should get someone in close.'

'I agree. And I think it should be me.'

He nodded. 'That was my thought, too.'

She downed the rest of her drink and hunted about for her shoes.

'You can't drive home after that gin,' Lars said. He put his drink down.

It was amusing that he was so punctilious about not breaking the law in small ways, considering what he was prepared to do in big ways. He was right though: no point in attracting attention.

'I'll get a taxi.'

'No.' He turned her face to his. He slid his hand down her arm and cupped her breast. She ran her hand over the fair hair that he always kept short. She lifted her mouth to his, felt the cool clinical taste of vodka on his lips. After a few moments he pulled away.

'We'll go upstairs,' he said.

Chapter Eight

So slow the hours.
So silent the moon.
Wide-eyed and restless
I lie awake
And ache for you.

You do not believe me?
Touch my pillow.
It is wet
With the traces of my tears.

That was written over a thousand years ago, but it could have been written yesterday, Lisa thought. Human heartache, the pain of lost love; that never changed. Not that it made the work of translation any easier. She had managed this much, but she just couldn't tell if it was any good or not.

The telephone rang.

She had the answering machine on so that she could screen calls. She was supposed to be working, after all, and anyway there was only one person whose voice she wanted to hear.

Her heart sank when she heard Stella.

'Lisa? Lisa? Are you there? Pick up, please. You can't keep avoiding me like this! If you don't get your arse in gear soon, I'll come over there in person and roust you out, I swear I will.' There was a pause as Stella waited for a response. 'Seriously, kid, I'm worried about you. Speak soon. Love you loads.'

Lisa propped her head on her hands and thrust her

fingers into her hair. She couldn't speak to Stella, not now.

It was Wednesday. Why hadn't there been anything from Jay?

She got a fresh piece of paper and began to write. The letter was short and simple, saying just that she was very worried and please would he get in touch straight away if only to let her know that he was OK. She sealed the envelope, addressed it, and stuck a stamp on it. She pushed her chair back from her desk and flexed her shoulders.

The nearest post box was up on the road and the climb was so steep that it was an hour's walk. She didn't feel like it but it would do her good. And Piki, too.

The dog ran on ahead of her, turning back now and then to make sure that Lisa was following. The narrow track led in and out of rocks and trees. It would be all too easy to slip on mud or wet leaves or trip over a tree root. And the mobile was useless here. Now that Lawrence wasn't at home to notice her absence, she was conscious as never before of how lonely a spot this was. Their nearest neighbours were farmers who lived a quarter of a mile along the coast. Not far as the crow flies, but she wasn't a crow. It took twenty minutes to drive up the track from Falling Water, along the main road, and then down the track to the farm.

A jay started out of a tree with a harsh whirring cry like someone winding a rusty old alarm clock.

Today was the first fine day after a period of heavy rain and the stream ran full and fast, laced with white foam. The tumbling water and wind in the trees made a constant rushing noise. It always made Lisa think of the poem by William Allingham:

Up the airy mountain
Down the rushy glen
We daren't go a-hunting
For fear of little men.

Lisa's Cornish grandmother used to tell stories of people being pixie-led. Lisa didn't believe in any of that, of course, but still she was glad to have Piki with her. Woods could be strange places.

She kept up a steady pace. By the time she got up to the post-box she was breathing heavily. She stood for a moment holding the letter then pressed her lips to it and put it in the box. It was done and all she could do now was wait.

She took a circular route down through the woods to where a stone bridge crossed the stream at the end of the garden. Lawrence had made the most of the natural beauty of the setting. There was a herb garden at the side of the house, but no formal flower beds. Instead there was the long narrow pond in front of the house, with a lawn off to the side and a wild flower meadow that marked the transition between the clearing and the trees.

She paused, shook her head, not quite believing what she saw.

Someone was standing by the pond, close in by the house. It was Lawrence. For a couple of heart-stopping seconds she was sure of it: the height and the build – the man moved again and the resemblance had gone. The thudding of her heart filled her entire chest. She took a deep breath.

The man strolled down the path by the window with his hands thrust into his pockets. He had the air of a man waiting for something he didn't relish, like someone pacing a dentist's waiting room. Lisa let her pulse rate settle before she called Piki to heel.

She was half way across the lawn when the man caught sight of her. He half-raised a hand in greeting. He moved towards her, then checked himself, as if he wanted to see her reaction before he committed himself. She knew him now and she wouldn't have been much more shocked if it *had* been a ghost. She hadn't seen Barry for over five years.

'What the fuck are you doing here?' she asked.

Her jeans were none too clean. Her shirt was a favourite: coral-pink cotton with mother-of-pearl buttons, but she was wearing it for the second day running and she was sweaty from the walk. Barry wasn't smart exactly. He, too, was wearing jeans, but everything was just right, from his highly polished brogues to his rimless glasses. His check shirt was tucked into a wide leather belt that showed off a flat belly. The floppy dark hair, long nose and round glasses gave him the look of a clever postgraduate. He was in good shape and had aged well. And yet something in his appearance *had* changed; she just couldn't put her finger on it.

'What are you doing here, Barry?' she asked again.

They were in the living room. He was standing by the window, thumbs in the pocket of his jeans, rocking on his heels a little. She hadn't asked him to sit down.

'I'm setting up a server farm for the company.'

She didn't know what a server farm was, but she wasn't going to ask.

He went on. 'Actually I'm taking over from someone who's sick. I'll be here a fair bit over the next few months.'

'I didn't mean what are you doing in England. I mean, what are you doing *here*.'

'The site's not far away, half an hour's drive, so ...' He shrugged.

She waited him out.

'Ok, Ok.' He lifted his hands in a gesture of surrender. 'I wanted to see how you were. Is that a crime?'

'Why didn't you ring me first?'

'I thought you might not agree to see me.'

'Too right.'

'I read about Lawrence – saw one of the obits. I'm

54

really sorry. He was a great guy.'

She nodded. She could allow him to be sorry. There had been a time when Lawrence and Barry had got on well together.

Barry looked around. 'You know, this place hasn't changed a bit.'

She looked, too. She hadn't noticed that everything was a little the worse for wear. Now she saw it through his eyes. The rubber plant was looking tired, it needed repotting. The pale leather on the long sofa had darkened in places. Here and there Ricky's wheelchair had worn the varnish off the wooden floor. It had all seen better days.

'I like that,' Barry said. 'The lived-in look. Where I live now nothing's allowed to get old – least of all the people.'

Was that a veiled criticism? She decided it wasn't. It was the kind of sardonic comment she used to enjoy from Barry.

'Is that all you came for?' She scrutinised him, seeing the deeper lines, the hair salted with grey. Now that Barry had reached middle age, he did look a little like Lawrence. For the first time it occurred to her that she might have married him because he reminded her of her father. It was a pity the resemblance was only skin-deep.

'Ricky can have the new equipment,' he said. 'The things you asked for. No problem.'

There never was a problem. The agreement between them had been tacit, but fully understood. Barry would provide everything that Ricky needed in material terms, as long as he wasn't required to see him. It had gone against the grain to accept her ex-husband's money, but she had gritted her teeth for Ricky's sake.

'You didn't come all the way from LA to tell me that.'

He looked away from her, out of the window. 'I want to see Ricky,' he said.

'Ha.' She gave a gasp of disbelief. 'You think you can turn up and see him just like that –'

'No, no, of course not – it doesn't have to be today. I knew I'd need to speak to you first. That's why I came when I knew he'd be at school.'

'It won't be today or any other day.'

He held up his hands in a gesture of surrender.

'You need time to think about it.'

'I want you to go.'

'OK, OK. I'll be gone, I promise, long before Ricky gets home. When will that be? An hour or so? Look, why don't we sit down, maybe have a cup of coffee? I'm not going to interfere, not if you don't want me to, but there are things I need to say. OK?'

She hesitated. Making coffee would at least give her a chance to think. 'OK.'

He flashed her a smile and that was when she knew what was different.

'You've had your teeth fixed,' she blurted out.

'Yeah, yeah, it kind of goes with the territory when you're doing business on the West coast. Like going to the gym. It's not enough to know your stuff. You have to look good, too.'

Now that she'd noticed, she couldn't take her eyes off them. 'Are they tax deductible?' she asked. 'They make you look like Tom Cruise.'

Barry grinned. He'd always been able to take a joke against himself. That was one of his good points.

'I'll make the coffee,' she said.

Her hands were trembling as she opened the coffee tin. God knows, she could do with some herself. While the kettle boiled she stood by the window gazing out, trying to relax and centre herself. She thought she had come to terms with the situation long ago. The occasional letters that they exchanged, the yearly bulletins about Ricky's health and progress at school, her requests for extra money for Ricky – a formality really because Barry always agreed, none of these contacts had raised the slightest flutter in her breast. But actually seeing Barry here in the flesh ... Her body remembered what she had forgotten: that they had once been lovers and together they had made Ricky.

The kettle turned itself off with a click. Lisa poured water in the cafetière and stood looking out of the window while it brewed. There was a flash of movement in the trees: a squirrel. It leapt from one branch to the next, and disappeared round the back of a tree.

Lisa pushed the plunger down firmly.

Lisa handed Barry a cup of coffee. 'I've thought about what you said. And I've decided it's better that you stay out of our lives.'

'But just keep on handing over the cash?'

'It's been good enough for you up to now.'

She saw the anger in his face and the effort with which he pushed it down. 'Sorry,' he said. 'I don't want to get into an argument. It *has* been good enough, but now it isn't.'

'Why now, after all these years?'

'When I read about Lawrence, I got to thinking. While he was alive, I knew that Ricky had someone – at least –'

'Someone to act like a father, you mean, the father that you decided not to be.' Barry flushed. 'OK. I deserve that. But at least I never tried to duck out of my financial obligations. Even in the early days when there wasn't a lot of cash.'

She had to grant him that. The irony of it was that Barry worked for fun, always had done, the money had come along as a by-product and he didn't really care about it. She didn't know how much he was worth exactly, but she did know that if he sold his shares in the company, he need never work again.

'Are you sure you're ready for this?' she said. 'He still drools, you know.'

Barry looked anxious. 'Really?'

She laughed. 'Actually, no, but you see how little you know about Ricky.' She

looked at her watch. 'He'll be home from school in half an hour. I want you to go.'

'There'll be difficult decisions to make now that he's getting older. Have you thought about what he'll do when he leaves school?'

'He's only just started his AS levels!'

'But he got good results in his GCSEs. He'll be thinking of a degree in computer sciences, IT, something like that?'

'There are special residential colleges,' she began. She shook her head. 'I don't want to talk about this. It's too late to come the concerned parent.'

Barry's eyes slid away from hers. He examined his hand, rubbing the cuticles of one hand with the fingers of the other. It was a gesture she hadn't seen before.

'OK.' He got to his feet. 'I'll contact you again – when? A week?'

'No.'

'A fortnight.'

'I'll see. And don't come here again without ringing first.'

She followed him out through the kitchen. He had his hand on the handle of the outside door, when he turned and said, 'I meant to ask you … '

'What?'

'Is there anyone? I mean, are you –?'

'None of your business.'

'But there's no-one else living here, is there? It's just you and Ricky, yes?'

'Barry! Just go!'

He nodded, as if she had told him what he needed to know. 'I'll e-mail you.'

She stood at the door and watched him climb into a

black BMW. He pulled out onto the track. He waved a hand, then picked up speed, and disappeared into the tunnel of trees. She watched him until he was out of sight. What did he *really* want?

Chapter Nine

Brisbane.

Population 1.6 million.

6.00 a.m. on a fine, sunny morning, temperature 22 degrees and rising. Already commuters were queuing at the Gateway Bridge toll booths. He planned to get to work early and then leave early so that he could drive down to the coast for a swim, have dinner at that seafood place near the jetty –

The doorbell rang.

Jay looked round at the window and for a moment couldn't understand why it was dark outside. He looked back at the computer screen: a car edged forward in the jerky style of the web-cam and sped out of view.

On the other side of the world it was a spring morning on Australia's Gold Coast. Here, in his house in England, it was eight o'clock at night on a chilly autumn evening.

The doorbell rang again. Of course, it would be Robert, on the dot as usual. Jay went over to the window and opened it, shivering as the cold air flowed in. If only it *were* 22 degrees and rising. He stuck his head out and saw Robert's face, sallow in the street light, looking up.

'Down in a minute,' he said.

Robert nodded. He never wasted words.

Jay had already set the table and lit the fire, so everything was ready when he let Robert in with the fish and chips. Robert always brought the food and Jay supplied the drink, beer with the meal and Scotch while they played chess. At half past ten they had a cup of tea and a chocolate biscuit. At eleven o'clock – again on the dot – Robert departed. It didn't matter what stage they had reached. The game in progress was simply abandoned and resumed at their next meeting.

Theirs was an unlikely friendship, but a fortuitous one. Robert had responded to the postcard that he had put in the window of a local newsagent offering accountancy services for small businesses and the self-employed. Robert had been one of Jay's first clients.

Jay had wondered if Robert were a little autistic, and when they started to play chess once a fortnight, he felt sure: Asperger's Syndrome, probably. Robert was at the high-functioning end of the scale. He lived alone and looked after himself. He had his own little business making and repairing stringed instruments. Tonight Robert was looking worried. He smoothed back the lock of greasy dark hair that hung over his forehead.

'What's up?' Jay asked.

'They only had one haddock. The other one's coley.' So that was it. Any break from routine troubled him.

'I'll have that,' Jay said. 'I like coley.'

Robert's face cleared. 'That's alright, then.'

With an air of relief he divested himself of his duffel coat. This wasn't retro-fashion, worn in a spirit of irony. It was a venerable garment that had survived from the first time round. Jay noted that his shirt, as usual clean but somewhat creased, was fastened on the wrong buttons. He refrained from pointing it out. Robert wasn't without social contacts: he belonged to a chess club, and even played the viola with some other gifted amateurs in a string quartet that gave an occasional public performance. But it had become clear to Jay that he had no close friends.

Neither did Jay. It was too dangerous.

He and Robert were like two men stranded together on a desert island, Jay, by his circumstances, Robert, by his personality. Robinson Crusoe and Man Friday; Jay wouldn't have cared to say which was which.

Robert rarely talked about his private life, never

enquired about Jay's. It was only this mutual reticence that made their friendship possible. Early on Jay had wondered if Robert, too, had something to hide. Had he been in prison? Was he a recovering drug addict? Maybe like Jay he had picked this seaside town as a good place to begin a new life. This had struck Jay as wildly funny until another possibility had occurred to him. What if Robert knew who Jay really was? What if he were a plant? But that way lay paranoia and anyway a few carefully judged questions soon put paid to any flights of fancy. Robert had a past, but he wasn't interested in talking about it. If a question was put to him, he would answer but in a slightly bemused way, as if he didn't understand why you were asking, but was willing to humour you.

Over supper they exchanged comments about local goings-on, the mess the council had made of the new traffic scheme, the new play at the theatre. Then they retired to the chess board.

Robert was much the better player. When they had first begun to play, he had surrendered a castle and a couple of pawns to make the contest more even. That had been reduced now to one pawn. Playing with Robert had raised Jay's game and it was his ambition to play him on equal terms and beat him. That was still some way off.

Tonight they picked up a game near the end. Robert had the advantage and it was check-mate in six moves. Robert gave a Jay quizzical look: he hadn't expected it to be so easy. Jay told himself to get a grip. They set out the pieces again.

There was a sound above their heads. Neither man looked up. A few seconds later, there was a pattering on the stairs and Barrington appeared. He headed for the kitchen where both men had left a bit of fish in his bowl. He was a grey tom, sleek and stout, who had come into Jay's life around a year ago, when Jay had come across him basking in the sun in the little walled garden beside the house. Barrington wasn't a stray; he was too prosperous-looking for that. He had a permanent home somewhere. But after a night of Barrington yowling outside his bedroom window, Jay had given in and provided him with a cat flap. Now he came and went as he pleased.

'Why do you call him Barrington?' Robert asked. He took a white and a black pawn off the board and held them behind his back.

'The name just came into my head. It seemed to suit him. It was a week or two before I realised that it's the name of a guest house on Eastborough.'

Jay touched one of the hands that Robert held out. Robert opened his hand to reveal a white pawn.

It wasn't the first time they had had this conversation. Far from it. They were like an old married couple, endlessly rehearsing the same topics.

Jay's fantasy was that Barrington not only lived in the guest house, but actually ran it and dropped in on Jay by way of relaxation. Cats have the potential for living a double life; dogs don't. It wasn't a thought that he could share with Robert, but Lisa would have enjoyed it. The sudden thought of her caught at his heart. He sighed.

The sound brought him to himself and he realised that his hand was hovering over the board with the pawn still in it. Robert was looking at him and frowning. He must be more careful.

He used the pawn in his first move and the game began.

'You know when you went to the Great Barrier Reef?' Robert asked, as he advanced a knight.

It was all Jay could do not to groan out loud.

It was sheer bad luck that Robert was obsessed with Australia. Jay's cover story was that he had spent a number of years as an independent financial adviser in Brisbane. It was plausible, given his training as an accountant, and dull enough to deter further enquiry. The same applied to Brisbane. It was large enough to have an extensive ex-pat community, but it didn't have the glamour of Sydney or Melbourne. Jay felt indignant about that. It was a fine city once you got to know it. And Jay did know it. Inside out. When he couldn't sleep he'd got into the habit of logging onto ourbrisbane.com. With the aid of maps and web-cams he wandered the city streets and explored the suburbs. He got to know its people through the profiles that were pasted up. Everything was there on the web, why, you could even call up a list of the new books in Brisbane Central Library. The city was so familiar now that there were times when he almost believed in his past life there.

'Yes?' he said, trying not to sound guarded.

'Did you go out to Lady Elliott Island or Lady Musgrave Island?'

Jay relaxed. He knew the answer to this. 'No, I didn't, but I always meant to. To see the turtles when they come ashore to breed.' Robert beamed at him. 'That's what I want to see. I'll have to make sure that I go at the right time of year.'

'Around November to January. That's the best time to go anyway.' Robert was fascinated by the wildlife and was saving up for a holiday there. At first Jay had thought that Robert's trip was imminent, then that it would take place in a year or two. As he had grown more familiar with the state of Robert's finances, he had begun to wonder if it would ever happen at all. Robert was careful with his money and wrote down everything he spent – Jay had never known anyone keep such meticulous records – but he didn't earn very much.

They went on with the game. Jay found his attention wandering, but he didn't suggest that they finish early. Best to stick to the routine, though he knew he wasn't giving Robert a run for his money.

After Robert had gone, Jay washed up and tidied the

kitchen as he did every night. Like dressing for dinner in the jungle, it was a question of maintaining morale and self-discipline. It was the same with alcohol. When he was alone, which was every night except for chess evenings, he drank half a bottle of wine. Never more. Rarely less. He would decant half and recork the remainder, using a special gadget to expel the air.

Tonight it occurred to him that he had grown more and more like Robert in his reliance on routine and the thought depressed him.

He went upstairs and booted up the computer. He called up a file labelled Australia and typed in 'Have not been to Lady Elliott Island or Lady Musgrave Island.' Robert was sure to ask him again.

He closed the file and sat back to turn things over in his mind yet again. He tested the plan, examining every link. He couldn't set it up on his own, that was always what he came back to and Robert was the only person he could ask. He would have much preferred not to involve anyone else, but Robert's role would be pivotal, even if it did amount to little more than being in the right place at the right time. He didn't see how Robert could come to any harm and it wasn't as if he was asking him to do something wrong, not really.

'It's nothing illegal,' he said aloud, wondering even as he spoke if that was true. There was such a thing as being an accessory after the fact, wasn't there?

There was a ping and a little red number one appeared on the bottom left of the scene.

He clicked on it. It was an e-mail confirmation of his flight to Hong Kong.

He moved on to ourbrisbane.com. There the sun was high and the day was fulfilling its promise. It was comforting to know that in another part of the world people were going about their daily business. If the weather continued like this, the weekend would be perfect for going down to the coast or maybe he would drive out to the West End, browse in the second-hand book shops, visit a Thai restaurant. Or just work in the garden. He had his eye on a house in the property for sale section, white picket fence, a view over the water ...

If he ever managed to get clear of all this, maybe he really would go to Brisbane. Perhaps even with Lisa. But no, he couldn't let himself hope that ...

There was a muted miaow. Without taking his eyes off the screen Jay patted the table. Barrington landed with a soft thud. He curled up in the circle of light from the desk lamp. Outside the stars edged across the velvety darkness. On the other side of the world the sun moved across a cloudless spring sky.

Far into the night the man and the cat kept each other company.

Chapter Ten

Lisa turned over in bed and stretched out a hand to the bedside table. Where there should have been a cup of tea her hand found empty space. She groped about. With a little jarring shock she remembered that Lawrence was dead. Never again would he get up early, make some tea, and leave a cup by her bed. This had happened before: her sleeping self sometimes forgot that Lawrence had gone. She squinted at her alarm clock. Five past seven.

She drew her hand back into warmth of the bed and rolled over onto her back, remembering with a sinking heart that today was her birthday. It was over a week since she had written to Jay and she had heard nothing. Surely today of all days he would find a way to be in touch. It had always been a joke between them that her birthday was on Halloween. He used to tease her about being a Scorpio, passionate and attracted to the dark side.

The phone on the bedside table rang. Lisa rolled over and snatched it up.

'Gotcha! At last!' said a triumphant voice.

Stella. Lisa had so much wanted it to be Jay that she couldn't speak.

'Lisa?'

'Yes, I'm here.'

'Sorry, did I wake you?'

'The alarm would have gone off in a few minutes anyway.'

'I wanted to get hold of you before you could get that bloody answering machine on.'

'I'm sorry. I should have got back to you –'

'Oh, never mind –' Lisa could see her waving a

dismissive hand. 'Now today, your birthday, right? I've booked a table at the Golden Pagoda for 1.00. We'll meet at the Health Club at twelve.'

'Oh, Stella –'

'I'm not talking no for an answer,' the voice warned. 'I've moved heaven and earth to free up a long lunch-hour. See you there.' And she was gone. Lisa put the phone down with a sigh. Stella meant well, and she might even be right. There was quarter of an hour before she had to wake Ricky. No good sitting about brooding. She got up, put on her dressing gown, and went down to the kitchen. She made a cup of coffee, and took it into the sitting room. The surface of the pond was as flat as a pane of glass. Mist was rising off it and drifting between the trees. This was the sort of day Lawrence had loved. And wasn't tomorrow All Saints Day, the day for remembering the dead? That had never meant much to her before. They did these things differently in Catholic countries and made a festival out of visiting family graves. Maybe that was healthier. She wished that Lawrence had a grave, somewhere that she could visit him and take flowers. His will had stipulated that he should be cremated and his ashes scattered on the stream so that they could be carried away and lost in the sea. He had spent some of his happiest hours out there fishing from his little cruiser. But the casket of ashes was still on the chest of drawers in Lawrence's bedroom. And that wasn't all that she'd left undone. There were all his personal papers, letters from her mother, other things; he had wanted her to burn them She didn't want to think about that now. Instead she turned her thoughts to Jay and let herself drift back to the first time they had met. Fate, really, or chance, whatever you wanted to call it. But if they hadn't happened to be in the museum on the same day ...

They'd exchanged comments briefly in front of a display case and she hadn't thought anything of it. Later the bell had rung for closing time. She had gone down to the entrance hall and Jay had been selecting postcards from the rack. He looked round and she saw what hadn't been visible earlier. The left side of his face around his jaw and chin, extending to his lower lip, was pitted and puckered with scar tissue. She looked away a little too quickly and busied herself picking out postcards of her favourite pieces.

The security guard unchained the door and let them out. Outside in Gordon Square the air was thickening into twilight. The rain had eased off to a drizzle. Jay put up the collar of his coat.

He said, 'There's a café round the corner that I often go to ...'

She hesitated. But what did she have ahead of her? A meal alone and a long evening in her hotel room or maybe a trip to the cinema.

There was an awkward little silence as they set off, but then they began to talk about porcelain and it was alright again. In the café he had asked if she liked florentines. When she said yes, he ordered some along with the tea.

She had caught herself glancing at his ring finger – no wedding ring – and pulled herself up short. This wasn't a pick-up. Or was it? It was so long since such a thing had happened that she wasn't sure. Perhaps he was just being friendly.

'Are you married?' he asked. His tone was matter-of-fact.

'Divorced. And you?'

He stumbled a little. 'No. I mean – I'm not married.'

He answered her questions briefly, he was some kind of accountant and travelled a lot, and deftly turned the conversation back in her direction.

She wondered about that now. Why hadn't she pressed him more? But she knew why. She didn't want him to be married.

She'd found herself telling him about Ricky and how once a month at her father's insistence she had a weekend away, sometimes with a friend, sometimes alone, as on this occasion. Again and again her eyes were drawn to his mouth. The damage wasn't much worse than the scars left by a bout of acne. What had caused them – a burn? A car crash? It didn't make him any less attractive. Far from it. She wondered what it would be like to press her lips to that mouth.

His eyes met hers. She felt herself blushing and looked away.

'Do you always spend your weekends off in London?' he asked.

'No, but I will be coming again next time,' she'd said, surprising herself. She hadn't known that until then.

The time came for them to leave the café. He was going to St Pancras to catch a train home to Derbyshire. She needed to go west towards Marylebone High Street. They said their goodbyes and she set off down the pavement. She'd gone about fifty yards when she heard footsteps behind her. He was jogging towards her.

'Your postcards. You left them on the table.' He handed the packet to her,

'Oh. Thanks.'

'Where will you be staying – when you come up again?'

'Durrants on George Street.'

He pressed his lips together and nodded, as if something had been settled between them. Then he turned on his heel and walked away.

When she arrived at the hotel a month later, there was a note waiting for her, and that was how it had begun.

A flash of movement in the garden brought her back to the present and her cooling cup of coffee. She had to look hard to distinguish the ghostly grey form of a heron at the end of the lake. She got the binoculars to have a better look. Lawrence had stocked the pond with trout and used to rush out, arms flailing, to frighten the bird away, but surely its strange, shy beauty was worth the tribute of a fish or two. In China, cranes are regarded as auspicious and that was what she felt about herons. Days when she saw one were days that went well.

She still had her binoculars trained on the bird when its head swivelled. It stretched its wings and, flapping heavily, rose in cumbersome flight. Lisa heard overhead the harsh 'fraank, fraank' of its cry as it settled into a powerful, stately flight and disappeared over the house.

Had something alarmed it? She swung the glasses towards the wood. There, almost concealed by the trunk of a tree, she saw a figure. She had swung the glasses past before she realised what it was. She swung the glasses back. She couldn't see it now. Perhaps she'd been mistaken, but she could see it in her mind's eye: a dark coat, and dark hair. Just a glimpse, but ... She moved the glasses. And then there it was. A shadowy figure, face indistinct, standing among the trees. Her heart lurched.

She went into the kitchen, thrust her bare feet into her wellingtons and shrugged on Lawrence's old coat. She unlocked the door. Piki was at her post by the back door and followed her out. She walked round to the front of the house with the dog at her heels. She scanned the wood. Now that she was outside it was hard to work out exactly where the man had been standing. Mist was drifting through the trees. Surely, surely that wasn't what she had seen?

Piki whined. Lisa glanced at her. The dog was gazing into the wood, every line of her body quivering. Lisa lunged for her collar, but too late, Piki shot off round the pond. She stopped stock-still, her head cocked on one side. She let off a volley of barks and bounded towards the trees, still barking. The hairs stood up on Lisa's arms. These weren't barks of warning, but of recognition. Piki

73

disappeared into the undergrowth.

There was scuffling and more barks, muffled now. By the time Lisa reached the edge of the wood, there was silence. She called Piki's name. There was no response. She took a few hesitant steps towards the place where she had seen the figure. If it had ever been there at all, it had gone now.

And so had Piki.

Chapter Eleven

'I thought it was Lawrence,' Lisa said.

Stella shook her head. 'Look, there are two possibilities: either you imagined it or there really was someone really there. I mean – we don't believe in ghosts, do we?' She patted her hair, still damp from the swimming pool. Her make-up was immaculate and her eyebrows were plucked into shapes that made Lisa think of spiders' legs. How different she and Stella were. Lisa couldn't remember when she had last plucked her eyebrows. Stella was so soignée, Lisa was so ... not.

The waiter arrived.

'Hey, Ed, you look more like Elvis every day,' Stella said to him. He beamed. And it was true, Lisa thought, at least as much as anyone Chinese could look like Elvis, which was actually quite a lot. The heavy, slicked-back, black hair was especially effective.

'I think we'll just have a selection of dim sum. That OK, Lisa?'

Lisa nodded. 'Including *char sui bao,* please.'

'Sure thing,' Ed said and disappeared in the direction of the kitchen.

The restaurant was part typical Chinese restaurant with lots of red plush and scroll pictures of waterfalls and mountains, and part shrine to Elvis. In the background the King was crooning 'Fever'. It took a second look at the photographs that thronged the wall to realise that at least half of them were Ed dressed in a white jump suit covered in diamante and tassels.

'Funny how Elvis impersonators sound more like Elvis than Elvis did,' Stella said. 'Actually Ed's pretty good.

It'll be a dark day for Cantonese cuisine in Barnstable if he ever turns professional. So, what happened about the dog?'

'She was chasing after *something*. She still hadn't come back when I left the house.'

'Rabbits?' Stella suggested.

'Didn't seem like that. You know, before Dad died, I'd have said for sure that I didn't believe in ghosts. But now ...' Lisa shook her head. 'I keep thinking he's in the house somewhere. I almost seem to see him out of the corner of my eye.'

'Have you got rid of any of his things?'

'I haven't even emptied the waste-paper basket in his room. His old gardening shoes are still by the back door.'

Stella nodded. 'You think he might still need them.'

Lisa hadn't expected her to understand. Stella was so practical and unsentimental, a red-hot business woman, who managed an all-female car dealership. They'd met at an Italian evening class. Theirs was an unlikely friendship, but they shared the same ribald sense of humour and they both liked swimming.

'It was like that when my mum died,' Stella went on. 'You can't rush it. You know the worst thing? An old apron hanging on a peg in the kitchen. It was a tatty old thing, but it was ages before I could bring myself to throw it out. Start small, that's the secret and begin with the stuff that you *know* is rubbish.'

Ed arrived with the jasmine tea.

When he had poured it and left, Stella said, 'What you said earlier? *This* time you were sure it was Lawrence. What happened *last* time?'

'Last time? Last time it turned out to be my ex-husband!' She told Stella about Barry's visit.

'You never did tell me why you split up,' Stella said.

Lisa shrugged. 'We hadn't intended to have children and then I got pregnant by accident. When it turned out to be Ricky, Barry couldn't hack it.'

'He cleared off?'

'It wasn't quite like that. He was away in the States a lot on business and then it was easier for me to stay with Dad. After a bit, we gave up the flat in London. At first, when Barry came back he stayed with us.'

'But after a while he stopped coming back.'

'We didn't actually get divorced until Ricky was about five.'

'Did he marry again?'

Lisa shook her head.

Elvis had moved on to 'The Girl of my Best Friend.' Lisa frowned. Something was nudging at her memory.

'He wants you back,' Stella decided.

Lisa couldn't help laughing. For Stella any relationship between a man and a woman had to involve sex in some form or other. She was a serial monogamist, whose men never lasted more than a year or two and she seemed to like it that way.

'Seriously,' Stella said. 'Did he ask if you were with anyone?'

Lisa hesitated.

'He did, didn't he? And what did you say?'

'Told him to mind his own business.'

'Umm. And *are* you with anyone?'

'No!' There was a time early on when she might have told Stella about Jay, but the moment had passed, and she hadn't. She hadn't told anyone, not even Lawrence, and of course not Ricky, though she'd wondered sometimes if Lawrence had guessed.

Stella was eyeing Lisa in a speculative way. 'I just can't believe that there hasn't been anyone since your marriage broke up. I mean, what do you do for sex?'

Ed had appeared behind her with a plate in either hand. He pretended he hadn't heard.

'Prawn dumplings and *char sui bao*. And Chef wants to know if chickens' feet are OK with you ladies?'

77

'Why not?' Lisa said, avoiding Stella's eye. They managed to wait until Ed was out of earshot before they started laughing.

'Seriously though,' Stella said. 'I did wonder about that bloke who drives Ricky to school … '

'Frank! You're way off the mark there. He's just a friend. Stella, you think everything is about sex.'

'Darling, everything IS about sex.' Stella picked up a prawn dumpling with her chopsticks. 'Or money. But look – putting that to one side, I've had a thought. You've already mistaken Barry for your dad once, what if it was Barry again this morning? You didn't really see his face, did you?'

'But why would he –?'

'Obvious – he wants to know whether anyone stays over –'

Ed turned up the music at the precise moment that Elvis launched into 'Such a Night.' Lisa drew in her breath. It was as if someone had punched her in the solar plexus.

Stella looked up from her plate. 'Are you OK?'

'Sorry, got to go.'

'You're as white as a sheet!' Lisa reached for her bag and fumbled in it for her purse.

'Uh, uh,' Stella shook her head. 'My treat. But, Lisa –'

Lisa was on her feet. 'Thanks. I'll see you next week at the pool.'

Stella was rising, too. When Lisa reached the door, she glanced back.

Stella was throwing her napkin on the table. 'Oh, Christ,' Lisa heard her mutter, 'You weren't supposed to leave yet.'

Lisa drove past the turning to Falling Water and pulled into the car park overlooking the great sweep of the Vale of Porlock. The Welsh coast had vanished and veils of rain moved across the sea.

She needed time alone, to think, to remember that first time with Jay in the hotel on the south coast. They were in his room, sitting on the sofa, waiting for room service. The conversation flagged, and she wondered what she was doing here, with this man she hardly knew, even started to wonder if she'd have to make an excuse and leave. And then she asked him what films he enjoyed.

'Mostly old stuff,' he said. 'Truffaut, *The Last Metro,* I watched that the other week and really enjoyed it. And *Rear Window.* And a film I've seen, oh, any number of times – my favourite film really, you probably won't know it ... It's a film from the fifties ...'

'Who's the director?'

'Max Ophuls –'

'It's *Madame de* ...' she said instantly.

He gave a laugh of surprise and delight. 'But how –'

'It's one of my favourite films, too. That part where they're dancing and there's no-one else left in the ballroom.'

'Yes! Even the musicians are leaving –'They were silent for a few moments, then she said, 'You know, in that film Danielle Darrieux was well over thirty.'

'Charles Boyer must have been fifty at least.'

'*And* the lover, Vittorio de Sico.'

'Love's wasted on the young ...' he said, looking into her eyes. His irises were blue, with darker streaks of slate grey. His arm went round her shoulder.

There was a knock on the door and they moved apart.

It was room service. The waiter laid the tea things out on the table and left. Lisa busied herself pouring out.

There was another silence. Lisa cast around for something to say. She noticed Jay's iPod on the table.

'What have you been listening to?' she asked.

'On the way here, Elvis.'

'*Elvis?*' She was surprised 'Oh. I see. Not cool?' He was laughing. 'Had me down as a Bach and Mozart man?

79

Well, I like them, too.' He shook his head. 'It's hard to explain about Elvis if you don't already get it. Here, listen ...' He picked up the iPod, held one of the earpieces to his ear, and fiddled with the controls. He handed her the other earpiece, and she put it to her ear. A moment's silence, then a driving, throbbing beat.

'Great backing band,' Jay commented.

And then Elvis singing 'Such a Night.' It was teasing, playful ... sexy.

She caught Jay's eye, he was grinning, and she, too, was smiling all over her face. Jay got up and pulled her to her feet.

The music filled her head and buoyed her up.

She shifted her weight from foot to foot, swung her shoulders. Jay was swaying, his eyes holding hers. He slipped an arm round her waist and she put her hand on his shoulder. Tethered by the earphones, they rocked to and fro, the iPod held between them. He pulled her in closer, and she relaxed into him, let him steer her round the room in a dance part jive, part tango. His hand was warm in hers, his body solid against hers. His lips brushed her cheek. When had a man last held her like this, she wondered, and then time slipped away. There was no room in her head for anything but the rhythm of the music and the dance.

'Such a night!' Elvis concluded. There was a long drum roll and the track ended.

They pulled back a little. Still in the spell of the music they stood looking into each other's eyes. She put her hand on his face, where the skin was rough and puckered. His lips sought hers and his arms locked round her. They toppled onto the bed.

Such a night indeed.

That had been three years ago, and now she was alone in a parked car with rain running down the windows, waiting to go back to an empty house.

At the end of *Madame de ...* the lovers die. Elvis's night of love turned out to be a one-night stand. Oh God ...

No use to ask herself now why she hadn't tried to find out more about Jay's past or his life away from her. She had known instinctively that if she pressed too hard she would lose him. But it was true, too, that she hadn't really wanted to know more. It suited her, because of the other part of the unspoken agreement. That Jay in his turn wouldn't make too many demands. That he would be content to let Ricky remain at the centre of her life. How many men would have been satisfied to play second fiddle like that?

She sighed and looked at her watch. More time had gone by than she had realised and she'd have to hurry to be back in time for Ricky.

On the way down the track she stopped to look in the mail box. Three white envelopes: the handwriting and the postmarks told her that one was from an old school friend in Shropshire, another from a cousin in Ireland. The hand writing on the last card looked familiar, too, and there was a London postmark. Jay? She ripped it open. On the front was a reproduction of a Chinese water-colour and inside was written 'best from Barry'.

Her heart sank and she was frowning as she drove off down the track. It was years since Barry had sent her a birthday card. Surely Stella couldn't be right about him? She shook her head, dismissing the idea. Hanging around her house? Stalking her? It just wasn't like Barry. At least not like the Barry she had known, but how well did she know him now? Dusk was falling. The darkness between the trees was almost tangible. When she reached the house, there were no lights on. Ricky wasn't home yet. As she got out of the car, she looked around, wondering if someone was out there, watching her. She called Piki, her voice sounding overloud in the silence, but the dog hadn't returned.

81

When she let herself into house, it seemed emptier than ever. As she stood there with her hand on the door, the silence closed in around her.

Tears pricked her eyelids. Better get a grip on herself, she didn't want Ricky to arrive home and see that she had been crying on her birthday. She picked up the kettle. It was warm. She laid her hand against the metal. Not just warm, but hot. It had boiled very recently. She wasn't alone in the house.

Common sense asserted itself. Since when did burglars settle down and make themselves a nice cup of tea? Ricky must be home after all, though surely Frank wouldn't have left him alone and why was the house dark?

She opened the door to the dining room and reached for the light.

Another hand got there first.

Chapter Twelve

She found herself looking into the smiling face of Peony. Behind her, sitting round the table were Ricky, Frank, Charlotte, and Stella.

Ricky grinned and pressed a button on his voice aid.

'Happy birthday,' Marilyn Monroe sang in her breathless, little-girl voice, 'Happy birthday, Mr President, happy birthday to you.'

The others joined in the chorus.

On the table were plates of sandwiches, smoked salmon and egg mayonnaise, bowls of crisps, and a sumptuous chocolate birthday cake with four-and–a-half candles on it, the half made by breaking a candle in two.

There was a bottle of champagne in an ice-bucket. Frank seized the bottle and drew out the cork with a flourish and a pop. Peony held out two glasses for the overflow.

'The candles,' said Ricky.

'I'll do it,' said Charlotte. She took out a cigarette lighter.

As usual she was dressed all in black and since Lisa had last seen her she had shaved her eyebrows. Narrow black lines were painted in their place and there was black eye-liner on both upper and lower lids.

'You look like Cleopatra,' Frank told Charlotte. 'Or Nefertiti.'

Charlotte grinned, flicked open the cigarette lighter, and lit the candles. Peony turned the lights off. The little flames, reflected in the window, hovered in the dusk above the lake. Lisa leaned forward, took a deep breath and blew the candles out.

Peony switched the lights back on.

'Charlotte made the cake,' Ricky said.

'I can't believe you've done all this …'

'Well, you did say that you wanted a surprise.' He was beaming, so pleased with himself that Lisa had a lump in her throat.

'And that's not all.' He gestured towards his wheelchair tray. There was a small oblong parcel wrapped up in shocking pink paper. Lisa opened it. 'Oh, Ricky, a new mobile.'

'It does everything, takes photos, internet access, *everything*.' Lisa couldn't help smiling to herself. This wasn't her idea of the ideal present, it was Ricky's, but that didn't matter. He was looking anxiously at her.

'Darling, it's perfect. You'll have to show me how it all works later.'

'As long as you promise to get rid of that piece of obsolete technology you've been calling a phone!'

Peony cut the cake into thick wedges and handed them out. Charlotte took Ricky's plate and a fork and organised them on his tray.

Frank handed Lisa a glass of champagne. He picked up one for himself and they clinked glasses. Lisa took a gulp of champagne. It had an instant effect, as if the sinews in her legs had been loosened.

Charlotte was gesticulating in a theatrical way and Stella and Ricky were laughing at something she was saying.

A sobering thought struck Lisa. Had she so few friends that Charlotte had been necessary to make up the numbers? Her life hadn't seemed empty with Ricky and Lawrence and Jay in it, and there had been her work, and Stella, but now …

'Have you met Charlotte's mum?' Frank asked in a low voice.

She shook her head.

'Ah, they're a lovely family. Her mum's a physiotherapist. She fosters difficult teenagers.'

Lisa gave Frank a sideways look. She found herself appraising him in the light of what Stella had said. The fair hair, scanty on top, the steel-rimmed glasses, the pink, pudgy face: he wasn't bad-looking exactly, he just wasn't her type. His wife had died about five years ago. In order to nurse her he had taken early retirement from his job lecturing in maths as the local FE college and now drove the mini-bus to keep busy. He was a decent chap, and lonely, she suspected, but they didn't have anything in common except their children.

That reminded her. 'How's Alice?' she asked.

His face lit up. 'Just had her home for half-term. She's loving it at Portland.'

His own daughter was a couple of years older than Ricky, and was more seriously disabled. She was at a residential college in the Midlands. That might be a good place for Ricky when he left school ...

Frank was saying something.

'Sorry?' Lisa said.

Frank cleared his throat. 'If you need anything doing around the house ... any little job ... '

He didn't meet her eye. Probably didn't want her to think he was making a move on her? Maybe he was! Though that thought wouldn't even have occurred to her if it hadn't been for Stella, damn her. She gave herself a mental shake.

'That's good of you, Frank. There isn't anything just at the moment, but I'll be sure to let you know.'

'Lawrence's cruiser. I don't know if you're planning to sell it.'

'Sooner or later, I guess.'

'I've got a friend who'd like first refusal – would give you a good price.' Her rational mind knew it made sense to sell. It was what Lawrence would have wanted. He

85

would have hated to think of the boat getting mildewed and neglected.

'If you'd like me to clear it out for you, just say the word … I know how hard it can be. After my Jenny died...'

The cruiser did need clearing out. Lawrence kept a spare set of clothes there. Books. Some of his fishing things ... But a voice inside her was crying, *not yet, not yet*. Frank must have seen that in her face. He put a hand on her arm. 'No hurry is there?' He made a show of looking at his watch. 'God, is that the time? Best be off.'

'I said I'd give Charlotte a lift. Come on, Cleo,' he called across the room. 'Your carriage awaits. Or do I mean your burnished barge?'

Charlotte put her tongue out at him.

He grinned at Lisa. 'Did *Anthony and Cleopatra* for O level many moons ago. "The barge she sat in, like a burnish'd throne, burn'd on the water ... Age cannot wither her, nor custom stale her infinite variety." Great stuff.'

Maybe there was more to Frank than met the eye.

Stella and Peony left, too. After the mini-bus had disappeared, Lisa lingered outside. She needed a few moments alone. The euphoria brought about by the surprise and the champagne was draining away. Her birthday was nearly over – and nothing from Jay.

A shape detached itself from the mass of trees and trotted across the lawn. Piki! She slunk up to Lisa, head and tail drooping, every inch of her eloquent of abject apology.

Lisa shook her head. 'Where've you been, you bad girl?'

The dog thrust a wet nose into her hand and followed her back into the kitchen.

Peony had arranged the birthday cards on the window sill in the dining room. Lisa saw that Ricky was looking at the

86

one with the Chinese watercolour.

'Who's that from, Ma?' She didn't say anything. He manoeuvred his wheelchair round the table and reached for the card.

'Oh, it's from …' his voice trailed off. Lisa hadn't encouraged him to refer to Barry as Dad. It implied a relationship that she felt didn't really exist.

Ricky was looking at her, expecting her to say something. That was the moment when she could have told him about his father's visit, but she didn't.

'Got homework to do?' she asked.

He nodded. 'Yeah, oh, and I need money for that trip.'

'How much?'

'The form's in my bag, and there's something that you've got to sign.'

She delved into the canvas bag that was always slung on the back of the wheelchair. 'Don't you ever clear this out?' she asked.

She took the bag off the wheelchair and tipped a litter of papers and pens onto the table.

'Hey, this Swedish one is mine,' she said.

'Don't take that one. That's my lucky pen.'

'Your lucky pen?'

'Well, maybe it isn't lucky yet, but I'm going to train it up.'

She balanced it on her palm. There *was* something attractive about it. She felt a reluctance to hand it over. A bit childish, but …

'Please,' he wheedled. 'I'll swap you: a pen with 'A Present from Blackpool' on it *and* one advertising Scotch whisky.'

'No deal, but I'll let you borrow it,' she decided. As she sorted through the papers, her eye was caught by an envelope that had come through the post and was addressed to her. It was a credit card statement.

'What's this doing in your bag?'

'Meant to give you that,' Ricky muttered. 'We took it out of the box as we came down … '

'Oh no, you didn't. I checked the box myself on my way down.'

She ripped open the envelope and took out the statement.

This was the card she kept in her office drawer and used for internet purchases. There shouldn't have been more than a hundred pounds on it, yet there was a balance of £5,482 outstanding. She scanned the list of items. They were mostly credited to something called Second Life.

She looked up at Ricky. His face was screwed up in a grimace that was all too familiar: a mixture of guilt and embarrassment at being found out.

'I can explain everything,' he said.

'I'm waiting.'

'It's an investment, really. You'll get it all back, I promise. You see, I needed to buy land –'

'*Land*!'

'Well, virtual land, and I'm going to build on it – I've already designed my own house – and then I'll sell it on –' The words tumbled out as he hurried to explain.

'You've spent £5,000 on a game! £5,000 of *my* money.'

'Not a *game*!'

'Ricky. You took my credit card!' Anger was seizing her and bearing her up like a wind. It was almost exhilarating. 'That is stealing!'

'I knew you wouldn't say yes. That's why I had to do it!'

'You'll have to pay me back!'

'I told you, when I sell the houses –'

She didn't know whether to laugh or cry at his naivety. 'No, Ricky. You'll have to pay me back now – it'll have to come out of the money Laurence left in trust for you.'

'Oh, fine –'

'And I'm banning you from the internet for a week! And after that a curfew of ten o'clock. From now on, I am going to keep a very close eye on what you're up to.'

'What!' He was outraged. 'It's private. I can't have you looking over my shoulder all the time. That's gross!'

'You should have thought of that before you abused my trust.'

Ricky spun the wheels of his wheelchair and scooted past her.

'Where are you going, young man?'

'Nowhere!'

Chapter Thirteen

And that, sadly, was the truth: there was nowhere for him to go. He couldn't storm off, slamming the door behind him, or take the dog out and walk off his rage. She thought of her own teenage years: the brooding walks, the hours spent sulking in the tree house. Even a single week without the internet was a huge deprivation for Ricky, because what else had he got –

Lisa shuffled the pack of cards and laid them out for a game of 'Miss Milligan'. A few hands of patience might help to settle her down. She was exhausted, but she knew she wouldn't be able to sleep.

After a few minutes she put the cards down. She couldn't concentrate. She kept remembering the raised voices, Ricky's face contorted with anger. If only Lawrence were here. They hadn't always seen eye to eye, but he would have known how to deal with Ricky. It was the kind of thing he was good at. Nothing had gone right since he had died. At times like this Lisa missed her mother, too, even though she scarcely remembered her. She had died when Lisa was only four. Lawrence had never married again.

The phone rang, making her start. Lisa looked at her watch. Eleven thirty. It was still her birthday. Could it be Jay?

It was a man's voice and for a moment she thought it *was* Jay. At first she couldn't understand what he was saying.

'Lisa, look, I'm sorry to bother you, but is Peony there?'

Her heart sank. Not Jay after all. It was Gavin, Peony's

husband.

'Lisa? Are you there?'

'Yes ... but Peony left hours ago.'

'She was going on to a client in Porlock after your party, but she was supposed to be home by half ten. I wondered if she'd stopped off at your place –'

'Do you think she's had a breakdown?'

'She'd have rung ... '

'You know what mobile reception's like out here. She might be struggling to change a tyre even as we speak.'

'I can't leave the kids ...'

Lisa hesitated. But after all, Ricky would be OK for half an hour on his own. 'Tell you what, I'll drive over the top and have a look.'

'You're a star.'

Ricky was reading Terry Pratchett in bed when she went in. He gave her a wan smile. She recognised it and knew what it meant: he *was* sorry, even though he wasn't ready to admit it. She told him what had happened. 'I won't be long. You'll be OK, won't you?'

'Oh, Mum ...' He rolled his eyes.

'I'll leave Piki here.'

'No, take her with you.' Still she hesitated. 'I won't be long.'

'Mum! Just GO. I've got the phone here if I need it. Which I won't.' Outside Lisa stood for a moment taking in the sounds and sights of the night. A full moon somewhere over the ridge was flooding the landscape with a pallid light. The wind was soughing in the trees. Far out in the Bristol Channel she saw the lights of a large ship.

Piki was thrilled by the unexpected treat and pranced at Lisa's heels. Before Lawrence died, Lisa had occasionally gone to an evening class in Lynton – Yoga, Local History – but she couldn't remember when she had last been out at night. She caught some of Piki's excitement at the novelty of it.

She drove up the twisting track to the main road, the beams of her headlight sending shafts of light between the trees.

Left to Porlock or right to Lynton and Lynmouth? If Peony had got stranded near Porlock, she could have walked down to the town where there was mobile reception. So it made more sense to go right towards Lynton.

Gusts of wind buffeted the car and tugged at the steering. The moon threw the shadows of bare gnarled beech hedges across the road. The road down to Lynmouth was notoriously steep. Lisa crawled down in second gear, turned into the car park at the bottom, and crawled back up. There was no sign of Peony.

She retraced her route back to the turn off to Falling Water. A few miles further and she breasted a rise in the road. The great sweep of the vale of Porlock came into view. The sea shimmered in the moonlight and lights glimmered on the Welsh coast.

She drove down to Porlock. It was only twenty to twelve, but most of the lights were out in the little town. She parked in the car park, got out her mobile and rang Gavin, hoping that he would say that Peony was there, maybe she would even answer the phone herself. She didn't and Gavin's voice was terse with worry. He said he'd ring the police. She restrained herself from ringing Ricky. He'd only think she was fussing and she'd be back in under fifteen minutes.

Peony couldn't have vanished into thin air on the road between Porlock and Lynton. She had to be *somewhere*. There was a pub, not far from the turn off to Falling Water. What if Peony had stopped there for some reason? She'd check the pub and then go home.

But when Lisa turned into the car park, it was empty and the windows of the pub were dark.

As she accelerated away a black-and-white shape

appeared on the road in front of her. She braked and the badger disappeared into the undergrowth. As she pulled away, she wondered if something like this had happened to Peony? Every now and then serious accidents were caused by red deer. She drove slowly back towards Porlock, with her eyes fixed on the road. It wasn't long before she found what she was looking for. On the right-hand side, just where a narrow road turned off to the Oare valley, there were skid marks. Someone had lost control of a car and had used the lane as a run-off.

Lisa pulled up and fumbled in the glove compartment for a torch. She got out of the car with Piki at her heels. She shone her torch down the lane, following the trajectory of the flattened grass on the verge. She began to run, the wind whipping her hair around her face and tugging at her clothes. Piki raced ahead of her. There were more skid marks, but still no car. Lisa shouted 'Peony! Peony!' and the wind snatched the words from her mouth. She swung the torch from side to side catching glimpses of twisted beech trees and patches of gorse.

Somewhere ahead, Piki was barking, a commanding staccato. Lisa caught up with her, the dog whined, and shot off down a shallow, leaf-strewn slope that ended in a cluster of trees. There was the scent of crushed grass. Lisa followed her, slipping and sliding on the leaves. The beam of the torch jerked wildly about.

She caught a glimpse of something white and her heart missed a beat.

There, wedged upside-down in the writhing branches of an ancient beech, was Peony's car.

Chapter Fourteen

They say all international airports look the same. Maybe so, but they don't all smell the same. There was the faintest scent of something spicy and familiar. Jay couldn't think what it was. Hoisin sauce? Five-spice? Or an amalgam of several different things?

It was 11.30 in the morning Hong Kong time, and he had been travelling for nineteen hours. He didn't like flying. Airports were dangerous places. You never knew who you might run into and the bigger the airport, the greater the risk. That was why he had flown from Manchester, changing planes at Frankfurt. Only a handful of other passengers had made the transfer: a couple with two young children and a group of three middle-aged women, over-dressed and over-made-up. He'd gathered from their conversation that they were going to Hong Kong for a weekend's shopping.

He caught the express train into the city, through suburbs of immensely tall, slender tower blocks. Tiredness and jet lag made everything seem at one remove, as though it were being unscrolled on a screen in front of him. Hot air, heavy with moisture, enveloped him as he left the station in the centre of Hong Kong. In Manchester it had been bitterly cold.

He got a taxi to a hotel in the Causeway Bay area.

It was a relief to find himself in his hotel room. He took off his money belt with its stash of Hong Kong dollars and locked it in the safe. He collapsed on the bed, intending to sleep for just an hour, but it was four o'clock when he woke up. He'd dribbled on the pillow and his mouth was dry. He got up and went over to the window. He was on the 21st floor. Far below in the narrow street traffic crawled along. Directly opposite were the windows of a dilapidated block of flats, their balconies crowded with junk and festooned with washing. There was a kettle and a basket of tea-bags, sachets of coffee, and so on. He made himself a cup of tea – Tetley, of all things – and that was comforting. He had a shower. By the time he left the hotel it had begun to drizzle and it was like stepping into a sauna. The evening streets were crammed with jostling crowds and bobbing umbrellas. Little shops and workshops and restaurants were open to the street. Fish swam in polystyrene trays of water on the pavement. The only place he'd visited that was so densely populated was New York, but New York had a kind of airiness, long vistas opening out in every direction. Hong Kong was closed in and claustrophobic.

He hadn't thought he could miss Lisa more than he already did. Now he knew his mistake. At home when the sun set and the moon rose they were setting and rising for her, too. Now she was half a world away under a different sky. And yet everything here made him think of her. How fascinating she would have found it all and what a useful companion she would have been with her command of Chinese.

He was too tired and disorientated to walk far or choose a restaurant. He went back to the hotel, ate a meal of decent Cantonese food from the buffet and went to bed early.

He dropped off almost immediately into a kind of half-sleep. Splinters of ideas and images were thrown up into his consciousness but he couldn't complete a train of thought or arrange the images into a narrative. He muttered in protest. He craved the oblivion of real sleep and at last he sank down to somewhere warm and dark. And oh, the inexpressible comfort and relief: Mia was sleeping beside him, they were in the house in Chiswick and he knew that in the next room Sam was asleep beneath his duvet with the design of planets and space-rockets. Everything was alright, it was fine, it was wonderful. Then in the way that things happen in dreams he was no longer in bed, but standing in the street outside Frida and Lars's house. It was an intensely still moonlit night and he could see that the front door was open. A feeling of dread was rising up from the pit of his stomach. He knew what was going to happen, but was powerless to escape from the dream. Against his will, his feet took him forward up the steps and in through the door. He climbed the stairs, his heart thumping to the rhythm of his steps, on and on, up and up, it went on forever and yet all too soon he had reached the top floor and another open door. He wanted to back away, but he was carried inexorably forward. Inside the room lay the body of a woman. Moonlight streamed through the window onto blonde hair streaked with blood. The beautiful carpet was soaked with it.

It was always at that moment that it struck him with the force of a blow: there was a killer on the loose and he had left Mia and Sam unprotected. He turned and ran down the stairs, but they stretched on and on, down and down; he ran and ran, but got no nearer to the bottom. Some part of his mind understood that he was dreaming and with a tremendous effort he willed himself to reach the door. He ran out into the street. The door to his house was open, wide open, and he knew what he would find inside—

'No! No! No!'

He was sitting up in bed, a hand to his heart, his whole body shuddering. He groped for the light – the wrong side of the bed – finally found it and the room was flooded with light.

He lay back down and let his heart rate settle.

He hadn't been the one to discover Frida's body – that had been the nanny – and it hadn't been a still moonlight night, either. It had been pouring with rain. And yet the dream was always as he had dreamt it tonight. He hadn't had it for months. It used to come almost every night, making him afraid to go to sleep. But he wasn't sorry that he had dreamed it tonight. It reminded him of what he had lost and of the justice that was owed Mia and Sam – and to Frida.

The next morning on the street outside the hotel he boarded one of the narrow, clanking trams going west and an hour later got off in the district called Sheung Wan. He consulted his street map and headed south to Hollywood Road. It was lined with furniture and antique shops of all kinds. He paused to look in one window and saw that it specialised in making coffins. Now that he looked more closely at the other shop windows he saw they too were offering coffins and wreaths and funeral paraphernalia. Everything the well-dressed corpse could require.

He walked briskly on until he found the number he was looking for.

The man pored over the photographs. It would not be easy, Jay knew that. The painting, the glaze, the mark, the weight, the condition of the foot rim, all these had to convince.

'Ah, very fine,' the man said, without looking up. He was dressed Western-style in a business-suit, his black hair sleeked back. His name was Li, a very common name, much the same as being called Smith in English. Of course he was only the middleman. '*Fencai*. How you say?' He clicked his fingers, searching for the word. 'Ah, yes, *famille rose*. Qianlong mark. Very good, very fine. And the date?'

'Around 1740, 1750.'

'Ah yes. One very like this was sold at Sotheby's in Singapore in the 1980s, I believe.' He lifted his head a fraction and caught Jay's eye. 'It is – how do you say it? –

ah, yes, museum quality. Indeed I think the purchaser donated it to a museum?'

Jay's heart gave a lurch. He kept his face impassive and held the man's gaze.

The man stared blandly back at him. Then he sat back in his chair and cleared his throat. 'We do not make fakes, I must make that clear. We make facsimiles; they are not intended to deceive.'

'I understand. Your man can do it?'

The man gave him a long look. What he saw must have satisfied him, for he nodded. 'He can. For the price we agreed. There will be differences, small, but ... mmm.' He hunted for a word. 'Significant, yes. Someone who is expert, even, does not see straight away, but after a time, yes. You understand?'

'That is precisely what I want. You know I want two copies?'

'That is understood.'

'I have my flight booked back to England for next Monday.'

'A week. It is enough.'

He spent that week as a tourist. What else was there to do? He caught the funicular railway to Victoria Peak up an incline so steep that gravity pressed you against the back of the seat. In the zoo he stood for a long time looking at the caged monkeys. One day he took an underground train to the end of the line to see the Hakka walled village. He was the only person there and wandered alone through the little white-washed rooms and the courtyards with their collections of furniture and agricultural equipment. After three attempts, he managed to find a taxi driver who understood enough English to take him to the Taoist monastery in the hills above the town. It was swelteringly hot and he moved from one patch of shade to the next. In the courtyard there was a furnace in which people were burning pretend money and garishly coloured paper cars and houses as gifts to the ancestors.

Jay thought about Sam, who would remain forever a tousle-haired ten-year old. Jay bought a paper aeroplane to send to him in the afterlife, and flung it into the flames, eliciting sympathetic nods and smiles from the other visitors.

Without a word Mr Li handed him a bowl and he received it in his cupped hands.

It was cool to the touch. The weight was right and the feel of it. He lifted it up to the light. It was translucent, of course, but it was the quality of the translucence that mattered – the exact tint of milky blue.

He traced the sinuous pattern of flowering peach branches. It was beautiful, the way they curled over the edge of the bowl in what was almost a trompe l'oeil effect.

'Remarkable,' he murmured.

He examined the foot rim. That was always the first place that he looked. If it looked too clean and unblemished, he was suspicious, but this had just the right amount of wear.

He was handling the bowl as if it had been made in the Emperor's factory over two centuries ago instead of in a workshop in Hong Kong last week. A thought struck him. If a fake is indistinguishable from the original, if no-one can tell the difference, then in what way is it less valuable than the original? Of course given time and the right level of expertise one would be able to tell the difference ...

Mr Li still had not spoken a word. Jay looked at him now and their eyes met.

For a moment they were simply two men united in their appreciation of a piece of fine craftsmanship.

'It is fine, yes?' said Mr Li.

'It's perfect.'

Chapter Fifteen

Lisa was down on her hands and knees, scrubbing the kitchen floor. Better to do something, anything, rather than sit at her desk, unable to work, unable to stop worrying.

Peony was hanging on – but only just. It was five days since the accident and she still hadn't come round. They didn't know how much brain damage there was. They'd transferred her to a special unit for head injuries in Bristol. And on top of that there was all the other stuff. Two broken legs, a broken arm and a fractured collar-bone.

Lisa sat back on her heels and wrung out the cloth in the bucket. She was so tired. Nights were a jumble of flashbacks and bad dreams. Those moments when she had clambered up to Peony's car had seemed to pass in slow-motion. When she saw Peony's face striped with blood, her leg trapped by the concertinaed car, Lisa had thought she was dead. Then she'd managed to find a pulse. And now she found herself reliving again and again the events of that night. She had only to close her eyes to see the throbbing light of the ambulance, saw Peony, eyes closed, lips blue, her body limp on the stretcher, Gavin walking beside her, hair dishevelled, face haggard.

But she had no memory at all of driving home after that, though she remembered looking at a clock when she got in. Two o'clock in the morning. Where had all that time gone? Lisa squirted detergent on the floor and bent again to her task.

And still nothing from Jay, still no answer to her letter, zero, zilch, absolutely nothing. For all she knew he could have vanished off the face of the earth. She rubbed ferociously at a grease spot. No Lawrence, no Peony, no

101

Jay – and without Peony she couldn't go looking for Jay – her whole world was falling apart.

Piki give a low growl.

Lisa looked up. She gasped. A man was standing in the kitchen door, silhouetted against the light. She jerked back and knocked the bucket. It tipped over sending a tide of soap suds across the floor.

'Oh, hell, sorry, I startled you.' It was Barry. 'Here let me help you with that.' He grabbed a teacloth, squatted down and began to mop up the water.

Lisa straightened up. 'What are you *doing* here?'

All at once, she wanted to cry.

He rocked back on his heels and looked at her. 'Hey, what's the matter? It's only a bit of water.'

'It's not that.'

'Is it Ricky?' He looked alarmed.

She blinked hard, fighting down the tears. 'No, no, he's alright. But what are you *doing* here? And why didn't you knock?'

'I did knock. No reply, and then I thought that seeing as how you were expecting me –'

'What?'

'You did get my e-mail?' Maybe she had at that. She couldn't remember. Lisa put her hand to her head. 'It's been a hell of a week. Ricky's nurse, Peony, she's had a bad accident.'

'Hey, I'm sorry. Will she be OK?'

'Too soon to know.'

'I could come back?'

'No, no.' *Let's get it over with.*

They both got to their feet.

'You don't look too good.' Barry said. 'How about I make you some tea?'

'No, no. I'll do it.'

She went over to the sink and filled the kettle. She plugged it in and stood looking out of the window, giving herself a few moments to compose herself. The Welsh coast had disappeared and rain was pockmarking the surface of the pond.

When she turned, Barry was sitting at the kitchen table. She sat down opposite.

'Are you sure you're OK?' he asked.

'I'm fine.' There was silence.

'Oh hell,' Barry said. 'Why don't I cut to the chase? Ricky'll be leaving school in a couple of years. Why shouldn't he study in the States?'

She stared at him.

The kettle reached the boil and turned itself off with a click.

'What are you *talking* about?'

'There are some great courses. MIT, North-Western –'

'It doesn't matter what the courses are like! This is Ricky we're talking about – he could no more just take off for the States than he could – oh, fly to the moon!'

'Are you so sure of that? Look, for Christ's sake, hear me out at least. 'I know what you're going to say –' he raised his hand, 'about him not being able to live independently. We could make that possible, or if not he could stay with me –'

Lisa couldn't stay silent any longer. 'You don't know what you're talking about,' she burst out.

'I can't understand your taking this attitude, Lisa. You worked so hard to keep him in mainstream education –'

'You haven't a clue. You haven't been in touch with Ricky for years and –'

'Actually that's not strictly true –'

'What?'

Barry spread his hands. 'I'll come clean. We've been in e-mail contact.'

She couldn't believe what she was hearing. 'Since when?'

'Since the beginning of the summer.'

'Behind my back! How dare you!'

'I didn't, at least – look, it was Ricky who made the first move. He e-mailed me the address of his website. I suppose he didn't tell you because he thought you wouldn't approve. And he was right, wasn't he?'

'Damn right he was!'

'I took a look, and liked what I saw. It went on from there. We've been e-mailing each other about once a week. Mostly technical stuff.'

So that was another reason why Ricky hadn't wanted her to see what was on his computer screen.

'Look, honey –' Barry began.

'Don't call me that!'

'OK, OK.' He put up his hands. 'So I behaved badly, I admit it, and I'm not proud of it. If it makes you feel any better, I'll admit that I might not be so keen to make up for lost time if Ricky wasn't a computer geek.'

'He's not a geek!'

'OK, OK, mathematically gifted, whatever. Looking at things long-term, who knows, there could be an opening for him in the business. But I don't want to get ahead of myself. All I want for now is to get to know him a bit better.'

'It's too late, Barry!'

'Suppose everything you think is true. That I'm a total shit and I'm only doing this because there's something in it for me. But just think about it: there's something in it for Ricky, too: opportunities that he won't get here. He's been dealt a pretty shabby hand and –'

'And not the least shabby part of it was having a father who couldn't stand the sight of him.'

That hit home. Barry flushed and then went white. She thought he was going to snap back, but he made a visible effort to control himself.

'You're so sure, aren't you, that it was all my fault that our marriage ended?'

'You abandoned us!'

'Every time I came home, it was less *like* home. I know Ricky needed you, but you squeezed me out. You and Ricky were in your own little world. I might have done more if –'

The phone rang. For a few moments they stood and let it ring.

Lisa said, 'I'd better take it – Peony –'

'There's no point anyway in raking it all over. I'll go now, but this isn't the end of it, Lisa. I have some rights and I intend to exercise them.'

He turned to go and as Lisa picked up the receiver, the door slammed behind him.

Chapter Sixteen

Lisa was still seething as she headed north on the M1 two days later. She didn't know whether she was angrier with Barry or with Ricky for going behind her back. She hadn't spoken to Ricky about it yet. She wasn't sure how to handle the situation. Ricky was already sulking about being deprived of the internet. A blazing row was the last thing she wanted at the moment with everything else she'd got on her plate. But she couldn't put it off indefinitely. Barry wasn't going to back off, she knew him well enough to be sure of that.

She spotted a police car up ahead and glanced at the speedometer. God, she was doing nearly ninety and she hadn't even realised! She put the brakes on and resolved to pay more attention.

One stroke of luck: it had been Frank on the phone. He had been ringing to tell her that quite by chance he'd met someone who was keen to pick up some part-time nursing. Her name was Karen, a really nice woman, well qualified, too. He had got talking to her in a pub a few weeks ago. Her mother lived in Barnstaple, had been ill, was convalescent now. She didn't need Karen's full-time attention, but Karen wasn't comfortable about going back home to Scotland just yet. The work with Ricky was exactly what she was looking for. Lisa had followed up one of her references, some London business man whose wife had required nursing, and he spoke highly of her.

It felt disloyal, somehow, taking Karen on, but Lisa was desperate to drive up to Derbyshire and it would be months before Peony came back to work – Lisa pushed to one side the thought that perhaps she never would. The brain scan had shown that the damage wasn't as great as the doctors had feared; on the other hand, she was still unconscious, no-one was quite sure why. They just kept saying that the recovery from this kind of injury was unpredictable. Gavin was beside himself with worry and Peony's mother had come down from London to look after the children.

Lisa turned off the motorway, drove through the market town of Chesterfield with its crooked spire, and struck out across the moors. She drove through Eyam, a picturesque little place. The name rang a bell. She turned up a winding road that led up on open moorland.

There was an information board by the side of the road. She pulled up and got out of the car. She was near Jay's house now. She needed time to compose herself and gather her thoughts. She looked around taking it all in. Jay must have seen all this hundreds, even thousands, of times. On the summit of the hill was a low, ruined building with a high chimney, the remains of some mining endeavour. A kestrel hovered, the only living thing in sight. She read the board. Eyam was the village that had cut itself off when plague had arrived in the seventeenth century. The population had been decimated but the neighbouring villages had been saved. This was Mompesson's Well where the villagers had left money soaked in vinegar in return for food and other provisions.

She drove on and found the turning she was looking for. The road wound down the side of a hill through plantations of conifer with glimpses of the valley spread out below. The road got smaller, until she was down to one lane with passing places and plenty of pot-holes. Any moment now ...

She turned a bend and her heart lurched. Next to a five-barred gate set back from the road there was a For Sale sign.

She pulled onto the verge and parked. She walked over

to the gate. It was green with lichen, and was secured by a heavy rusted chain. But the padlock itself, positioned so that it wasn't visible from the road, was shiny. She locked the car and climbed over the gate. Good job she was wearing jeans and sturdy shoes. The track wound into the wood. It was muddy, the ruts filled with water. She inhaled the creosote aroma of pine-needles, sharp and penetrating.

Her heart thumping, she made her way up the track, turned a bend, and found herself in a clearing.

And there it was: Deepdale Lodge, a narrow tower of grey stone, three stories high. She spotted in the distance some tumbled walls, the remains of a chimney. There had once been a big house and this tower had been built as a folly, an eye-catcher. Somewhere there was the trickle of a stream and she heard a bird calling.

To one side of the house was an area of flattened grass. There were oil stains in the middle, not recent by the look of them. There was no car in sight.

She went up to the house and rattled the door knocker, but she wasn't really expecting anyone to be there. She didn't think anyone had been there for a while. The house looked withdrawn and lonely. Through a little window beside the door she saw a stone-flagged floor, a kelim rug in faded colours, a coat tree from which hung an old raincoat and an anorak. They didn't look like things Jay would wear.

A stone spiral staircase with a rope hand rail wound up out of view. A door opened off to one side and when Lisa followed the wall round she saw a window of frosted glass: a lavatory or a bathroom.

She went back to the front door and tried it. It was locked. What now? She looked at her watch. One o'clock. Karen was staying until eight, so Lisa should leave by three thirty, just to be on the safe side. Should she go to the estate agent's and see what she could find out there? She walked round the tower and found the remains of a walled garden: tangled rose bushes, overgrown bushes of lavender and rosemary. Against the garden wall was a ramshackle shed with a door so warped that she struggled to open it. There were a few rusty tools, flower-pots, shelves and shelves of ancient Kilner jars containing nuts and screws. Was this the sort of place where someone might hide a spare key? She remembered a holiday she had had with Lawrence, years ago in a house in Cornwall, lent to them by an architect friend. They had been given instructions that the spare key was hidden in the garden shed in a jar of screws. She examined the glass jars, turned them this way and that. There were a couple of dozen at least. *Well, Lawrence, where is it? If you're there somewhere, why don't you nudge me in the right direction?* Her eye fell on a jar half full of long nails. She took it outside, unscrewed the lid and spread the contents across one of the flagstones.

There in the midst of the nails was a long-shafted key.

She went back to the door of the house. She hesitated. It felt wrong to be doing this, but she had to know what had happened to Jay.

She took one last look around, and put the key in the lock. She took a deep breath and turned the key. It engaged readily, but the door was stiff. She gave it a firm push and stepped inside. It was cold and the air felt stale, unused. She had a bad feeling about this. She closed the door behind her, feeling like one of those bold girls in fairy tales: Goldilocks or Bluebeard's wife. Or maybe Alice in Wonderland.

She pushed open the door she had seen through the window. It was a bathroom, a very small one with a half-length bath. It was completely bare: no towel, or bathmat, not even a sliver of soap. She turned the tap on the basin. Nothing came out. The water must have been turned off.

She was half-way up the spiral staircase before some instinct told her to lock the front door behind her. She did that, went back up the stairs, and pushed open the door at the top. At first glance it was a perfectly ordinary room, with a carpet, curtains, a table by the window, a sofa and some easy chairs, and a kitchen area to one side. But the smell: musty didn't begin to describe it, the air was heavy with damp and decay. Cobwebs hung from the cornice and dust lay like fur on the furniture. On the mantelpiece was a row of china ballerinas. Dusty as they were, she could see that they were crudely modelled and the painting was out of register.

She walked over to the window and saw a view across a valley dotted with sheep. The window sill was strewn with the tiny cigars of mouse droppings. The hems of the flimsy cotton curtains were uneven where they had been nibbled away.

She looked back at the room: no magazines, no books, no photos in frames, no pictures on the walls, no stereo equipment, no TV. She followed the spiral staircase to the next floor. There was a metal-framed bed with a bare, stained mattress and a few dusty cardboard boxes. The floor was bare except for an ancient rag rug. Over by the window she could see rotten floorboards. She lifted the flap on the nearest box, raising a little cloud of dust. It was full of newspapers, the top one a yellowing copy of the *Daily Express*. 'Iraq invades Kuwait,' she read. The summer of 1990. Ricky had been a baby then.

She made her way back down to the ground floor. She stood in the hall, fingering the key in her pocket. Jay didn't live here. No-one lived here. So why had he given her this address?

She noticed something that she had missed on her way in: letters backed up behind the door. That explained why the door had seemed stiff. She crouched down and picked them up. A spider ran out, making her start. The bottom items were sticky with cobwebs. They were all circulars, junk mail, addressed to the occupier, none bearing Jay's name. How long had it taken for this to accumulate? Two months? Three? Still squatting, she fanned them out on the floor and caught sight of the white corner of an envelope and a stamp. She pulled it out. Her heart leapt when she saw Jay's name on the envelope. The next moment she recognised the hand-writing.

It was her own letter, unopened.

She didn't have time to take in what this meant. As she straightened up with the letter in her hand, her eye caught a flicker of movement through the window by the door.

A woman in a suit, carrying a clipboard, was coming up the track towards the house.

Chapter Seventeen

'It was a close call,' Lisa said. 'I got out through the bathroom window. It stuck and I thought I wasn't going to make it. I could actually hear her unlocking the door as I climbed out. I thought I was going to have a heart attack!' Stella was staring at her open-mouthed. Lisa couldn't help enjoying the effect she was having.

'I was going to just sneak away and then I thought, the place is up for sale, I bet that woman's an estate agent – and she was. I pretended that I'd just arrived, said that I'd seen the sign and I'd stopped to have a look. I thought she might be able to tell me something about Jay.' It was the following day. They had already done their twenty lengths of the pool and they were in the Jacuzzi.

Stella was wearing a halter-neck swimming costume and her hair was captured under a cap covered in pink petals – she looked like a fifties starlet.

'Let me see if I can get my head round this,' she said. 'For the past three years you've been having an affair with this man, this Jay McCallum, and you've kept it a secret all that time?'

Lisa nodded. 'At the beginning I didn't know it was going to go on for three years and then ... the secrecy was part of the excitement. I can understand that.'

'That was some of it, but also ... it was something that was mine, just mine, nothing to do with the rest of my life.'

'Lawrence and Ricky were in one compartment, Jay was in another?'

Lisa shook her head. 'Ricky and Lawrence weren't in a compartment, they were my whole life, my *real* life. Jay was – I don't know – a holiday? A respite? To start with at least.'

The health club was in a big hotel high up in Lynton and the Jacuzzi was in a bay window overlooking the sea. Hundreds of feet below Lisa could see a section of the beach, the shingle so dark a grey that it was almost black. 'But once a month,' Stella said. 'Was it enough?'

'For a whole weekend, I had his undivided attention. We talked more in a weekend than lots of couples do in month. And between times, we read the same books, watched the same DVDs. He told me that every night he listened to the shipping forecast and that he always thought of me then. So I started listening too …'

'Ah, the things we do for love …'

'And that wasn't all …' This was harder to put into words. She stared down into the foaming water. 'All the tedious stuff, the practical stuff, you know, who does the washing up or collects the dry-cleaning, or arranges for the plumber to come … all the stuff that clogs up your life, that spoils things: we didn't have to bother about any of it.'

There was a rueful half-smile on Stella's face. 'Why do you think I never got married? I've always preferred my men in small doses.'

'We made love, we talked, we went for walks …'

'I bet the sex was terrific?'

Lisa thought of the times when they'd fallen into bed and only surfaced for dinner at midnight. She smiled.

'Yeah, I can see that it was.' Stella grinned. 'Look, this house in Derbyshire. Had you written to him there before?'

Lisa shook her head. 'If I needed to change an arrangement we'd made, I'd ring his mobile phone, but I didn't do that very often.'

'He didn't have a landline? That's pretty bloody strange.'

114

'He said he was away on business such a lot that he hadn't bothered. And I think he did travel,' Lisa said, remembering the gifts of perfume – duty-free? – and the Marimekko scarf.

'What does he do for a living?'

'Something to do with money, an accountant, a financial consultant. He didn't talk much about that, either.'

'Did he ever talk about friends or relatives?'

'Not really. But then neither did I.' Lisa thought back. 'He did mention some distant relatives once – he used to visit them in mid-December – that was the only time he couldn't meet me –'

'Did he mind being seen with you in public? Did you eat out in restaurants or go to visit places?'

'We didn't go out much –'

'He's married,' Stella concluded.

'No!' Lisa said, louder than she intended.

Stella raised her eyebrows.

'OK, OK, I wondered about that, too, at the beginning,' Lisa admitted. 'Of course I did. But he said he wasn't and I believed him. What married man would be able to get away for a weekend every month, no questions asked? He never rang anyone when we were together. And he worked around me and my commitments. If I needed to change things there was never a problem.'

Outside storm clouds were massing on the horizon and it was growing darker. The coast of Wales was visible only as a phantom outline. 'Did the estate agent shed any light?' Stella asked.

'She'd never heard of him. The house had belonged for as long as she could remember to an old lady called Mrs Brayfield, and even she hadn't lived there for years. She went into a nursing home, but she hung on to the house, hoping that she'd be well enough to go back one day.'

'OK.' Stella stretched her arms along the rim of the

Jacuzzi. 'Let's think this through. Could he be a relative?'

'The old lady didn't have anyone close. She died a few weeks ago and left everything to a charity. The estate's being handled by a solicitor.'

Stella pondered. She shifted her shoulders to let the water jets massage her back.

Curtains of rain were sweeping in from the sea. Two surfers carrying their boards were emerging from the waves. At this distance they looked like ants carrying grains of rice.

'Can you be absolutely sure that *anything* he told you was true?' Stella said. 'Do you even know that he gave you his real name?'

Lisa stared at her.

'Did he use credit cards? Cheques? Please don't tell me he always paid in cash? Oh Lisa. He did, didn't he?'

The silence stretched out between them. Rain slapped the window.

'You just think he's chucked me, don't you?' Lisa said. Stella's face was full of sympathy. 'Oh, darling … 'The beach was lost in veils of rain and the shrubs in the hotel garden tossed and shivered. The storm had arrived.

Stella glanced at the clock over the swimming pool. 'I've got to go. I'm going to be late back to the office. I'll ring you later.'

She hoisted herself onto the edge of the Jacuzzi and water streamed off her. She said, 'In my experience these things hardly ever come out of the blue. So often there are warning signs, just little things that you didn't want to see at the time. It's only when you look back that you realise.'

116

Chapter Eighteen

Rain was hammering on the roof of the car. This wasn't the weather to be negotiating the hair-pin bend up from Lynmouth and anyway what Stella had said had shaken Lisa. She decided to sit out the worst of the storm in the hotel car park. Sheets of rain slid down the windscreen, blurring the view. She felt a sense of vertigo. If Jay wasn't Jay ... it made him seem strangely insubstantial, as if he might not have existed at all. What if he was really Michael? Or Stephen? Or Edward? Unthinkable ... The single syllable had suited him, had sounded so well on her tongue, whether she was calling his attention to something, or murmuring it in bed. She had never suspected for a moment that Jay wasn't his real name, but now that Stella had sown the seeds of doubt ... She slumped down in the car seat. Lord, she was tired. The rhythm of the rain on the car roof had a lulling effect.

She thought of what Stella had said about warning signs. Had there been anything? It seemed to her that the last few times they had met, he had been as loving as ever. But that question Stella has asked about going out together in public: something *had* changed, something that hadn't seemed important at the time. On the last few weekends they had hardly left the rented cottage they were staying in. Jay always booked them and they tended to be in rural, out-of-the-way places anyway. But in the past there had been the odd trip out to a restaurant or a National Trust house. Recently, nothing. Oh, they had gone out for walks, but not to any kind of public place where there might be lots of people. When exactly had that happened? About six months ago, she thought. What was the last place they had visited? She searched her memory. An Elizabethan manor house. Yes, that was it. The home of one of those Catholic families who stuck with the old religion after the Reformation. Priest holes everywhere. Beautiful garden, too. Jay had bought her a lavender plant at the garden shop.

She had suggested an outing once or twice after that, but Jay had never been keen.

She closed her eyes and let her thoughts drift back. That day at the manor house had been perfect. The weather for one thing. She could feel the sun on her skin and there was just a little breeze. They'd had lunch in the café before they looked round the house. In her mind's eye, she saw an awning and flowers in pots. What did they eat? She could almost taste – what? – bread, a sandwich. Maybe egg, yes, and something fishy, egg and prawn. How odd that she could remember that.

The warmth of the sun, Jay close beside her, her hand in his: some of the strain left her as she sank back into the past.

They'd gone into the house. Impressions flooded in: the cool dimness of the interior of the house, the firm, smooth feel of a banister, uneven floorboards, the scent of lilac through an open window. Jay was holding her hand. She wasn't really looking at him, he was just there beside her, and they were looking at things together. Jay was fascinated by one of the priest holes. It was so carefully constructed and so clever. It was a double one – so that anyone searching would think they'd found it, but then there was a second one concealed further back.

After that they'd gone out into the garden. There were swans on the moat and a border where flowers and herbs were planted together. She could smell lavender. And Jay said that he'd buy her a plant at the garden shop and then they'd have a cup of tea. She sat on a bench outside the shop to wait for Jay and turned her face to the sun. After a while she heard his footsteps crunching on the gravel.

When she opened her eyes she had to squint. He was smiling down at her and he had got the plant.

But something had gone wrong with the day. It was as if a cloud had passed over the sun. Jay was pale. She asked him if he was alright and he told her that he'd got a headache, too much sun, would she mind if they went back to the cottage and had tea there? He put out his hand to pull her to her feet. It was a hot day, but his hand was cold and clammy.

Lisa opened her eyes. She had sunk so deep into her memory that she was almost surprised to find herself in the hotel car park. The rain was easing off. Time to go. She shivered and turned the key in the ignition.

She drove slowly home, mulling things over.

Later, back at the cottage, he'd said he was fine, it was just the heat. But it *was* after that they'd stopped going out to places. It hadn't seemed odd at the time, but now she wondered ... Was there more to be remembered about that day? She had a feeling there was, but it wouldn't come through trying.

The road home rose up over bare grassy headlands and down into tunnels of gnarled beech trees. There were pheasants everywhere. They simply stood about in the road – waiting to be shot, as Lawrence used to say – only scurrying to the side of the road when Lisa slowed right down and sounded her horn. Lawrence ... it stuck her that it was the first time she had thought of him that day.

She parked in the carport, and looked at her watch. An hour at least before Ricky came home. There was time to take Piki out.

She set off towards the headland, the dog romping ahead. She let herself relax in the rhythm of the walk, enjoying the freshness in the air and the way the sunlight glinted golden off the autumn leaves, wet from the rain.

Don't struggle to remember, she told herself, let it

119

unwind in front of you, just be there, sitting on the bench with the sun on your face.

Jay pulls me to my feet, and we're walking along arm in arm and we're walking past the entrance to the plant shop and we're walking faster now, Jay wants to get back to the car and – there was something nudging at her memory. Had she missed something?

OK: back to the bench. Jay's holding my hand. I'm getting up. We're moving off, my attention's on him, I'm worried about him, and now there's the door of the shop, we're picking up speed. There's someone in the shop-doorway. A woman. Young or old? Not young. Not old. Middle-aged then and she was tantalisingly near to remembering something else –There was a cracking sound, like a firework going off. Gun shots: someone was out shooting pheasants. Piki came racing up, tail between her legs.

Lisa frowned. Those shots were too loud. They were closer than they ought to be.

As she walked home she tried to summon up the memory of the woman in the doorway, but it was no good, she'd lost her train of thought. She'd have to let it go for now.

All evening, while she cooked pasta for Ricky, while she watched a DVD with him, she had the feeling of something hovering on the edge of her memory, something just out of sight.

She read in bed for a while, her red cashmere cardigan wrapped around her shoulders for comfort. When it got to the time for the shipping forecast she switched on the radio.

She settled down in bed with her face against the cardigan. It was the most beautiful garment she owned. Jay had bought it in a shop specialising in Scandinavian design. She remembered him wrapping it round her and drawing her close to kiss her. She had felt cherished, protected. She closed her eyes.

'Low 100 miles southwest of Iceland 972 moving steadily southeast and losing its identity. Developing Atlantic low moving rapidly northeast ...' Was Jay out there somewhere, listening to this and thinking of her? She felt a pang of longing for him. Were those good times all over? She couldn't bear to think so.

'Expected Fair Isle 964 by 0600 tomorrow ... Dogger ... Fisher ... German Bight ...'

From nowhere the memory came. The woman standing in the doorway. The face was still a blur, but – 'she had grey hair.' Lisa spoke aloud in surprised discovery. It was long and she was wearing it in a plait, curling down over her shoulder.

And with that visual image came some other knowledge, not recalled since that day. The woman had looked ... well, how had she looked? There was something about the way she was standing. Puzzled! She was *puzzled*. But why?

Had Jay given her the wrong money or had he walked off without his change? Lisa half-expected the woman to say something, but she didn't and they walked on.

Lisa held her breath, willing the memory not to slip away. And then she had it. The woman looked as if she had seen someone she thought she knew, but was wondering if she had made a mistake.

Chapter Nineteen

Ricky beckoned Lisa into his room, while Karen was making a cup of tea in the kitchen.

'I don't like her,' he hissed.

'Shush. She might hear you.'

'Even if she did, she wouldn't understand what I'm saying.' His voice was full of scorn. True enough, but surely he couldn't hold that against the woman. It was always the way when anyone new came into his life. He'd just have to rely on his voice aid for a while longer.

'You'll get used to her,' Lisa said firmly, 'and she'll get used to you.'

'I don't want to get used to her.' She wasn't Peony: that was the real problem.

Lisa had been to see Peony and to talk to her, as the doctors said that it helped. There was always someone by her bedside, but as the days went by and Peony didn't regain consciousness ... Lisa gave herself a mental shake. Better not go there – the doctors were still optimistic ... at least, they said they were ... She had got into the habit of texting Gavin every morning. It was easier than trying to speak to him, when he was so often in the ward.

Ricky shot a sideways glance at her. 'Why aren't you going for one of your weekends? Why have you stopped doing that?'

'I just need a day this time, OK?'

'What are you going to do?'

She almost said you don't tell me everything – you didn't tell me about e-mailing your father – so why should I tell you what I'm doing? She stopped herself just in time. She knew she couldn't put it off much longer, but this wasn't the right moment.

Ricky returned to the attack. 'I don't see why I need to have anyone here. I mean, I wouldn't be on my own. Charlotte's coming over.'

'Charlotte couldn't drive you to Barnstaple,' Lisa pointed out.

'But her Mum could.'

'Oh, Ricky.' She rubbed her temples. She had a three-hour drive at least to get to the National Trust house, longer if she got caught up round Bristol. 'I can't deal with this now. The woman's here. I can't just tell her to go away. I'll think about it for next time, OK?'

'You won't! I know you won't.'

'I'll think about it. I will, I promise.'

His silence was eloquent.

'Look, I've got to go.' She dropped a kiss on his head. 'Have a good time shopping.'

He didn't reply, just swung his wheelchair round to his computer screen.

She looked back from the door, hoping that he'd relent and say 'Hasta la vista, baby,' in his Arnie voice.

He didn't.

Lisa sighed. She went to look for Karen to say goodbye. The funny thing was, Lisa hadn't really taken to her either. She wasn't sure why. She was easy-going and amenable, was perfectly happy to take Ricky shopping –

Lisa opened the kitchen door. Karen was washing the breakfast things and that was nice of her – it wasn't really her job. She turned to smile at Lisa. She was mid-thirties, Lisa guessed, with toffee-coloured hair cut in a bob and a smooth, freckled face.

She wasn't wearing a nurse's uniform, of course – that wasn't necessary – just an unremarkable, rather dowdy skirt and jumper. But with them, Lisa was amused to note, she was wearing a pair of extraordinarily sexy shoes, black suede with pointed toes and kitten heels. That was rather endearing.

It was just after midday when Lisa found herself looking in through the window of the plant shop. A middle-aged man wearing jeans and wellingtons and a sloppy sweater was moving some pots around. There was no-one else in the place.

She went in and browsed. Not much point in buying something for the garden at this time of year. She lingered by a tray of cacti and selected an interestingly knobbly one. Ricky might like it.

When she took it over to the till, the man straightened up from his work and came over. He had ginger hair and an open, friendly face.

'Filthy weather,' he remarked. 'We close today. Shouldn't be surprised if you're the last person I serve this year.'

The chatty type: good. As he handed her the change, Lisa plunged in.

'I was wondering – there's a woman who used to work here – I don't know her name, but she has a grey hair, a plait.'

He paused and she felt the touch of his fingers, rough on her palm. 'You must mean Margaret? She left a few months ago.'

'I don't suppose you know ... ?' Lisa's voice trailed off.

The man was already shaking his head. Something had changed. It was as if a shutter had come down over his face.

'She emigrated. New Zealand. She wanted to be near her daughter and the grandchildren. Do you want this in a bag?' He gestured to the cactus.

Lisa's heart sank. Another dead end. 'No thanks, I mean, yes. I'd better, it's a bit prickly.'

'Can I help in any way?' he asked.

Lisa considered. Well, what was the harm?

'I thought she might know someone I'm trying to get in touch with. I met him here last year and he gave me his address and phone number, but I lost my address book, too. I think Margaret knew him and I just wondered –'

He shook his head. 'Not something I can help you with, I'm afraid.'

It had always been a long shot. Lisa shrugged and smiled. 'Well, thanks anyway.'

She walked off in the direction of the house, scarcely thinking about what she was doing. It was a cold, gusty day with fast-moving clouds overhead. She wandered around the garden. The only things in bloom were some late chrysanthemums and Michaelmas daisies. A few withered roses clung to the bushes.

She sat down on a bench and gazed at the house. She hadn't the heart to go inside. The day when she had wandered here with Jay was part of a different life, a happier life, buttressed as it had been by Lawrence and Peony.

She was chilly and it was a long drive home. Better have something to eat before she set off. She went to the tea-room, got soup and a sandwich and some tea. She sat near one of the patio heaters. Even so a cold draft played round her ankles. She was late having lunch and the place was deserted.

Would she have to accept that she'd never know what had happened to Jay? Would she still be wondering about it on her deathbed? And wasn't it time she gave her full attention to her other problems? Sooner or later – and it had better be sooner, before Barry took things into his own hands – she would have to have a proper talk with Ricky. Lawrence's death had left a father-shaped void and what was more natural, really, than that Ricky should want to know more about his real father, should want to impress him, even? But it was quite another thing for Barry to come barging in, thinking he could take over …

126

A great weariness settled over her. She felt so alone.

She had eaten the sandwich without noticing and she didn't see the man from the plant shop until he was standing next to her with a cup of tea in his hand.

'May I?' He gestured to the seat opposite.

'Please do.'

'I'm Miles, by the way.'

'Lisa.'

'I was wondering – it might be nothing to do with your friend, but after you'd gone I remembered something. When was it exactly that you were here?'

'Last May.'

He nodded. 'Must have been about then. It stayed in my mind because there was something strange about it. Probably doesn't have anything to do with what you were asking about …'

'Tell me anyway.' He tore open a sachet of sugar and tipped it into his tea. 'This bloke came into the shop. Margaret served him. I was doing something out at the back.' He tore open a second packet and tipped it in. Then a third. He noticed Lisa watching. 'I've always had a sweet tooth. Anyway, when I came in, he'd gone and Margaret was looking upset. Apparently she'd said to him, "Don't I know you from somewhere?" and he said, no. She said she hadn't realised at first because he didn't used to have a scar. "But if it's not him, it's his double." And just as she was telling me about it, she went as white as a sheet. I've never see anything like it, no word of a lie.'

He took a gulp of tea. Lisa waited.

'I said something silly, you know, like was he a long-lost lover? But she wasn't really listening.'

'She didn't say who she thought it was?'

'Nope. A few minutes later she said she'd made a mistake and it couldn't have been who she thought it was. And then she said she wasn't feeling very well and she'd have to go home early.'

Lisa thought this over. Perhaps Margaret *had* made a mistake, but Jay had been upset, too. She didn't know what to make of this. Miles was saying something.

'Sorry?' she said.

'And that was the last time I saw her.'

The hairs went up on the back of Lisa's neck. 'What?'

'She was due to go on holiday anyway – went off to visit that daughter I mentioned. And then she rang up from New Zealand and said she'd decided to stay out there. A few weeks later I happened to drive past her house and there was a for sale sign up –' He shrugged. 'I do miss her. We worked on our own a lot, used to chat all the time. I've got a new assistant, a young lad, willing enough, but it's not the same.'

Lisa thought of Jay's reaction to the meeting with Margaret. She *had* recognised him and he had recognised her. And it was a meeting that had dismayed them both. So why had Jay risked visiting a part of the country where he might run into Margaret? Unless …

'Had Margaret always lived around here?' she asked.

'No, only a couple of years or so. She retired here. Used to live in Wiltshire. And I remember her mentioning Chiswick once.'

He pushed his chair back to the table. 'Better get back. You never know, someone might actually want to buy something.'

He got to his feet. 'We said we'd keep in touch and I really thought we would. We were good friends.'

He was moving away from the table, when Lisa said, 'Wait a minute. You say you haven't heard from her. Do you mean, nothing at all?'

'Not a dicky-bird. Not so much as a postcard. Nada, nothing, absolutely zilch.'

Chapter Twenty

Lisa turned off the motorway and headed along the A39. The road wound along the coast and there were steep drops down to the sea. She was gripping the steering wheel too tightly: her knuckles were white. She didn't like this drive at night. She made herself relax and switched on the CD player. There was a disc already in there. Willie Nelson was singing 'Everywhere I Go.' There was a sweetness and an honesty in his voice that made her think of Jay. That was ironic, given that what he had told her had turned out to be a tissue of lies.

All her anxiety about Jay's disappearance had centred on her fear that something had happened to him. Now she was wondering if there was something sinister about it. If there was something sinister about Jay? Had that woman been *afraid* of him? It occurred to Lisa that marriage might not be the only reason why a man might want to conceal his true identity.

Someone was driving behind her with their lights full on and had been for some time. She squinted into her rear-view mirror. She reached a stretch of open road and slowed down so that he – she was sure it was a he – could overtake. He didn't. All the way past Minehead he hugged her back bumper. She turned off when she got to Porlock and drove into the public car park. She didn't want him following her up that gradient. She'd wait here for a few minutes.

She checked her mobile phone and found a text from Gavin asking her to ring him as soon as possible. Without giving herself time to dread what she might hear she punched in his number. He answered right away.

'Gavin?'

'Lisa! It's alright, she's come round, and Lisa, she recognised me.'

Lisa had been holding her breath. She let it out now. 'Thank God. When –?'

'A couple of hours ago. But the doctors say she should make a full recovery. They might be able to move her from intensive care to a high dependency ward in a day or two.'

'When can I visit?'

'Soon. I'll let you know.'

'Did she tell you how it had happened?'

'She doesn't remember anything after leaving Porlock. That's common apparently, when someone has had a serious accident. The police are still examining the car –' He broke off and she heard someone speaking in the background, then he said, 'They're telling me I can go back to the ward now, I'd better –'

'Of course. Give her my love.'

'Will do.' A weight had dropped off her, how heavy a weight she only now realised. As she started the car, she found she was humming along to Willie Nelson – one of her favourite songs: 'Always on My Mind.'

By the time she turned off the road to Falling Water, it was almost six o'clock. She had been on the road for three-and-a-half hours. Her shoulders were stiff and sore from the strain of driving. As she went on down through the tunnel of trees, she looked forward to a hot bath and a stiff drink.

She turned the last bend in the track.

There was a police car parked outside the house.

She pulled to a halt. Later she found she had left the car slewed across the grass verge and she didn't remember how she got to the house.

She opened the kitchen door – it wasn't locked – and she could see through into the dining room. Ricky was there in his wheelchair. Her hand went up to her heart.

Thank God! He looked at her with an expression that she couldn't decipher. As she moved forwards she saw that Karen was sitting on the sofa with her hands clasped together, her face impassive. A uniformed policeman was sitting beside her. Her thoughts flew to Peony. But Peony was going to be alright –

The man got to his feet.

'Mrs Brown?'

She nodded mutely.

'I'm sorry to have to tell you that Ricky here has been arrested for shoplifting.'

A shop assistant had seen Ricky putting a pack of batteries into his bag and he had tried to leave the shop without paying. The policeman was kind. The shop didn't want to press charges. Things wouldn't be taken any further. Ricky should look on this as a warning.

The policeman left and while Lisa was talking to Karen, Ricky sloped off to his room. Karen was pretty decent about it, all things considered, she even said she'd be willing to look after Ricky again – 'He's a nice kid' – though maybe it wouldn't be wise to go shopping again. She'd been in a different part of the store. 'Ricky and his friend seemed fine. And then when the security bloke stopped us on the way out, I got the shock of my life.'

When Karen had gone, Lisa stayed in the kitchen for a few minutes to give herself time to get a grip. Piki was lying by the back door, head on paws. She knew that things had gone awry with her people. She looked up at Lisa and whined.

'You and me both, old girl,' Lisa said.

She straightened her shoulders and went to hunt out Ricky.

'What I don't understand is where Charlotte was in all this?'

Ricky was lying on his bed, propped up on the pillows. Lisa was sitting at the foot.

131

'Charlotte didn't have anything to do with it! I told the policeman that.' It came out as a wail. 'Why does everyone think it must be down to Charlotte? Just because I'm in a wheelchair it doesn't mean I can't be a criminal, does it? They haven't even charged me and I know why. Wouldn't look great, would it, prosecuting a *cripple*?'

All at once she wanted to laugh. But that would be fatal. And anyway he was right. Of course they would have thought about the adverse publicity. She bit her lip and looked down in an effort to compose herself.

'What does it take,' he said, 'for people to take me seriously? To treat me as if I was just another person?'

'Make no mistake,' Lisa said quickly. 'I take this very seriously.'

'Honestly, Mum, it's got nothing to do with Charlotte. If you want to know the truth, she's been telling me it was wrong and that I'd get into trouble.'

struck her in the way he had put this. 'Ricky – when you say "Charlotte's been telling you" – d'you mean this wasn't the first time?'

She knew from the way his eyes flicked away from hers that she'd hit on the truth.

'Ricky!'

'The top drawer in my desk.'

She went over and pulled it open. Inside was a pair of socks still clipped together, a paperback novel by Terry Pratchett, an Atomic Kitten CD in its cellophane wrapper and a large bar of Green and Black plain chocolate.

'Is this everything?' she asked.

He nodded.

He shouldn't have taken them, of course he shouldn't, it was very wrong, and she was furious, and yet ... and yet ... there was pathos in the modest scale of the theft. He could easily have afforded these things out of his pocket money. He hadn't even used them. It was as if he had known he would have to return them one day.

'We'll have to take them back.' She saw the look of alarm on his face. 'Or pay for them at least.' Maybe she was letting him get away with too much, but what was she going to do? Call the policeman back?

'Mum? Please?'

'You won't do this again.'

'No, no, I promise.' He winced. His hand stayed down towards his leg.

'Cramp?' He nodded. She moved further up the bed and put both hands round his calf. She pressed her thumbs in and felt the muscles tight and knotted beneath her thumbs.

'It was exciting,' he said. 'Mum, you don't know what it's like.' He gestured towards the wheelchair. 'It's as if I'm in a cage. Sometimes I just want to break out. To *do* something, anything.'

She went on massaging his leg with rhythmic, circular movements. She thought of when she had been a teenager, a little younger than Ricky, spending long hours lolling around in her bedroom, reading and re-reading copies of *Jackie* and Superman comics. Days of such ennui that she had longed for something to happen, even something calamitous, to relieve the boredom. Riding lessons had helped. So had long walks with their elderly Labrador. Ricky didn't have those outlets. 'It was easy,' Ricky said scornfully. 'I felt like it served them right, the people in the shops, they'd look at Charlotte or Peony instead of me, as if I was stupid or deaf or something. Because I'm in a wheelchair, they don't think I'm a real person.'

'But why didn't you tell me you were feeling like this?'

'*You* don't tell *me* everything, do you?'

She looked up. 'What do you mean?'

He looked her straight in the eye. 'Why haven't you told me about your boyfriend?'

Her hands fell away from his leg. She stared at him, dumbfounded.

133

'Oh, come on, Mum.' He grinned. 'Me and Lawrence, we were onto you ages ago. I asked Lawrence, what do you think Mum does on her weekends off? I asked if he thought you had a boyfriend.'

'What did he say?'

'He said, "Don't you think she deserves a little corner of her life to herself?" And then he said, "She's still a young woman." And I was like, yeah, right. I mean, forty isn't *young*. But that meant he thought you *did* have a boyfriend.'

Lisa was opening and closing her mouth like a goldfish. She pressed her lips firmly together.

'It's alright, Ma,' Ricky said. 'I mean, it took a while to get used to the idea, but I'm cool with it now.'

Surprised as she was, there was still a part of her that could be amused at Ricky's air of nonchalance. It gave her the energy that she need for a counter-attack.

'While we're exchanging confidences,' she said, 'perhaps you'd like to explain why you didn't tell me that you've been e-mailing your father for the last six months.'

She had the satisfaction of seeing *his* mouth fall open.

Chapter Twenty-one

'Can Dad come for Christmas? Can he? Please?'

'Hold your horses! I've said that he can come round and take you out. That'll do for now.'

They were in the kitchen, eating pasta, and there was an open bottle of wine between them. It was nine o'clock and they had both got their second wind.

Ricky nodded. She could see he was making an effort not to show his feelings, but his face was glowing with excitement. She felt a pang of jealousy. It wasn't fair, when Barry had been absent from their lives for so long, though that of course was *why* Ricky was so thrilled.

She found herself telling him about Jay and her efforts to find him. If the aim had been to get his attention, she certainly succeeded.

'Maybe he's a secret agent!' Ricky's face was alive with interest. 'Like Sydney in *Alias*! His cover was blown and he had to disappear.'

She couldn't help smiling. Ricky had seemed so grown-up when she was telling him about Jay, but this was such a *Boy's Own* idea.

'Yeah,' she said, 'and maybe he's Superman. He's had to fly off to some far distant planet, light years away, or – wait, Lex Luthor has attacked him with a piece of Kryptonite and he's too weak to pick up the phone!'

'Oh, Mum.' He rolled his eyes. He put down his fork and leaned forward. 'Seriously, why shouldn't he be a member of MI5 or something? Someone has to be.'

She picked up her glass of wine and took another sip. Well, he was right, wasn't he? It was beginning to seem as likely an explanation as any.

'It might just be that he's married,' she said. 'Even if it isn't to Lois Lane.' Was she getting drunk? She was amazed to find herself talking to Ricky like this.

'No. He wouldn't go to all this trouble just for that. The address in Derbyshire was a ghost address!' His eyes were shining. 'Not his real address,' he added kindly, in case she might not have understood. 'He actually lives somewhere else.'

'Well obviously … '

'Yes, but have you thought that we might be able to work out where he really lives?'

She sat back and stared at him. 'How do you mean?'

'Well, not the exact address. I don't mean that. Not yet, anyway. But I bet I could narrow it down.'

'I don't see … '

'Easy. He didn't want you to know where he lived, right? So it won't be near the address he gave. And it won't be near any of the places that he went with you either. If it was me I'd leave, oh, I don't know, a fifty mile exclusion zone, *at least* fifty miles, but that'll do to be going on with.'

He punted the wheelchair away from the table.

'Come on.'

'But where are we going?'

'To my computer, of course. And bring that bottle of wine with you.'

'Somewhere up here – that's my best guess. North of the Humber, east of Leeds. Yorkshire, or Northumberland, maybe.'

Lisa looked over his shoulder at the computer screen. 'As simple as that …' she murmured.

'Did he have a Yorkshire accent?'

'No. He didn't really have any particular accent at all.' She stepped back and sat down on the bed. 'It's very clever, Ricky, but … '

136

'Doesn't get you very far, does it?' he agreed. 'But there'll be something we can do, you can bank on that.'

She watched his face in profile as he stared at the screen. He thrust his chin and bottom lip out in a way that she recognised. For a moment he looked just like Barry.

'There isn't a problem that can't be solved,' he said. 'It's just a question of having enough data.'

Lisa sighed. Yes, he was his father's son alright. 'But that's our problem, isn't it?' she said. 'We haven't got enough data. We haven't got *any* data. It's going to take more than a lucky pen to solve this problem.'

'It wasn't lucky after all. It stopped working and I chucked it out.'

Quite suddenly she felt pole-axed, she could scarcely keep her eyes open a moment longer. It had been a long, long day.

'I think I'll go to bed.'

'You do that, Mum.'

'Don't stay up too late.'

He waved a hand.

She was at the door when he turned his head. The sweetness of his smile tugged at her heartstrings.

'Night-night, sweetie.'

'Night, Mum.'

She was woken up by Piki pressing a reproachful nose into her hand. She looked at the bedside clock and couldn't believe what she saw. Ten o'clock. Ricky usually slept late on a Sunday. She never did.

The events of the previous day came rushing back: the trip to the Midlands, Ricky being arrested for shoplifting. Oh God ... yet in spite of it all something had changed for the better. It was months since she and Ricky had talked so openly – and then there was the way he had tried to help. Of course there was nothing he could do, but the very fact that he wanted to ... And the business with Barry was out

137

in the open.

She got out of bed and looked out of the window. The weather had cleared and there had been a frost overnight. The air was so crisp and clear that you could almost pick out individual houses on the Welsh coast. She pulled on jeans and a heavy sweater. While the coffee was brewing, she checked on Ricky – still sound asleep. She poured herself a cup of coffee, thrust her feet into her wellingtons and went out into the garden with Piki at her heels.

The brilliant light and the chill in the air were intoxicating. Her spirits lifted. She felt a rush of energy. There was something she should have done months ago ... She went back in the house. She picked up the telephone and punched in Frank's number, pausing before the last digit. She took a deep breath and pressed the button.

At the other end the phone rang and rang. Finally it was picked up. Frank sounded breathless. 'I was out in the garden, sweeping up leaves,' he explained.

She spoke without preamble. 'You said you'd clear out Lawrence's boat. Please – would you do that?'

His answer was equally direct. 'Of course. I'll come and get the key, shall I?'

'They keep a spare at the boat-yard. I'll ring ahead and let them know you are coming.'

She hung up with a sense of achievement. So it was as easy as that. What next? She remembered what Stella had said that day in the Chinese restaurant. 'Start small, that's the secret, and begin with the stuff that you *know* is rubbish.'

Lawrence's office was on the first floor over the kitchen and dining room. She climbed the spiral staircase and opened the door. She stood on the threshold looking in. It was just as he had left it on the day he had walked out to his death, even down to the Rotring pen beside his drawing board. Except ... the sunshine lit up a layer of dust on the window sill and the air had that stale, undisturbed feel. And the objects themselves – the jar of pencils, the Alvar Alto vase on the windowsill – looked forlorn and faded as though they knew their owner was dead.

She went in and opened a window. Cold air streamed in, dispelling the stuffiness. She picked up the waste paper basket and stirred the contents around: discarded envelopes, circulars, nothing personal, nothing of any importance.

She went outside, collecting a box of matches on her way through the kitchen. She walked to the far side of the pond where there was a brick-paved area for barbeques and bonfires. She crouched down, took a ball of crumpled paper out of the basket, and cradled it in her palm. A flash of memory: she saw Lawrence's broad, blunt-fingered hand crushing a sheet of paper into a ball and lobbing it at the waste paper basket. A sense of the warmth of that hand, of his strong masculine presence flooded her, and she felt the familiar pang of longing. It was followed by a new thought. Lawrence had grown old, but he had stayed strong. He had gone before his muscles had wasted and his sight had dimmed.

She tipped out the contents of the waste paper basket. She struck a match and lit the edge of one piece of paper and then another and another until the match burned down almost to her fingers. She sat back on her heels and watched the blue and yellow flames eat into the paper.

When it was almost consumed she stood up and went into the house and up the stairs to Lawrence's study. She took the box of her mother's letters out of a cupboard. When she got back, the fire had gone out. She got some newspaper from the kitchen, scrunched up a few sheets and began again. The air was completely still and she had to blow gently to get the fire going again.

She took a letter out of the box. She stretched out her hand and was about to surrender the letter to the flames when she paused. She didn't intend to read the letters – Lawrence hadn't wanted her to – so why was she hesitating? Just to hang on to the possibility of reading them? They were all that was left of her parents' love – but no, that wasn't true. She was left and so was Ricky. She tossed letter after letter into the fire. The flames reared up, releasing sparks and smoke. Tears rolled down her cheeks and she knocked them away with the back of her hand.

She gazed into the flames, losing herself in them, her face glowing from the heat. The blackened paper was crimson at the edges. Feathers of burnt paper rippled and wavered in the draft of the fire.

The fire was dying down. She pulled some more letters out of the box and tossed them on the flames. And that was when it came to her. The house in Derbyshire. She hadn't really thought things through. The old lady's executor, her solicitor, would have access just as she, Lisa, had access to everything that belonged to Lawrence. She had been so shocked to find out that Jay didn't live there – that no-one lived there that it hadn't occurred to her to wonder why he had chosen that address. At random? Hardly. Maybe at one time his post had been delivered there.

She went into the house to look for the estate agent's card.

She struck lucky. There was a mobile number and though it was a Sunday, she caught the woman actually in the office, catching up on paperwork.

Lisa pretended she was interested in buying the house and asked for details to be posted to her. The woman was enthusiastic and told her that Mrs Brayfield's solicitor – 'He's her executor' – was keen to get on with winding up the estate. He'd be prepared to accept any reasonable offer.

'Which solicitor is she using?'

'Let me see.' Lisa heard the rustle of papers at the other end. 'It's Miller, Mr Jay Miller. Not a local firm. He's based in Newark.'

Chapter Twenty-two

Lisa arrived ten minutes before the match was supposed to finish.

There were so many players surging up and down the field that half the time Lisa couldn't even see the ball. She knew virtually nothing about the rules. A few vague terms floated around in her head: 'kicked into touch' 'scrum' and she remembered Stella telling her that she was a fly-half.

And where *was* Stella?

A huge woman was barrelling down the side of the pitch with the ball clutched to her chest. Lisa had never seen thighs like that before – at least, not on a woman. And it wasn't just her thighs, the woman was big, really big, Rubenesque was the word that sprang to mind, and what a subject the rugby match would have been for Rubens ... all that movement and heaving flesh.

Stella appeared out of nowhere and launched herself at the Rubens woman. She wrapped her arms round the woman's thighs and the woman toppled over with a crash like a tree being felled.

A roar went up from the spectators.

Someone else snatched up the ball and raced down the pitch, weaving from side to side. Lisa watched open-mouthed as the ball was passed to a stocky girl who took it the last few yards over the touch-line.

A shrill blast of the whistle. The game was over. The people standing nearby began to cheer and Lisa joined in.

Stella was on her feet now, leaning forward with her hands on her thighs, breathing heavily, her face freckled with mud. She looked up, saw Lisa waving and gave her the thumbs up. She gestured in the direction of the changing rooms to indicate that she'd see her there as they'd arranged.

'I nearly fell off my chair,' Lisa said. 'But then of course I realised that she hadn't said "Jay". It was the initial "J". I looked him up on Google. He's got a website. The J stands for Jonas. But still, Jonas Miller, Jay McCallum.'

'Same initials. You're thinking it's more than a coincidence?' Stella had showered and washed her hair and was sitting before a mirror smoothing foundation onto her face. 'Funny name, Jonas. Jay might be short for that. Or Jay might be a nickname.'

'If Jay is a false name, he might have chosen it because it begins with the same letter as his real name.'

'Worth checking out. Definitely. What are you going to do?'

'Well, my first thought was that I'd just ring Miller's office and ask to speak to him. And then something else occurred to me: even if he isn't Jay, he might *know* Jay. He might have arranged for Jay to collect his mail from Deepdale Lodge. I think it's better if I go and see him. I could make an appointment and say that I want to make a will or something like that.' Stella put the top back on the tube of foundation. 'If this man *is* Jay and if he's married or he's dumped you, he'll get in touch fast enough, he won't want you just turning up at his office. It'll be painful, but at least you'll know.'

'And if he isn't, I'll see what I can get out of him.'

'Good plan.'

'Only one thing. I'm not sure what to do about Ricky.'

'You've got that woman, haven't you, that nurse?'

'He doesn't like her – I suppose I could insist – but that's not my only problem.' Lisa told her about the shoplifting. She watched Stella's reaction in the mirror. She seemed to be frowning. She pressed her lips tightly

142

together, her shoulders began to shake.

'Stella, you're laughing!'

'Sorry, but – you just looked so serious! You haven't spawned a master-criminal! I mean, doesn't everyone pinch things from Woolies when they're thirteen or fourteen?'

'I didn't!'

'I bloody well did.' She opened a little square box, took a brush and swept it over the contents. 'Don't worry, I imagine this'll be the end of it. As long as … '

'As long as what?'

'As long as you can cut him some slack.'

Lisa stared at her. 'You mean I should give him *more* freedom – after what's happened?'

Stella brushed blusher onto both cheekbones before she turned to look at Lisa. 'Can't you see it from his point of view? Poor little bugger. He doesn't have many ways to rebel, does he? He can't hang around the bus shelter sharing a packet of fags with his mates.' She turned back to the mirror and rummaged in her make-up bag. 'He can't go out clubbing all night. Like I did.'

Losing patience, she tipped the lot out and selected an eye-shadow palette. She took out a little foam applicator and started stroking pale, pearly shadow over her eye-lid.

'Who's with Ricky right now?' she asked.

'Charlotte came over. They're working on this photography project.'

'I like that girl,' she said absently. She squinted into the mirror. Lisa watched the dark brown eyeliner go smoothly on. She wouldn't put on this much make-up for a party, let alone for a quick drink in the bar. 'Look,' Stella said, 'I can see that you might want someone on call.' She flicked up her eyelashes with her mascara wand. 'Hell, I don't mind dropping in after work for an hour or two myself, but why not get Barry on board? He wants to be more involved. Call him on it.'

143

'What if Barry can't hack it this time either and it ends in Ricky being rejected all over again?'

'Ricky's what? Sixteen? Seventeen? He can make his own mind up, perhaps?' Stella shovelled her make-up back into the bag. 'Come on! I need a drink.' She turned to face Lisa. She had a strange lop-sided look.

'Stella …'

'Mmm?'

'You've only done one eye.'

Chapter Twenty-three

The man with the paunch took a sip of wine.

'They don't do you badly here,' said his companion.

'No, indeed,' said the man with the paunch.

He pushed his heavy black-framed glasses up his nose. Actually the wine was execrable. But it didn't matter what he thought. His companion was getting through it alright and that was all that mattered. He'd had him pegged as a drinker from the first – the broken veins on his nose told their own story – and that was a stroke of luck. So was the fact that Martin was near the end of his career. He had been head of Applied Art for over twenty years, and before that had been assistant keeper. He'd never worked anywhere else. He'd grown sloppy and over-confident, was inclined to take things at face value.

'Well, James, here's to your new book,' Martin said and raised his glass again. *When you choose an alias, it's best to choose a name that's not too dissimilar to your own.*

Jay raised his glass. 'Oh, you know how publishers are. It won't be out for a year or two.' *Actually it won't ever be out.*

This was the last day of his week-long research trip to the museum and he had suggested lunch in a nearby Italian restaurant as a thank you. He encouraged Martin to go on talking, quietly filling up his glass from time to time, playing the assiduous host. They worked their way through avocado vinaigrette, cannelloni, green salad, tiramisu, and coffee. Martin drank four-and-a-half glasses to Jay's one, confirming Jay's suspicion that he was a boozer. He was holding it well, but it was sure to have an impact.

Jay picked up the bottle.

'There's just a drop left,' he said, and tipped what remained into Martin's glass. 'Let's finish with a grappa, shall we?'

'Why not?'

It was two-thirty when Jay caught the waiter's eye and nodded for the bill.

On the way back to the museum he noted that Martin's steps remained firm. The only outward sign of the amount he had drunk was a tendency to garrulousness. That was just fine. Outright drunkenness was not what Jay was aiming for, just enough to take the edge off things and produce that crucial blurring of judgement.

They made their way up the broad shallow steps between the columns of the portico. Jay was breathing heavily. This lack of fitness was part of the persona he adopted and the funny thing was that the disguise – the paunch in particular – made him feel that he really was fat and wheezy. He understood why actors were so concerned with getting the details of costume and appearance right.

At the entrance the security guard glanced into his bag. Like Martin, he had grown used to Jay and the search was perfunctory.

Martin led him through the rotunda and along a gallery of nineteenth-century watercolours to the staff entrance. He keyed the security code into the key pad beside the door. He didn't bother to block Jay's view – another example of his sloppiness – not that it really mattered. Jay had discounted this as a way in. During the day it was unthinkable and coming in at night, circumventing the alarm systems, would have been too problematic.

Martin took down a bunch of keys from the board by the door and clipped them to his belt. Together they walked through the main office, Martin nodding to his colleagues, through a pair of double doors, down a staircase, along a corridor through the conservation

146

department – it was a labyrinth down here – and they were in the storage area. They stopped by a row of pegs. Jay removed his laptop, paper and pens, and a bottle of mineral water from his large leather bag and left the bag there along with his coat.

Further down the corridor Martin stopped and selected another key. The door swung back to reveal a large, windowless room with floor-to-ceiling shelves around three sides. It contained much of the museum's collection of oriental ceramics, one of the finest outside London. An Aladdin's cave, Jay had thought when he had first set eyes on the storeroom, truly fabulous. They were only able to display a fraction of the collection and the ceramics Jay was supposed to be researching were in store at the moment.

And there was no CCTV camera. Security was simple, but effective. No member of the public was ever left in here alone. Normally a more junior member of the curatorial staff would be supervising Jay, but staff shortages and illness had given him Martin and he was glad of that. He wouldn't have wanted to blight the career of someone just setting out. They had spent the week working at two tables that abutted each other, Jay taking notes for his book – supposedly – and Martin correcting the proofs of the catalogue of a forthcoming exhibition.

Jay arranged his paraphernalia on the desk, Martin took down the Jiaqing vase with a chrysanthemum pattern that Jay had been looking at before lunch, and they began work again. After a quarter of an hour, Jay asked to see the *famille rose* Qianlong bowl, the one decorated with flowering peach branches. Martin put back the vase, took down the bowl, and placed it on the table. At the sight of it Jay's heart beat faster. Not long to go now. He drained the inch or two of water in his bottle.

Ten minutes later he stole a glance at Martin. His eyelids were drooping. Excellent. He looked at his watch.

Half past three. It was time.

Jay leaned forward, took his glasses off, and supported his head on his hand. He gave a little groan. It wasn't a loud noise, but in the settled silence it seemed to Jay absurdly theatrical.

Martin's eyes jerked open. 'Are you alright?'

'A bit dizzy … '

Martin looked alarmed. He got to his feet and came round the table. 'Can I help? A drink of water …'

Jay nodded. One thing, he didn't have to pretend to feel hot. Like most public buildings, the museum was over-heated and he was sweltering in his fat man disguise. He could feel that his face was flushed.

Martin's eyes went to the bottle of mineral water and took in the fact that it was empty. Jay knew what he was thinking. It was just a few steps along the corridor to the conservation department. He could be there and back with the bottle filled in two minutes.

'I'll have to lock you in,' Martin said.

'Fine.'

Jay listened as the key turned in the lock. The door was too thick for him to hear Martin's footsteps retreating down the corridor. He forced himself to count to ten before he made his move.

'The quickness of the hand deceives the eye,' he muttered.

As a child, he had spent hours trying to make pennies disappear through his fingers. Then, as now, practice had made perfect. When Martin opened the door a minute later, the scene that met his eyes was apparently unchanged. Jay was still sitting at the table. The *famille rose* bowl was still in front of him.

To Jay the air was electric with tension, but Martin seemed to notice nothing. He passed the bottle of water to Jay.

Jay sipped the water. It was cold and he was glad of it.

148

Sweat was prickling his armpits.

'Better?' Martin asked.

'Much better. Never agrees with me, eating a big meal at lunch-time.'

He wanted to go now, was longing to be outside in the cool December air, but he forced himself to stay on, pretending to finish his work. It was four o'clock when he allowed himself to fold down his laptop and told Martin that he was ready to go.

The most dangerous moment was approaching. Martin gathered up his papers, knocked them against the table to straighten them, put them in a box file. Jay watched out of the corner of his eye as Martin picked up the bowl with both hands and turned away to put it in the empty space on the shelf. Jay held his breath. If he were to look closely at it now ... but he didn't. Seconds later they had left the store, Martin locked the door behind them, and they went back through the maze of corridors. Jay felt drunk with relief. He had to make an effort not to talk too much.

Martin insisted on coming all the way to the main entrance with him. Those last few minutes were longer than all the rest put together. Martin was inclined to linger on the steps, stretching out their goodbyes, reluctant to let him go now that the time had come. Jay muttered something about his train, shook Martin's hand and set off down the street. The back of his head tingled with the consciousness of Martin's gaze. He expected to hear running feet at any moment. Surely he couldn't have got away with it? At the corner he looked back. Martin was standing on the steps. Jay raised a hand in salutation. Martin did the same and turned to go back into the museum.

Jay walked round the block to the city library. He pushed open the swing doors and went up the escalator to the local history section. From there it was stairs or the lift to the reference section. He took the stairs. He had reconnoitred on more than one occasion and knew that half-way up there was a landing and a corridor that led to a little-used gent's lavatory. He went in and locked himself in the last cubicle. He put the lid down and sat on it. The adrenalin had drained away and with it his sense of elation. He felt weak, and the blood was throbbing in his ears.

On a ledge over the door he had left a bottle of surgical spirit, laid flat so that it wasn't visible from ground level, and a roll of cotton wool. He removed the bushy eyebrows and the wispy beard that had covered his scarred chin. He pulled his jumper over his head and unbuttoned his shirt. It had taken a long time to construct the paunch which fastened with tapes around his waist and over his shoulders. There was a slit secured with Velcro. He opened it up and took the Qianlong bowl out of the padded interior. He turned it this way and that, his fingers trembling a little. There was something, some quality of the glaze, that distinguished it from the copy that was now sitting in the storeroom in the museum, but the similarity was remarkable. He folded the packing round it and put it back in the padded bag. He came out of the cubicle and opened the door that led out into the corridor. He poked his head out. No-one was in sight.

Back in the gents he opened a cupboard stocked with cleaning materials and reached in behind the spare toilet rolls. His hand closed on the wooden carrying case that he had left there that morning. He packed the bowl in it and put the case in a plastic bag that he took from his leather bag. The leather bag was reversible, and with the sandy suede side out was unrecognizable from the one he had taken into the library. His coat was reversible too. His jeans were nothing special. No-one would give them a second glance.

He stuffed the paunch into his bag and pushed the jumper down on top of it. He took off the heavy spectacles with the plain glass. He took a tube of hair gel out of his pocket and slicked his hair back. He surveyed himself in the mirror. James had gone, never to return.

He looked round to check that he hadn't left anything. Then he took a deep breath and walked out of the gents. There was no-one around on the stairs. He walked down and left the library. His car was parked a few blocks away on the top of a multi-storey car park. He packed everything away in the car and got out his mobile phone.

There was a fine view of the city and he gazed out over it as he made his call. The first was to the news desk of the local TV station. He told them that an extremely valuable Chinese bowl from the Qianlong period – yes, Qianlong, he spelt it out – had been stolen from the museum. He hung up without giving his name or any more details, then did the same with the local newspaper.

And then it was time to make the last phone call, the one he had been dreading. Martin would be clearing his desk, getting ready to leave for the weekend ... He hated having to do this. But he had gone too far to turn back. Only when Lars read of it in the newspapers would he be convinced that Jay really had the bowl.

He punched in Martin's number. He could actually see a corner of the museum from here. He listened to the ringing tone. Had Martin left already? – but no – the phone was picked up.

As soon as he heard Martin's voice, Jay said. 'Go to the store room and look at the Qianlong *famille rose* bowl.'

'What? Who is this?'

'This is James. Go to the store room and look at the base of the Qianlong *famille rose* bowl. And don't think you can conceal this. I've informed the local paper and TV station. I'm sorry, Martin, more sorry than I can say, it's nothing personal, though I don't expect you to feel that.'

He hung up before Martin could say anything.

Fifteen minutes later he was on the motorway heading north.

151

Chapter Twenty-four

The doorbell rang and when Lisa opened the door Barry was standing outside with a bunch of flowers. They were pink freesias and smelled glorious. He had remembered that they were her favourite flowers. He looked for all the world like an anxious suitor. And in a way he was, but it wasn't Lisa he was wooing.

'DVDs,' he explained, holding up the plastic bag in his other hand. 'You said Ricky likes *Buffy the Vampire-Slayer*, didn't you? I've got the lot here.' He handed her the flowers. 'Oh, and did you know you've got a chip on your windscreen?'

'Oh no!'

'Low down on the passenger side. Best not to take it on the motorway until you've got it fixed.' Barry fished out a set of car keys. 'Take the BMW.'

'What about insurance?'

'Covered. It's a company car.'

'Surely you can't just –'

'Of course I can. I'm the boss, remember.' He tossed her the keys.

'Well, if you're sure.'

'I'm sure.'

She hesitated. She didn't like being beholden to him, but ... 'Thanks then. You'd better come and meet Ricky.'

She took him into the living room where Ricky was waiting, his wheelchair angled towards the door. Lisa saw Ricky as Barry must see him: legs at a slant, head tilted to one side, the clawed hand. She knew how nervous Ricky was. If Barry didn't make a success of this, she would kill him. He'd agreed not to mention his idea that Ricky might

153

study in the States, at least not yet. Maybe he'd change his mind when he realised what looking after Ricky meant – and she hoped that he did. Of course part of it was that she didn't want to lose Ricky, she knew that, but it wasn't *just* that. It wouldn't work and it was better for Barry to realise that now.

'Hey, Ricky.' Barry's tone was natural, casual.

Ricky's face lit up in a smile. 'Hey,' he said in his own voice, a mark of favour.

Lisa hadn't been aware that she had been holding her breath, until she let it out. It was going to be OK.

Barry fumbled in the pocket of his overcoat. 'I thought maybe … your mum said your old one's broken …' He brought out a package.

'Wow, an MP3 player!'

'This is the best on the market right now. I've got one myself.'

Moments later they were deep in technicalities.

Lisa might as well not have been there.

Once she had got used to the BMW, she started to enjoy herself. It handled well and it ate up the miles. More than once she found herself pushing ninety on the motorway and had to rein herself in. She felt like a different person behind the wheel, more powerful, more confident. She remembered the pleasure that she used to take in driving, the sense of freedom. There was a trip she and Barry had taken in the early days of their marriage, driving down the coast of California. Golden days. They had been free spirits. *They* weren't going to be tied down by domesticity and children. It was soon after that trip, that Lisa had got pregnant. They'd talked about abortion, but it hadn't seemed right somehow. They *were* married after all. Barry hadn't put any pressure on her either way. At the time, she'd thought that was a good thing, but now she wasn't so sure. Maybe that had made it easier for him to duck out afterwards. And later – had she let him off the hook too easily? If she'd insisted that he looked after Ricky more, would he have got to feel about Ricky as she did? She pushed that thought to the back of her mind.

It was an easy journey and she arrived in good time. She found a car park beside the gaunt, river-side ruins of Newark Castle. As she set off on foot for the centre of town it began to spit with rain. She made her way up a narrow street to a spacious market place, dominated by a massive church with a tall spire. Branches of Starbucks and Toni and Guy jostled against old-fashioned family butchers and charming Georgian houses. The place had a sleepy, provincial air.

No-one had rung her back from Miller's office, so almost certainly he wasn't Jay. It was that *almost* that was giving her butterflies in her stomach.

The appointment was for two. She had over an hour to kill. She decided to look at the office from the outside. She went on down Church Street. The solicitor's office was in an attractive Regency terrace. She walked briskly past it with her umbrella held low. She had only a couple of seconds, but it was enough to take in the spider-web fanlight, steps that led up to the white-painted door – and a well-polished brass plate that confirmed what the website had told her: Jonas Miller was a sole practitioner.

Her spirits rose when she saw that a little further down the street there was a cafe. The street curved so if she sat near the window she would see the entrance to the office. People would be going out for lunch or to get sandwiches and she might be able to spot Jonas Miller. She went inside and ordered a cup of tea and a toasted cheese sandwich. While she was waiting for it to arrive, the door of the solicitor's office opened and down the steps came a woman wearing a navy suit with a skirt that was rather too short. A secretary or maybe a legal assistant? She came trotting down the street, opening her umbrella as she went.

She slowed down, hesitated – Lisa held her breath – was she coming in? Yes, she was!

She went up the counter. Lisa examined her covertly. She was about thirty with long dark hair tied back in a pony-tail, revealing gold stud earrings, and she was wearing a blouse with a pussy-cat bow.

The waitress arrived with Lisa's sandwich and a glass of sparkling mineral water. She greeted the woman at the counter. 'Hi there, Helen. What can I do for you? New job panning out OK?'

'Good, thanks. Can I have prawn mayonnaise on brown and a cappuccino. Also a cheese and pickle roll and a latte, all to take away. The boss is having lunch at his desk today – and so am I.'

So that was that.

Lisa nibbled at her sandwich, too nervous to eat properly. The place was getting busier, and people were waiting for a table. She paid her bill and went to the ladies and touched up her make-up. Outside it was raining hard. She put up her umbrella and walked down the road away from the market place. The rain grew heavier. Round the next bend was a church. She tried the door. It was open and she went inside.

It was empty except for a woman at the far end arranging flowers. Lisa sat down in the first pew. It wasn't too late to change her mind, to just go back to her car and drive home. What if Stella was right and Jay had given her a false name because he was married? What if he had decided to end his affair with Lisa in a particularly heartless way? She didn't believe that of him, couldn't believe that of him, but that didn't mean it wasn't true.

The smell of dusty hassocks and damp hymnbooks was comforting, though apart from weddings and funerals, she hadn't been at a church service since she used to sing in the school choir. Lawrence was an atheist and a humanist.

He had encouraged her to form her own ideas about religion, but the influence had been there. As a young woman, full of confidence in her strong, beautiful body, she had felt immortal and later, after Ricky was born, it would have been hypocritical to turn to a God that she hadn't wanted when all was well.

Lawrence's death had changed things: at times she felt as if she was on the brink of some momentous discovery. But would a church service take her any closer to it? She doubted it ...

'Are you alright?'

She hadn't heard the woman approaching and now she was standing beside Lisa. Lisa looked up, took in close-fitting jeans and an Arran sweater. The woman had a yellow rubber glove on one hand and was carrying a pair of secateurs.

'I don't mean to intrude,' the woman said. 'You just looked so sad.'

'I'm fine. Really. I just needed somewhere quiet to sit and think.'

'I'll leave you to it then.' On impulse Lisa said, 'The thing is, I might be about to make a God-almighty fool of myself.' The woman sat down next to her and put the secateurs on the bench. She seemed in no rush to speak. The silence settled round them.

The woman said. 'The Bible tells us to be "as wise as serpents, as innocent as doves". I've always liked that.'

'But what does it mean?'

'Maybe that we shouldn't be naïve, but we shouldn't be cynical either. Though if I had to plump for one or other, I'd rather be a fool than a cynic any day.'

Perhaps the woman wasn't the leisured middle-class housewife Lisa had taken her for. 'Are you the vicar's wife?'

'No.' She grinned as if Lisa had made a joke. 'I *am* the vicar.'

As Lisa walked back down the hill she remembered something she'd pinned up on the wall of her room when she was an undergraduate. 'Work like you don't need the money. Dance like there's no-one watching. Love like you've never been hurt.' Another memory from those days came back, so sharp and vivid that it brought tears to her eyes. She'd been taken in by a hard-luck story and had lent money to someone who had no intention of paying her back. She'd told Lawrence about it.

'I've been such a fool, Daddy.'

'Yes,' he'd said, ruffling her hair. 'But you're my kind of fool.' She had reached the office now. A sign on the door said, 'Please walk in.' She did, and found herself in an outer office where the secretary she had seen in the cafe was sitting at a word processor. The woman got to her feet to greet Lisa. 'Mrs Brown? Mr Miller will see you straight away.'

The secretary opened the door and she stepped into the room. She didn't know whether to be disappointed or relieved.

The man sitting behind the desk was a total stranger.

Chapter Twenty-five

Jonas Miller looked exactly as Lisa imagined a typical country solicitor would look. The broad face was ruddy, suggesting time spent outdoors. He was wearing a three-piece suit in a fine tweed, a tattersall check shirt, and a plain, narrow, olive-green tie. There was a red carnation in his button-hole. She almost expected to see a watch chain. When he stood up, his jacket swung open to reveal a brilliant scarlet lining. Maybe not so typical after all.

He held out a hand. She saw that it was red and seamed with scar tissue as though he'd had a bad case of sunburn or maybe eczema. The skin was rough under her fingers, but the firm grip inspired confidence.

'Now, I understand you want to talk about making a will.' The pale blue eyes were shrewd.

She nodded, realising as she did that she hadn't thought any further than this moment. The will had been a pretext, but she'd better go through with it and why not? She ought to make a new will. Lawrence had been named as Ricky's guardian in her old one ...

'OK, let's begin with some basic details. Your address?'

She gave him her address. He raised his eyebrows, clearly wondering why she had come all this way when there were plenty of solicitors closer to hand.

This was her chance.

'I'm planning to move into the area. It's not a problem, is it?'

'Not at all.'

'And also – you were recommended to me.'

He smiled. 'That's always good to hear. May I ask who

that was?'

'Jay – Jay McCallum.'

He frowned as if in an effort of memory. He shook his head. 'Not a name that's familiar.'

Lisa thought of Ricky's detective work on the computer. Surely there was nothing to it, but was it worth a try – 'I don't think he actually lives round here – I think he said Yorkshire –'

Was the pause that followed just a beat too long? Perhaps she was imagining it, but she got the impression that she had taken him by surprise. If so, he had been off balance only for a moment.

'Jay? That's not a very common name. I don't think '
'We were introduced at a party. I might have got the name wrong. He's a tall man, and he's got this scar by his mouth – a burn, I think. It's quite distinctive.'

The solicitor pursed his lips and shook his head. 'I don't think ... no, I'm sure I don't know anyone like that.'

She was making too much of this, she knew that, but still she plunged on. 'I told him I needed a good solicitor and he gave me your card.'

'Must have been someone I met briefly somewhere – an agricultural show, something like that. Is he a farmer?' He was relaxed now, in command of the situation.

'I don't think so.'

'Well, anyway.' He spread his hands to indicate that she was here now and they should get down to business.

She explained about Ricky and about Lawrence's death necessitating a new will. He went through her affairs with a thoroughness and a focus on the task that impressed her. He recommended that she appoint two guardians who would be responsible for Ricky until he came of age or later.

'All things being equal,' he said, 'I tend to feel that twenty-five is quite early enough for most people to come into an inheritance. If you agree, we could think about

160

setting up a trust fund until then.'

She was taken aback. She hadn't thought of Ricky running his own affairs, even at twenty-five. She hesitated.

Miller had been taking notes. When she didn't speak, he looked up.

'I think you said that there's no mental impairment?' Miller said.

'No, no, there isn't. But I need to think about who would be good trustees. And I'll have to talk to Ricky.'

He didn't express any surprise that she hadn't done this already. He simply said, 'When you're ready, give me a ring, and I'll draw up a rough draft for you to consider.'

The meeting was almost at an end. She decided to have one last try. As she stood up to leave, she said, 'You know it's funny, I was sure that man who recommended you, said you were *his* solicitor.'

'Perhaps you misheard the name,' he said as he got to his feet.

'But in any case you said you didn't know anyone with a scar like that.'

He smiled and there it was again. Something just slightly off kilter, like a scent so faint that it's there for a moment and gone.

'That's right. Bit of a mystery, but it's brought me a new client, so I'm not complaining.' He stretched out his hand to shake hers again.

A few moments later she was walking out of the front door. Half way down the street, she looked back. She saw Jonas Miller was standing in the bay window of his office. He turned back into his office when he saw her looking. She got the impression that he was glad to see the back of her.

If he *had* been Jay at least she'd know. As she drove down the motorway she kept worrying away at the meeting with Jonas Miller, going over and over it, getting nowhere. She

161

was sure that he knew something. Was it that he wouldn't tell her, or that he couldn't? Did solicitors have a duty of confidentiality, like doctors and priests? Just as with the woman in the plant shop, she'd reached a dead-end. What on earth could she do next?

A few years ago she had taken Ricky to an aquarium with one of the largest shark tanks in Europe. You couldn't see the whole of the tank from any of the viewing stations; the distortions of the water and the glass added another element of uncertainty. They had waited there for ages without really seeing anything, now and then glimpsing the flicker of a tail or a shadow in the dim depths of the tank. It was like that now. She was catching hints and glimpses of something. Except that, no, it wasn't quite like that. It was more as if other people could see what was in the tank and all she could see was their reaction to it.

She gave herself a mental shake. Get a grip, she told herself. Think things through rationally. Were there any practical measures she could take? There must be something. Could she hire a private detective? But what could he do that she hadn't already done? Fingerprints? DNA? Even if she could get those off something Jay had given her – a book maybe – they'd be useless unless they could be matched against a database and there'd only be database if Jay had a criminal record. Even a private detective wouldn't have access to that. Maybe Ricky could hack into –

She shook her head. She was losing touch with reality.
She turned into the track to Falling Water. She wasn't far from home when she saw a flash of white a little way ahead, put on her brakes and came to a halt. Caught in the headlights was a rabbit, a young one. She flashed her headlights, but it was too frightened to move. It stayed frozen in place. She got out of the car and walked towards it. The lights of the car fell across the track throwing each

blade of grass and fallen leaf into brilliant relief. When she was almost close enough to touch the rabbit, it came to its senses and shot into the undergrowth. There was still some daylight in the sky, but darkness lay between the trees. The shir-shir of the waves on the beach came faintly up. The smell of damp leaf-mould filled her nostrils. Down below there was a glint of light from the house.

There was a rustling in the undergrowth, too loud to be a rabbit. Her rational self dropped away: she was a creature in the darkness of the forest and somewhere close by was another creature. She stood stock still, every sense on the alert.

There was a sudden burst of pop music and a dog barked. Someone must have opened a door in the house below and let Piki out. The barking got louder and nearer. Piki loped towards her and then everything was alright.

She let Piki climb into the passenger seat and got back into the car herself.

But as she drove on to the house, she couldn't quite shake off a sense of foreboding.

That visit to the aquarium: just when they'd been about to give up, the shark had risen up in front of them, huge and solid, inches away from the glass, the empty eyes staring into theirs.

Chapter Twenty-six

The day was cold, but Sandra was sweating as she walked up the path to the house in Chiswick.

It had been bad enough losing her job looking after Ricky. How could she have guessed that the little toe-rag was shoplifting? It just hadn't occurred to her that someone in his condition would be up for it. And now the man she had in place there had rung her to say that Lisa had gone off in her ex-husband's car. After Lisa had changed phones, they'd put a tracker device on her car instead and they'd kept tabs on her that way. But now they didn't know where the fuck she was.

She rang the doorbell and stood there nibbling at a bit of loose skin on her finger, as she waited for Steve to examine her on the CCTV.

She had a bad feeling about this. She and Lars had been on a roll for so long that she'd forgotten that once things started to go wrong, it was all too easy to let them get away from you. She had to put a stop to this right away.

The door clicked open. She hung her coat in the lobby, and made her way up the stairs to the first-floor drawing room. Steve was sitting on one of the window seats, so that he could keep an eye on the road. He looked out of place, as if he was the wrong scale for the room. He always wore a suit, a good one, but no cut could disguise his bulk. The material strained over thighs like hams. Mr Muscle, that was how she thought of him. Lars was sitting on a sofa, the phone next to him and a book – a sales catalogue – open on his lap. She remembered that there was an important sale of Chinese porcelain that day. Lars usually attended in person, but it was best not to take any chances

165

with Jay on the loose, so he would be bidding by phone. He looked up and frowned: he'd realised that it must be serious if it warranted her coming to the house in the morning. She grimaced to indicate that, yes, it was serious.

The phone rang. As Lars picked up the receiver, he gave her a curt nod: he'd deal with it later.

She sat down on a chair behind the sofa and glanced over his shoulder at the sales catalogue. Lot 165 – almost the last – was marked. Lars had told her about it: Chinese, of course, a little eighteenth-century bowl decorated with dragons, a pair to one he'd already got.

Lars switched on the loudspeaker. The sound quality was excellent – he sometimes took conference calls here – she could hear people clearing their throats and shuffling their feet. The bidding for the previous lot began. She listened with half an ear.

Over on the window seat Steve had opened a book, something by Andy McNab, but she could tell that he wasn't really reading it. His eyes strayed constantly to the street outside. Since they had stepped up the security, Lars was rarely out of his sight. Sandra had sometimes wondered about Steve's private life. Eventually she had concluded that he didn't have one. Working for Mr Lorenson, as he always called him, that was his life. She had absolutely no doubt that Steve would take a bullet for Lars if it ever came to that. The bidding for lot 164 was drawing to a close. 'Here with me at ten thousand five hundred,' the auctioneer was saying. 'Any further bids? No? Then I'll sell.' And the gavel went down.

'Lot 165,' the auctioneer announced. 'Dish with overglaze enamel decoration, Qing dynasty, Yongzheng mark.'

Lars stirred in readiness. Sandra had been to auctions with him and could visualise the scene. The first time it hadn't been at all what she'd expected. She'd been surprised that you could just walk in off the street. Hardly any security, nothing to stop some villain with a sawn-off shotgun just strolling in. And the people – they hadn't looked like money – mostly men, a bit shabby, tweed jackets, the odd leather jacket, and a few women – they tended to be smarter. Most of the people at auctions were dealers, Lars had said. The telephone bids were taken by people from the auction house sitting at tables on one side.

She hoped Lars was going to be successful – she needed him to be in a good mood. The auctioneer opened the bidding at £20,000. 'Yes,' Lars said to the woman on the other end of the line. She didn't answer, but she must have nodded or raised a finger, because someone in the sale room raised the bidding to £20, 500.

It began to go up in stages of £500. There were several people bidding.

When it reached £30,000, Lars hesitated. Sandra saw that the bidding was going above what he wanted to pay. He could afford it, of course, it was small change to him, but what collector likes to pay over the odds?

'With the phone,' the auctioneer said.

'Yes,' Lars said and they were off again, the bidding mounting rapidly to £35,000. People were dropping out now.

'Here with me at £36,000,' the auctioneer said. Sandra wanted to nibble the skin on her fingers. She stuck her hands under her thighs.

Lars was hesitating.

'In the room. Against you on the phone.'

Lars opened his mouth to speak.

The door burst open and Brigitta came hurtling in. 'Daddy!' She slammed into Lars's knees and he dropped the phone. It went spinning across the floor. His face contracted and his hand went up. Sandra flinched, waiting for the sound of the slap that would send the child reeling. But before the hand could descend, Steve had plunged across the room and scooped Brigitta up. By God there was nothing wrong with his reflexes! He carried her, wailing, from the room.

'Any further bids?' came over the loudspeaker.

Sandra scrabbled under the sofa for the phone. She heard a tiny voice saying, 'Hello, hello?' as she snatched it up and tossed it to Lars. He caught it one-handed and put it to his ear. He went on bidding as though nothing had happened, but Sandra saw that his hand was trembling.

Brigitta's sobbing grew fainter as Steve took her back upstairs to her nanny. His voice was a low, soothing counterpoint. He'd always been good with the kid.

A few moments later the bowl belonged to Lars.

He hung up and without speaking went over to the window and stood looking out. Steve came in and sat down again. Lars looked round, and Sandra saw that he had regained his composure. The incident wouldn't be mentioned by any of them. Lars hated losing control and he never admitted to being at fault. It would be as if it had never happened. All the same, when Sandra explained the situation with Lisa, he simply nodded and she knew she was getting an easier ride because of it.

'We'd better get a trace on the ex-husband's car,' he said. 'We need more people. I'll call in a few favours.'

'Excellent.'

He nodded slowly.

Sandra saw that there was more to come.

At last he said, 'You know, I'm disappointed in Lisa. She's trying hard to find our man, but I wonder, is she trying hard enough?'

In Sandra's view the poor cow was trying like fuck, but she didn't say so.

Lars went on. 'Perhaps we could focus her mind a little more. The son ... she's a devoted mother, you said ...'

'Too devoted. Spoils him rotten in my view. Are you thinking ... ?'

He nodded.

168

No need to spell it out. They understood each other.

Sandra thought it over. Lisa hadn't got another nurse for Ricky yet. That increased the chance of catching him alone and vulnerable. And if they could get the ex-husband out of the way ...

'Leave it to me,' she said.

Chapter Twenty-seven

Lisa opened the black, plastic bin-liner. It was almost full. There were several copies of *Yachting World* on top and underneath she could see the edge of a dark blue jumper. It was Saturday evening and Frank had just showed up with the things from Lawrence's boat. At the sight of that jumper – so old and familiar and just so *Lawrence* – her breath caught in her throat. How could this still be here, when he had gone? She wanted to pick it up and bury her face in it.

She closed the bag. 'I'll sort these out later.'

'Sure,' Frank said.

His voice was sympathetic, too sympathetic.

'Thanks, Frank, I really am grateful.' She tried to sound it.

Go, please, just go, she implored him silently.

'And the boat could do with a lick of paint here and there – I'd be happy to –'

Dear Frank, he never knew when to let well alone.

'I'm really grateful, but – can we leave it for now?'

'Of course. I'll be off then.'

I'm being an absolute cow, she thought. 'No, don't rush off,' she forced herself to say. 'I'll put some coffee on.'

'I won't, thanks. I'm meeting some mates in the pub.'

'You're sure?'

'Absolutely.'

'And, Frank – thanks again.' She managed a smile.

He smiled back. 'No problem. I'll be round on Monday for Ricky.' She thought at last he was going, but then he turned back. 'Been meaning to ask you. How's Peony? God, that was an awful thing. Lovely woman.'

'I spoke to her husband just half-an-hour ago. She's improving, but she's still in intensive care. Still doesn't remember what happened.'

This time he really did go. The moment she heard his car start, she reached into the bag and pulled at a sleeve of the jumper. The bag tilted sideways, spilling stuff onto the floor. She snatched up the garment and held it against her face, closed her eyes, and breathed in through her nose. She caught something, a scent that was quintessentially Lawrence, and also something oily. But when she tried again, only the oil remained.

She was standing there with her face buried in the jumper, when she heard Lawrence's voice. 'See you later, alligator.' On the edge of her vision was a dark shape in the doorway.

Her head shot round and her hand flew up to her chest.

That was what Lawrence used to say when she was a little girl.

But it was only Ricky.

'My God, you gave me a shock!"

'Sorry, Mum. I cued in the wrong thing.' He looked ready to cry. Her heart was pounding. She let out her breath. 'It's OK. I didn't know you'd got Lawrence on your voice-aid.'

'Not much. Just that. And that thing he used to shout – "what the blue blazes!"' They exchanged smiles, remembering. Lawrence had had a pretty short fuse at times, but there was never any malice in it. It had been a good thing, Lisa thought, that he hadn't let Ricky get away with too much. The smile faded from Ricky's face. 'D'you think I should wipe them?'

'Not unless you want to.'

'What's all this stuff on the floor?'

'Frank brought it all back from the boat. Did you want me for something, love?'

He nodded. 'There's something I want to talk to you

172

about.'

'Just let me deal with this, and then I'll be with you.'

'OK, see you in a minute.' He turned and went away.

Lisa folded the jumper and put it to one side. Her fingers trembling a little, she began to sort through the things on the floor. All the paraphernalia that accumulates on a boat, maps, flares – out of date by now – sun block, a few old paperbacks ... Those hot summer days the three of them had spent on the water seemed so long ago, part of another life. Ricky used to love it and she wondered if she had done the right thing in deciding to sell up. But it wouldn't be the same without Lawrence. Best to let it go –

'Mum! Come on!'

She stuffed everything back into the bag and went to see what he wanted.

Ricky was staring at his computer screen. Looking over his shoulder, she saw a photograph of a building composed of grey slabs.

'What's that?' she asked.

'Dad's new server farm. He's going to show me round tomorrow.'

So he was Dad now, was he? Lisa bit back the retort that sprang to her lips. She leaned forward and looked over Ricky's shoulder.

'It looks like a bunker,' she said.

'It *is* a bunker. A nuclear bunker. They're converting it. It's got staff quarters and Dad's actually staying there. How cool it is that! Look, you can take a virtual tour.' Rick clicked on the mouse. An isometric diagram sprang up.

'It's like a prison!'

'Well, it does have to be high security.'

'I'm not quite sure what a server farm is exactly.'

'Oh, Mum.' He rolled his eyes, but she knew he enjoyed explaining things to her. 'Look. I'll make things simple for you. Imagine that you log onto a website, let's say Marks and Spencer, well, they have to be sure that it's always going to be accessible and they have to be sure that if you want to buy something or download something, you're always going to be able to do that. So they have their system backed up, and that's basically what a server farm does.'

She had to hand it to Barry. This was the perfect choice for a father and son date. She still wasn't sure what they had done that first time. Ricky had been vague, had muttered something about 'just hanging out', and she hadn't wanted to press. It must have been a success, though, if he wanted to see Barry again so soon. She wasn't sure how she felt about that –

Ricky was going on. 'And big companies and government departments have to be able to rely on them to keep their data secure. It's way cool,' he concluded, with a sigh of pleasure.

'And that was what you wanted to tell me about?'

'No, no, it wasn't actually. The thing is, I've had another thought about Jay.' Lisa sighed. They'd gone over and over the trip to Newark and got nowhere. She almost wished she hadn't told Ricky about Jay. Just when she was coming to accept that she had reached a complete dead end, he was becoming more and more obsessed.

'I was watching CSI yesterday and I thought, you know, the first rule of forensics? Every contact leaves a trace. All those times you met Jay – there must be something that he left behind that would give us a clue. What about all those presents he gave you?'

'Don't you think that had occurred to me?' she said gently. 'I've looked at them all, and there's nothing.'

'But I haven't looked,' he said. 'I might see something that you didn't.'

He was smiling up at her, eager, hopeful, longing to make things right for her.

'OK,' she said. 'I'll bring them down.'

Books, CDs, DVDs, silk scarves, a pretty silver-and-turquoise bracelet, bottles of scent, more books, all spread out on Ricky's bed. There was such a lot when you saw it all together. Thank God there was no sexy underwear. The books and the DVDs were one of the reasons why she'd felt sure that Jay wasn't married. Even when they were apart they had shared so much, and surely these weren't the kind of things that a man gives his mistress? On Ricky's instructions, she had looked in all the CD and DVD cases, had held up all the books and fluttered the pages. No tell-tale receipts, no nothing.

Ricky was frowning. 'That *is* everything?' he asked.

'I think so ...

'I hate him! I hate him,' Ricky burst out. 'How could he do this to you? Give you all these things and then just disappear without a word!'

'Maybe he didn't do it on purpose,' she said. 'Maybe he had a heart attack and dropped dead, and no-one knows to contact me.'

Ricky's face contracted and she saw that he was on the verge of tears. This couldn't just be about Jay.

'What is it, love?' she asked.

The tears spilled over. 'I miss Granda so much.'

It was a long time since he had used that childish name. Lisa felt her own tears well up. 'Oh, so do I, so do I,' she said.

She knelt down and put her arms around Ricky. He leaned into her.

After a while she said, 'We've still got each other,' and he nodded.

A full moon hangs high in the cold night sky,
They say it gleams the same everywhere,
But could it be that many miles away

175

Wind and rain are spoiling the night?

This poem by Li Qiao had always been one of Lisa's favourites. Reading it now in bed, it seemed so apposite. Even if Jay were alive, there was no way of knowing whether he saw the same moon that she did, whether he was even in the same hemisphere. How well you covered your tracks, she thought. Maybe I'll never know what's happened to you. It was getting late. She closed the book and put it on the bed-side table, reached over and switched on the radio. She shivered and reached for her cashmere cardigan. As she settled it round her shoulders, she realised that she had forgotten to put this with the rest of Jay's gifts. And yet of all the things he had given her, this was her favourite. But she felt sure it had nothing to tell her, except that Jay had once loved her. All the same she shrugged it off her shoulders and examined it carefully. It had been a belated Christmas present last year and Jay had mentioned that he had bought it in a shop that specialised in Scandinavian goods. She looked at the label. 'Sylvie Hessedahl, Sverige.' That meant Sweden, didn't it?

She got out of bed, went through into her study, and switched on the computer. She called up Google and typed in Sylvie Hessedahl. A website came up with a picture of a model in a turquoise sweater. There was a list of options in English. Lisa clicked on 'Points of Sale'. 'Sold exclusively on line and in the shop on Stora Nygatan, Gamla Stan, Stockholm,' she read.

Gamla Stan? Gamla Stan? Surely that was familiar? Where had she seen that before?

When it came to her, she jumped up as if she had been prodded.

She ran downstairs and flung open the door to Ricky's room. He was lying in bed listening to a taped book and looked up, startled.

'What did you do with that pen?' she demanded.

Chapter Twenty-eight

'There I was in my pyjamas, rummaging in the dustbin at midnight,' Lisa said. 'I did manage to find it in the end.'

It was the following day and she had finally managed to get Stella on the phone.

'So, what have we got then?' Stella said. 'We've got the pen … '

'And it's nothing to do with Lawrence. I looked up the Hotel Gamla Stan on-line and it's only been open five years. That job Lawrence had in Sweden, that was well over ten years ago.'

'And you think it got into your house how, exactly?'

'I can't be sure, but I suppose Jay picked the pen up in the hotel, found it in his pocket when I needed one, and handed it over without realising what it was.'

'And when you'd used it, you absent-mindedly dropped it in your handbag, yes, that could work. And then there's the cardigan … '

'That might or might not have been bought in person from a shop near the hotel. He might have bought it on-line. But he did tell me he had bought it in a shop specialising in Scandinavian goods. He didn't say that the shop was actually in Stockholm.'

'He didn't say that it wasn't either. And he's never available in mid-December, so that could fit with him being in Stockholm.'

'Still it's not a lot, is it?'

'It's more than you had before,' Stella pointed out. 'But I agree, it is a bit of a stretch to assume that's where he'll be sometime in the next week or two.'

'Of course Ricky's all for me flying out there. He's

convinced that I'll find Jay at this hotel. But really ...

'Where's the problem?'

'Where's the problem? Well, there's Ricky for one thing –

'Barry's the obvious answer there, isn't he?'

'Well ... '

'Lisa, what is it with you and Barry? It's beginning to look like the real deal, isn't? Ricky's with him at the server farm, right now, isn't he? If Barry wants to make up for lost time, more power to his elbow.'

Lisa didn't want to talk about that. 'Well, maybe, but it's not just Ricky ...' Her voice trailed off.

'Yes?' Stella prompted.

'Ricky had all these ridiculous ideas – that Jay might belong to MI5 – '

'Someone has to!'

'That's exactly what Ricky said, but, Stella, it might be worse than that, what if he's a criminal? I can't really believe it, but ...'

'But people always say that.'

'Exactly. "He's such a *nice* man, he couldn't possibly be a mass murderer." But Stella, why was he so careful to make sure that I wouldn't be able to find him? Surely it can't just be that he's married? And the one person I feel sure knew Jay – that woman in the plant shop, Margaret, she left without leaving a forwarding address ... was she *frightened* of him?'

'You think she left the country to get away from him?'

'Oh, I don't know. Tell me honestly, Stella, d'you think I'm paranoid?'

'No,' Stella said, 'No, I don't. There's something fishy alright. And maybe the trip's not such a great idea. Pandora's Box and all that. But, Lisa, could you really miss up the slightest chance to find out what's happened to him? I know I couldn't.'

The chat with Stella had helped in a way, but it hadn't really resolved anything. Lisa couldn't settle to anything. She went out into the garden.

It was a frosty morning, so brilliantly sunny that her eyes watered and the sky was a deep, burning blue.

The lawn was overgrown and there were dead leaves everywhere. She stirred the nearest drift with her toe. How beautiful they were, little works of art. She picked one up: it was a magnificent combination of crimson, gold, and ochre and had its own unique configuration of spots and veins. When it had been alive it had simply been green like all the others.

There was a scuffling behind her. Piki had followed her out and was gazing mournfully up at her. Lisa bent down and ruffled the fur on her head.

'Time to get down to work,' she told her.

She set to with a will. She couldn't remember when she'd last worked up a sweat and it did her good. By lunch time she'd raked up a large pile of leaves for composting. She stopped only for a hunk of bread, a piece of cheese, and a banana. It was mid-afternoon when she straightened up with a groan. She was going to regret this in the morning.

She strolled round the end of the lake, shrugging her shoulders and massaging the small of her back to ease out the kinks. Piki followed her. They set off down the winding path across the grass to the headland. By the time Lisa and Piki got to the tree-house a few twinkling lights had appeared on the Welsh coast and a daytime moon hung low over the horizon. The light had almost gone. Lisa sat down on the spiral staircase and Piki flopped down beside her. Out of nowhere came a memory, something she hadn't allowed herself to think of in years. Ricky had been around a year old, the age that most children are beginning to walk, and up until then Lisa had simply lived from day to day, coping with things as they

179

came, not thinking about the future. When Lawrence had suggested converting the tree-house into a study, it had suddenly hit her: the realisation that of course he was right. Ricky would never climb into the tree house. And there was so much more that he would never do. He would never go roaming through the woods, never run along the beach feeling the sand between his toes. He would never dance the night away or freewheel downhill on a bicycle.

The pain she felt was as much for herself as for Ricky.

She couldn't take it. She'd just packed a bag and gone, leaving Ricky with Lawrence. She went to London and booked herself into a cheap hotel. She was gone three days. Then she realised that Ricky was still Ricky and of course she loved him. She had gone back full of guilt and more determined than ever to devote her life to Ricky.

It was true, wasn't it, that from that day on, she had had less time for Barry? She had been so anxious to make things up to Ricky –

She must have heard something without immediately registering it. One moment she was gazing out over the Bristol Channel, lost in her memories, the next moment, she was alert and uneasy. And Piki had heard it too, a low grumble was sounding from deep in her chest. The dog rose slowly to her feet and turned her head to look inland. Lisa followed the direction of her gaze. Dusk had gathered among the gleaming trunks of the silver birches. Deeper in where the trees clustered more thickly there was a clotting of the dark.

Piki whined and her head shot round. She'd heard something in a different part of the wood, and a moment later, Lisa heard it too: a car coming down the track. She saw its lights.

Barry's BMW came round the bend and drew up beside the house.

When Lisa looked back at the wood the darkness had gone.

Penne carbonara. Carbonara was one of Ricky's favourite sauces, and it was always penne, or maybe fusilli, never spaghetti or tagliatelle, because that was harder to manage with one hand.

Lisa tossed some sea-salt into the water and turned up the light under the pan.

It was dark outside now, but with the house locked up and Piki asleep under the kitchen table, she felt safe enough. She had gone with Piki to see if anyone was lurking in the wood, while Barry was getting Ricky out of the car. And of course there was no-one there. There had been *something* because of the way Piki had reacted, but it was probably a deer. They were very shy and it would have slipped away when it heard the car.

She got bacon and a carton of cream out of the fridge.

For Ricky's sake she had asked Barry if he wanted to stay, but he had made an excuse. He was too smart to outstay his welcome.

Behind her was the clatter of cutlery as Ricky set the table in his slow, methodical way. The radio was on and she was listening with half an ear to the evening news as she chopped the garlic.

Ricky was saying, 'When you go in, they lock one door behind you before they open the next. They have to guard against terrorist attacks and hackers and stuff like that.'

'… extremely rare Qianlong bowl of the type known as *famille rose* …' came from the radio.

Lisa paused in her chopping and turned her head to listen. 'One of the most daring thefts of recent times …'

'Mum, Mum! You're not listening!'

'Yes, I am.' She reached up and switched the radio off. 'What was it …?

'I *said*, they have multiple power sources; for instance, they'll have feeds from two different substations in case one fails.' She had always loved the smell of garlic, both musky and sharp at the same time. It made her think of

181

sex. And of Jay ...

She tipped the garlic into the frying pan.

'It's fantastic. The kids at school won't believe it. They've got two 11,000 volt HV feeds. Do you know how much power that is?'

When she turned to put the salad on the table, she saw a folded-up piece of paper at the place Ricky had set for her.

'What's this?' Ricky was grinning at her.

'A present. A Christmas present.' She opened it and ran her eye down the page. Stansted. Skavsta. She didn't understand.

'I've booked you a flight to Stockholm,' Ricky said. 'And a room in the Hotel Gamla Stan.'

'Ricky!'

'The airline ticket's non-refundable so you'll have to go!'

A thought struck her. 'Where did you get the money for this?'

'It wasn't very much,' he mumbled.

'Did Barry pay for this?'

'No! I did and I earned the money myself. The thing is – I've made £500 selling virtual property on Second Life – I *told* you I knew what I was doing.'

She was staggered. 'Really? You made £500?'

He laughed out loud at the sight of her face. '"Really!"' he shrugged. 'And you don't have to worry about me. That's all sorted, too. I've asked Charlotte to stay over. Her mum said she can be on standby for the first two days, she's happy to do that if you don't mind – then they're going away for a winter holiday – and then Dad'll take over.'

'You didn't tell him about –'

'No. Just said you'd like it and I wanted to give you a treat and he said – the garlic's burning.'

'What?'

'The garlic!'

Only now did she notice the acrid smell. She snatched the pan off the heat and dumped it in the sink. It sizzled and sputtered.

'What did he say?' she demanded.

'"Way to go, kid."' Ricky switched on his voice aid. 'I think you'll find,' said a gravelly voice, 'that I've made you an offer you can't refuse.'

Chapter Twenty-nine

For mile after mile only darkness lay outside the windows of the coach.

The cheap flight with a budget airline had arrived at Skavsta airport sixty miles south of Stockholm. By the time the coach reached the outskirts of the city it was late afternoon and a huge ochre moon hung low on the horizon. The thrill of arriving in a foreign city at night was soon followed by a sinking of the heart. Maybe after all she was doing something remarkably stupid. Even if Jay was at the hotel – and really, was it likely? – there was no guarantee that he'd be pleased to see her. The thought of a rebuff made her cringe inwardly. But even worse would be to draw a complete blank.

The coach stopped at the railway station. She got a taxi. It crept through the rush-hour traffic across the series of islands that make up the centre of the city. Lisa saw great expanses of water covered in ice, glimpses of imposing eighteenth-century façades painted yellow, ochre, and pink, high roofs laden with snow.

The hotel was in a narrow street near the southern tip of Gamla Stan, the old city. An elegant seventeenth-century doorway was flanked by small braziers holding lighted candles. There were butterflies in her stomach as she went in.

She'd thought carefully about what she would say. When the young man on reception asked her if it was her first time in Stockholm, she said that it was, but the hotel had been recommended by a friend who often came in December. She mentioned Jay's name. Lisa watched the man's face as he searched his memory. The man wanted to help, she could see.

'I'm sorry, no, I don't recall,' he said at last. 'But maybe he is booked in.' He looked at the register, turned a page or two. 'No, sorry, no-one English except for you. A quiet time of year.'

Lisa's heart sank. 'You're sure?'

He spread his hands. 'Quite sure, Madame.'

He was looking at her curiously and she forced herself to smile and shrug. 'Never mind.' A stately little lift, decorated with mirrors and a small chandelier, took her up to her room on the fourth floor. She dumped her bag on the floor, threw her coat on the bed, and sat down next to it. Now what? In other circumstances she would have enjoyed this pleasant room decorated in grey and blues and hung with gilded mirrors and tinted prints of country houses. But she felt a sense of futility. There might be other people here who'd remember Jay. But it was a slender chance and if he wasn't actually staying here, what use would it be? She'd come on a fool's errand. How was she going to fill in three days? How was she going to fill in this evening, even? She switched on the TV. A man with a three-piece suit and bouffant hair was saying, 'My client refuses to testify unless you can guarantee immunity from prosecution.' She channel-hopped, pausing for a few moments on Donald Duck dubbed into Swedish, then a National Geographic programme about otters, before settling on CNN as company in the background. She opened the mini-bar and found only a bottle of Seven Up, an orange drink called Zingo, two bottles of sugar-free Pepsi and a can of beer, which she noted was only 2.2% proof. Not much comfort there.

She looked at her watch. Seven o'clock. She could use up some of the evening by finding somewhere to eat and exploring the old city.

Outside the cold was somehow different from the cold at home, drier, more invigorating, like a splash of cold

186

water in the face. Snow lay piled up by the walls of the narrow streets and what remained underfoot was firm. She lingered, looking at the brightly lit shop windows with displays of traditional knitwear, of silk and linen, of amber and silver jewellery. She looked for the shop belonging to the designer of her cardigan and found it. She stood for a while looking at the sweaters and cardigans on display – they really were beautiful – and was astonished to see how much they cost.

The tall buildings and narrow streets were funnels for the wind. It was bitterly cold and she pulled the collar of her coat closer round her neck. She climbed higher through the steep alleys into the heart of the old city. Almost every window of the five- and six-storey buildings was lit by a seven-branched candelabra and it took a close look to see that the candle flames were really electric. The past seemed to press in around her. She wouldn't have been surprised to see a cloaked figure whisking out of sight. She looked round, hoping to catch a view down to the water, and felt a frisson when she did indeed see a figure in a dark coat stepping into a doorway. She went on and when she glanced back again the street was empty. She hurried on, feeling an urge to get out of the cold, to be in the company of other people.

She emerged on a street with more shop windows and – hallelujah! – a restaurant: Ruby's Bistro and Grill. She looked through the window to see if it was a place where she'd feel comfortable on her own and it was. The waitress saw the guide book she was carrying and welcomed her in English. Lisa ordered the dish of the day – baked salmon on mashed celeriac – and a glass of red wine. While she waited, she leafed through her guide book. Her meal arrived. It was good. She ate the food slowly, mopping up the sauce with bread, but it was still only nine o'clock when she left the restaurant.

A pewter sky pressed down, but the street was lit by

electric lanterns bracketed to the walls and was luminous with light reflected from the snow. She walked down to the quay, where a fifty-foot Christmas tree, trimmed to be perfectly conical, stood spangled with lights. She looked across the glittering water to the other islands on which Stockholm stood. A cold wind was blowing from the east – out there in the dark lay the choppy waters of the Baltic Sea, then the forests and lakes of Finland, beyond that the vast expanse of Russia.

She turned and walked south. The craggy cliffs of Södermalm rose up ahead, spires and cupolas outlined against the sky. As she crossed a square near the tip of the island, something moved on the edge of her vision. A man, silver-haired, wearing a camel overcoat, a respectable business type, unsteady on his feet, was staggered towards her, muttering something in a slurred voice. She walked quickly on, her heart beating fast. He was too drunk to pursue her, and she soon left him behind.

She was relieved to reach the hotel, but she wasn't ready to go up to her room yet. A little bar opened off the lobby. A nightcap might help her sleep and she wanted some company. She went in and looked around. There was no-one there, but as she hesitated, a willowy blonde woman appeared and gave her a welcoming smile.

'What can I get you?' she asked with scarcely a trace of an accent. Did everyone in Sweden speak perfect English?

'I'd like something that's typically Swedish,' Lisa said.

'That would have to be beer or schnapps.'

'Schnapps, please.'

Lisa watched the woman pour the drink. She wondered if it would be worth asking again about Jay. The woman put the little glass of schnapps in front of her.

'You are here on business?' the woman asked. 'No, no, just a winter break. A friend recommended this hotel. Actually I wondered if I might run into him here,' Lisa said. She touched the icy liquid to her lips.

'Ah, yes?' the woman said, but she shook her head when Lisa mentioned Jay's name.

But what if that wasn't the name he had used?

'He's got a scar here, like a burn mark.' Lisa touched her own face.

The woman narrowed her eyes, frowned in an effort of memory. Then her face lit up.

'But yes, I remember him. Not the name, but I remember. A sad Englishman with a scar. Yes, he came into the bar, just like you did tonight, and asked for a schnapps. He was cold and wet. And I can even tell you the date. It was St Lucia's day. Do you know about that?'

Lisa shook her head.

'That's a special day here. At school they choose someone to be St Lucia and last year it was my daughter – she wore a wreath of candles in her hair and handed out coffee and cakes. It's a great honour. I told your friend and he was so interested, such a nice man. He told me he comes every year to Stockholm to visit the Skogskyrkogården on that same day.' She saw the look of incomprehension on Lisa's face. 'Oh, I'm sorry,' she said. 'Yes, Skogskyrkogården, in English that would be the Woodland Cemetery. It's in the south of Stockholm. A famous place. A World Heritage Site. Many, many people are buried there.'

The T-bana train from Slussen passed an expanse of frozen water on which seagulls stood around, like people at a cocktail party. It slid underground and emerged in a prosperous suburb of wood-boarded houses painted copper, yellow and ochre. Rocky outcrops were dotted with spruce and leafless birch trees. Everywhere there was snow. Lisa got off at Skogskyrkogården and several other people got off with her: an elderly couple and a girl carrying a copy of a novel by Ben Elton.

The road that led up into the cemetery was flanked by

tall granite walls. The ice was treacherous and she had to tread carefully. Before her rose a stark stone cross against a sky that was almost as white as the snow on the ground. On her left was a long, low building: the crematorium. To the right was a saucer-shaped hollow with a long narrow plinth in the centre, black against the snow. She thought of human sacrifices before she guessed that this was a place to hold outdoor funerals. Beyond the hollow the ground swept up to a mound topped by a little grove of trees.

She went on along a wide curving road that swept round past the crematorium and along the edge of a frozen lake. All around dense woodland crowded in. The trees were mostly conifer and the foliage began high up, so that the bare trunks rose like columns. The graves lay in lines beneath them. A solitary magpie started up and skimmed the trees.

And it was at that moment that the true magnitude of the task dawned on her.

The place was immense. It stretched out in all directions as far as the eye could see. This wasn't a conventional cemetery with long open vistas. This really was a forest. You could wander for hours. Even supposing that it had been Jay in the bar – after all, he wasn't the only man in the world with a scar – and supposing the woman had remembered correctly and he would be here tomorrow on St Lucia's day, the 13th December, wasn't it hopeless really? Thousands and thousands of people were buried here. Even if she could find a register of burials, she had no idea whose grave Jay would be visiting. A parent? A friend? A lover, even? Innumerable little lights flickered low on the ground. She looked closer and saw that they were candles protected from the wind by lantern-holders. Some graves were decorated with fir cones and wreaths of evergreen. It was so homely – and so touching: the dead had not been forgotten or left out of the Christmas celebrations. She thought of Lawrence and tears prickled

190

her eyes.

She wandered among the graves, pausing here and there to read the dates and the unfamiliar names. There were no monuments, no statues of angels, no mausoleums, just rows and rows of simple headstones.

She found herself approaching a shallow flight of steps that led to a large area surrounded by evergreen bushes. In the centre was a headstone engraved with cursive gold script. A heart-shaped evergreen wreath had been propped up against it. This must be someone important. When she got close enough to read the words, she smiled. Just two words: Greta Garbo.

Lisa sat down on a bench and looked around. Far off through the trees a small bus came into view. There must be a road then. The bus stopped some way off and let off an elderly man carrying an evergreen wreath.

Lisa walked to the bus stop and managed to work out from the notice that the bus ran every half hour during daylight hours in a loop that took in the T-bana. She was in a cemetery so big that it had its own bus like the ones at the airport that take you from your car to the terminal. She stamped up and down for a few minutes to warm her feet and then sat down on the bench to wait.

It was a minute or two before she realised that she wasn't alone. About two hundred yards away a woman was standing among the trees, her dark slender figure almost merging with them. She seemed unaware of Lisa's presence. She was looking down at a grave, as if lost in contemplation. As Lisa watched, the woman lifted her head and gave a little nod, as if she was saying good-bye. She turned and walked towards the bus stop. She was wearing a fur hat, like a pale, soft aureole, a long black coat with gilt buttons, and carried a large burgundy leather bag that matched her boots. Very chic, very expensive. Something in her demeanour told Lisa that she wasn't young. As she came closer Lisa saw that skilful use of lipstick and eye make-up didn't disguise the fact the woman wouldn't see sixty again, or maybe even seventy. Lisa caught a whiff of an expensive perfume. She recognised it: Chanel No 19, one of her favourites.

She said something in Swedish.

Lisa shook her head. 'I'm sorry,' she said.

'You are English, yes?'

Lisa nodded.

'The bus, do you know how long?'

'Ten minutes or so.'

'Ah, good. I walked from the T-bana, but it's so cold. I catch the bus back.'

She sat down on the bench and regarded Lisa with interest. 'You are here visiting a family person?'

Lisa hadn't thought she'd need to account for herself and she stumbled over her explanation. 'No, no. I'm a – I'm interested in landscape architecture.'

'Oh, *ja*, Asplund. A great man, a great architect. This is a wonderful place.'

'And you? Who – ?'

'I come to visit my husband. I have my place here, too, and one day I will join him.' She spoke in a matter-of-fact way. 'When you get to my age, it's quite all right, you know. I've had most of my life and it's been a good one.' Lisa thought of Lawrence.

'Do you have children?' she asked.

'Oh, *ja*, and grandchildren, too.'

She told Lisa about them, one doing well at university in Lund, another taking a year out to travel.

Presently the bus came into view and Lisa fumbled for her purse.

'No, no,' said her companion, putting a hand on Lisa's arm. 'It's free.'

So it really *was* like the courtesy bus at the airport.

Lisa stood back to let the older woman board the bus. There were eight or nine people in the bus, mostly elderly

192

women, and there was plenty of room. The woman took a seat on one side of the aisle and Lisa took a seat on the other. She had enjoyed the brief contact, but it had been enough and she needed to think about her next move.

Everyone disembarked at the T-bana and the woman disappeared into the station. Lisa walked back to the entrance of the cemetery and up to the open space near the crematorium. She looked at her map: there was a short cut to the station if you cut across to the right past the hill that was crowned by a grove of trees. And that was how she discovered something that the lie of the land had hitherto concealed: a steep flight of snow-covered steps led to the top of the hill and a walled enclosure.

By the time she headed back to the T-bana twenty minutes later she had settled on her plan for the next day.

Chapter Thirty

She arrived at the cemetery around nine-thirty, just as it was getting light. She had stopped in Södermalm the previous day and bought a thermos flask and – with some effort – a hand-warmer. The hotel had filled the thermos with coffee and had provided a packed lunch. As she left for the T-bana, puny flakes of snow were making their way down from a pale grey sky. The receptionist had told her that it was minus three outside, but it felt colder than that. Good thing she had packed as if she was going to the Arctic. Her coat only just fastened over the layers of vests and jumpers. She looked as solid and chunky as a chessman.

She had toyed with the idea of hanging about all day at the T-bana station – but what if he didn't come by underground? – or of simply riding around on the cemetery bus all day, but it would be too easy to miss him. If he came by car or taxi, she was probably snookered anyway. And probably he wouldn't come at all, the whole venture was crazy, off the wall, but some solid core of bloody-mindedness wouldn't let her quit, now that she was here.

The walled enclosure on top of the mound gave the best view of the cemetery. From this vantage point, she could cover both the main entrance and the side entrance which led via a narrow path to the T-bana. She could see the road that wound into the forest and directly ahead of her was a long, narrow vista cutting through the lines of trees. She still couldn't see more than a fraction of the cemetery, but it was the best she could do.

It would be dark by three o'clock, so she had around

five hours to wait. She walked up and down, clapping her palms together to keep the circulation going. A man came up the path from the main entrance, pushing a bicycle, a mode of transport that hadn't occurred to her. It was hard to make out people's features at this distance, but he was too tall to be Jay. All the same she watched him until he was out of sight. It was company of a kind. Next came an older man with a young woman and a child bundled up in a pushchair: a husband, daughter and grandchild on their way to pay a Christmas visit to the wife and mother? She watched them out of sight with a little sense of yearning.

The day wore on. It seemed never-ending.

Around midday she badly needed a pee, and walked down to the crematorium, where there were some public loos. She was as quick as she could be which wasn't very quick, cold fingers fumbling with layers of clothes, like a small child struggling to use the loo.

She climbed back up the mound. It was getting colder. It was about two o'clock when she heard a sound and turned to see a man in a black overcoat and a homburg hat walking briskly up the steps towards her. Her heart stopped and the next moment raced on, but he bore only a passing resemblance to Jay. He crossed the enclosure, glancing at her without curiosity, it seemed, went on down the other side of the mound, and headed into the long, tree-lined avenue. She watched the dark figure growing smaller. The air was tinged with blue, the first sign of approaching night.

She looked back and Jay was walking past the crematorium. Her heart leapt. How could she have mistaken the other man for him even for a second? He turned left now and strode down a path into the forest. He would be out of sight soon. She hurried down the steps. He was walking faster now and she broke into a trot. While she was still circling the lake, he vanished into the trees. She slid on some ice, and struggled to keep her balance.

When she reached the trees, he had gone.

The lights on the graves trembled in the gloom. There was a movement off to the right and there he was, making his way deeper into the forest. She set off after him. He turned at a right angle along a line of graves and she lost sight of him again. When she reached the place where he had turned off, she saw him about a hundred yards away, kneeling by a grave with a trowel in his hand. She stood for a moment or two, getting her breath back. He took something from his pocket. She set off towards him. He leant forward and placed something in a small hole in the ground and covered it up.

She slowed down, reluctant to intrude on this private moment. She even felt a moment of regret. It wasn't too late to back off, to turn and walk quickly away, but then he looked up and it *was* too late. Her feet carried her on towards him. Without taking his eyes off her he rose slowly to his feet.

His eyes were wide with surprise and he stared at her without speaking.

She stopped a few feet away. The silence stretched out. She had time to appreciate the strangeness of the situation: two lovers reunited in the kingdom of the dead.

How she made the leap of intuition she would never know. The words sprang unbidden to her lips. 'How long have you been dead?' she asked him.

'It's more than five years now,' he replied.

She looked at the headstone and read the names engraved there.

Jonathan Redcliffe 1967-2004
Mia Carlsson Redcliffe 1965-2004
Samuel Carlsson Redcliffe 1994-2004
'You're Jonathan ...'
He nodded.
'And the others? Your wife? And your son?'

197

But he wasn't listening. He was looking over her shoulder, scanning the lines of trees.

Now she, too, was looking around. Some way off an elderly woman was tending a grave. There was no-one else in sight.

'Could you have been followed?' he asked.

'Followed?'

He seized her hand. 'Come on!'

He began to walk very fast, threading his way through the graves. His sense of urgency was infectious. She found herself struggling to keep pace with him, half walking, half running by his side.

'But, Jay –'

'We've got to get out of here. We'll talk later.'

She tugged at him. 'What's all this about?'

He stopped abruptly and turned to face her. 'What am I thinking of? Your mobile phone! You've got it with you?'

She nodded.

'Give it to me.'

As she handed it over, she wondered if Jay had gone off his head? Of all the things she had feared, that hadn't been one of them, but –'He read her mind. 'I'm not mad. I'm not paranoid.' He took her hand and held it to side of his face. She felt the puckered skin uneven under her fingers. 'They did this to me. And they killed Mia and Sam.'

She stared at him. Could this really be happening?

'Who is – who are –'

'I'll tell you everything. But later –'

He opened the phone and took out the sim card. There was a waste bin not far away. He tossed it in. Her eye was caught by a movement. She saw a man coming down the hill from the crematorium, a man in a black overcoat and a homburg hat. He was trying to run, but was slipping and slithering on the icy path.

'Jay!' She pointed. Jay turned to look. 'Oh, my God.'

198

'The bus!' Lisa said. She could see it some way off, winding through the trees.

'Come on!'

'But, Jay!' He set off at a run. Lisa jogged after him. She could see the bus-stop now, but would they reach it before the bus got there? She looked round. The man had reached the shelter of the trees. The ground was clear there and he began to run between the graves, really running, legs and arms pumping like pistons. Ahead of her Jay had realised that she wasn't with him. He was beckoning furiously. She panted after him, sweating in her layers of clothes. She was afraid that if she fell over she would never get up again.

The bus was only a few hundred metres away, but they weren't going to make it.

Jay was waving at it. She thought the bus was going to go sailing on. Then she saw that it was slowing down and Jay was jogging towards it.

She put on a spurt. The bus stopped and the door opened. Jay put one foot on the step to stop it closing. She felt sick, but all she had to do was keep going.

She had almost reached the road, when she tripped over a tree root, and went sprawling. The breath was knocked out of her body. Then Jay was hauling her up. He got behind her and propelled her into the bus. She caught the bus driver's eye. He looked quizzical, but he didn't say anything. The pneumatic doors closed behind them with a hiss and the bus moved smoothly off.

The bus was nearly full. Jay led her down the aisle to the back seat. They sat down, both still breathing heavily. Jay twisted his neck to look out of the back window. She turned, too. The man in the black coat had stopped near Mia and Sam's grave.

Jay murmured something under his breath. It sounded like 'lucky …'

She reached for his hand. His fingers closed round hers.

The flat was on the tenth floor of a block high up in Södermalm. They arrived there by a circuitous route involving two buses. They had scarcely spoken during the journey. As soon as they were inside Jay closed the door of the flat and took her in his arms. They stood locked together, her head on his shoulder, his cheek against her hair. He was gripping her so tightly that she could hardly breathe.

'I've missed you so much,' she heard him murmur. She pulled away and looked into his face. 'I thought I'd never see you again.'

'I know. I'm sorry.'

'What's all this about, Jay? Are you a criminal?'

He stared at her as though he didn't know what the word meant. Then he started to laugh.

She pulled away from him. 'This isn't funny! What the fuck's going on? In the cemetery – was that a policeman?'

Immediately he sobered up. 'No – no, it wasn't. And I'm not a criminal. At least –' He shook his head. 'No.'

'But you're in danger? We should go to the police.'

'No police,' Jay said. 'I've got to make you understand. They can't help us. They couldn't prevent Mia and Sam from being killed.'

'Then what the fuck is going on?

'Look, I'll tell you everything, but let's get out of Stockholm first.' Lisa looked around. The place was small, just one main room with a sleeping gallery and a bathroom and a kitchen opening off on either side. It was comfortable in a modern Swedish manner, lots of glass and pale wood and framed flower prints. There was a solid wall of books, mostly English titles. Lisa caught a few names: Ian McEwan, Doris Lessing, Margaret Atwood.

'Is this your flat?' she asked.

He shook his head. 'Belongs to Annica, Mia's second cousin. She works for Médecins Sans Frontières. She's in the Sudan.'

Through the window Lisa saw the snow-covered roofs of Stockholm, luminous under a moonlit sky. Vast stretches of inky water glittered in the lights of the city. A big ship, decked with lights – a ferry from Finland? – was moored at the quay-side. She couldn't see her hotel, it was tucked out of sight, but she could see the street that led to it.

She had at last found Jay, but at what cost? What had Stella said about opening Pandora's box? There was no going back now. She felt strangely detached. Was this shock, or what? Jay was on the other side of the room, stuffing clothes into a holdall. 'It's better if we get right away,' he said.

'But – my things?'

'Ring the hotel. Say you've been called home unexpectedly and you've gone straight to the airport. They can parcel up your stuff and send it on.'

There was so much she wanted to ask him that she scarcely knew where to begin.

'Why did you just disappear like that?' she asked. 'Why didn't you contact me? And why didn't you tell me about your wife? And that you'd had a child?'

'I'll tell you everything, I promise. But it's a long story and I'll feel better when we're out of Stockholm. I don't *think* they know about Mia's cousin, but we can't be too careful –' He went into the kitchen and took a plastic carrier bag out of a drawer. He opened the fridge and took out a piece of cheese wrapped in cling film. 'We'd better take all this with us. Annica won't be back until May.'

'But where are we going?'

He stared at her, as if he scarcely saw her. His expression changed and he put down the bag. He went over and put his hands on her shoulders.

'Look, I'm sorry. I'm so used to being on my own and deciding everything. There's a house I sometimes use out

201

in the country – an old friend of Mia's. I'll borrow Annica's car and we'll go there.'

'But – the snow –'

'Not a problem. They're used to it here. They clear the roads and the car's fitted with snow tyres.' Jay put his arm round her and pulled her close. 'Please trust me,' he said. He kissed her, but after a few seconds he pulled away.

'Who's looking after Ricky?' he said. The question was like a slap in the face. Jay saw her register the shock. He said quickly, 'He's probably perfectly OK but – you'd better ring him. Use the phone here.'

Chapter Thirty-one

Ricky manoeuvred his wheelchair over to the window to watch Charlotte and Piki going down the path. Light from the setting sun sent a gleaming track across the sea. He loved the view from his window. All the leaves had gone from the trees and he liked them best like that. You could see so much further. He had a feeling for landscape that he couldn't describe and didn't really want to. It wasn't very cool, but Charlotte felt it, too. It was one of the reasons why they had chosen to do the photography project together.

He sat for a few moments more, just luxuriating in the knowledge that he was alone in the house. It hardly ever happened.

He turned to the computer, his hand moved over the keyboard, and image after image appeared on the screen. They had set up the camera so that they would get a slanting view across the lake. They had taken the latest photograph that morning.

He brought the picture up to the screen, and leaned forward, scanning it inch by inch. In a strange way the picture was more real than the actual thing. It must be because the lens could take in more detail than the naked eye. When he zoomed in, he seemed to plunge into the frost-covered garden. The sun had only reached half way across the lawn and the rest was still white with frost. There was something he couldn't quite make sense of, a shape on the grass, or rather a line of shapes. He frowned. Surely those couldn't be footprints? He took the picture up to the point where the pixels started to dissolve and then brought it back to the point of highest definition. They did look like footprints. Maybe from when Charlotte took Piki out this morning? But no, because they didn't go up to the house. The marks on the grass were in a loop that came out of the wood and returned to it. Was it a deer? Maybe ...

He sat back and rubbed his eyes with his knuckles. When he looked again, he still couldn't make up his mind.

He turned his wheelchair and looked out of the window. He couldn't see the marks at all from here. The angle was wrong.

It would be getting dark soon. There was just the faintest hint of twilight in the air.

Piki came galloping up the slope from the headland. A few moments afterwards Charlotte's head bobbed into view. He watched her come up the path. She was wearing Doc Marten boots and a long, black, velvet coat with lots of buttons that she'd bought on E-bay. On her head was a ridiculous knitted hat with fingers sticking up from the top, like a glove. What he liked about Char was the way she always lived up to her idea of herself. She didn't give a damn about what other people thought. Dad had dropped in the previous day and he liked her, too, Ricky could tell, and that was cool.

Charlotte was scowling as she came in. Even through her dead-white make-up he could see that her cheeks were flushed from the cold and she brought a breath of the chilly outdoors with her. She flourished a Marlborough cigarette packet.

'Honestly – the way some people behave. They come out here to enjoy the countryside, you'd think they'd be careful not to litter it up.'

'You'd think they'd be too smart to smoke as well.'

Charlotte poked her tongue out. 'OK, wise guy. I'm going to give up, actually.'

She tossed the packet in the bin. She rubbed her hands together. 'Ok, it's the last night before your Mum gets back. Here's what we're going to do. I'll cook a proper meal. Not frozen pizza, I'm going to do pasta and we won't have it in the kitchen. I'll set the table and everything.'

'We could have some wine. There are some bottles in the kitchen.'

'Hey, cool. But won't your Mum mind?'

'Nah.'

'And then how about a DVD?'

'Buffy again?'

'Buffy again.'

When the phone rang, he flipped the loudspeaker switch.

'Ricky?' It was his mother, her voice high and anxious. 'Mum! What's the matter?' He could sense her taking a breath, composing herself. 'Nothing, nothing's the matter, I'm fine. Are you alright?'

'Course. I've been having a great time. How are you doing? Did you find him?' She cut across him. 'Look, love, I can't chat now, but the thing is, I've changed my mind about you being there on your own.'

'Oh, what?' He knew he sounded like a petulant kid, but he couldn't help it. 'I'm sorry, sweetheart, it's a disappointment, I know, I'll make it up to you. I'm going to ring Dad and get him to come over.'

'Oh, Mu–u-um.'

'Ricky,' she said in that steely tone that meant business. 'I've made up my mind and that's that. 'Charlotte came into the room with an open bottle of wine.

'Mum! I've got to go now.'

'And Ricky, have you locked the house up properly?'

'Yes!'

'Check for me, please.'

'I said "yes!"' He hung up.

'Supper's ready,' Charlotte said. 'Was that your mum? There isn't a problem, is there?'

'She wanted to make sure that we've locked up

properly.' He wouldn't tell her just yet that his dad was coming over. It would only spoil the atmosphere.

'I've done that.'

'Did you bolt the door?'

'Yep.'

'Cool. Let's have some music on. We can turn it up as loud as we like.'

Charlotte had cooked penne and had chopped the courgettes and the tomatoes into small pieces so that he could eat with just a fork. It wasn't a big deal, she just did it, and he appreciated that.

She had found a tablecloth somewhere and some candles.

'Hey,' he said.

She smiled and shrugged, meaning it wasn't a seduction scene or anything like that. They'd agreed a while ago that they wouldn't have sex. He would have liked to, just so that he knew what it was like. Still she was his best friend and it might have spoilt that. But maybe she was having second thoughts. The idea was exciting, frightening, too …

He brought his wheelchair up to the table. Piki flopped down beside him with her head on her paws. Charlotte switched off the lights so that the room was lit only by candlelight. Darkness pressed against the window. Far away on the Welsh coast pinpricks of light glittered.

The wine was a rioja. Ricky looked at the label. 14 per cent proof.

'I chose it because it's got such a pretty label,' Charlotte explained.

Ricky wasn't used to drinking much, though he used to have the odd beer with Lawrence. Charlotte wasn't used to it either. She disapproved of those girls at school who went out binge drinking and ended up showing off their knickers and being sick in the gutter. But wine wasn't like

206

drinking vodka or alcopops, was it? It was a proper grown-up drink and they were having it with a meal, like they did in France.

Having their wine in tumblers made it easier for Ricky, but it was difficult to keep track of how much they were drinking. The first glass went down fast.

'Wow,' Charlotte said. 'This wine's going to my head like – like –'

'Like wine!'

They giggled.

Ricky couldn't remember the last time he'd enjoyed himself so much. Everything was going right, the stuff with Dad, Mum cutting him some slack. Then he remembered that she'd back-pedalled on that, and that Dad was coming over. Still he wouldn't be here for at least an hour.

Piki whined. She got up and went over to the window, her tail giving the kind of half-wag that meant she was uncertain about something.

Charlotte turned to watch Piki. 'What's that?'

'What?

'Outside. I thought I saw something.' Ricky turned his wheelchair. He couldn't see anything, except his reflection and Charlotte's at the table. The candle flames floated in the darkness.

Piki gave a low rumbling growl.

'A fox, or a badger,' Ricky said. 'They sometimes come right up to the house and raid the bin.'

'It's a bit spooky, those big windows and the dark outside.' She was right. 'We could lower the blinds,' he said. 'In the living room, too.' Charlotte jumped to her feet. She pulled down the blinds in the dining room and went through to the living room. Ricky turned his wheelchair to watch her. She pulled the switch. The blinds were still descending when the telephone rang. Charlotte went to answer it.

Ricky groaned to himself. It would probably be Mum on his case again.

'No, she isn't here,' Charlotte said. 'Do you want to speak to Ricky? It's Gavin,' she said to Ricky and switched on the loudspeaker.

'Hey there, Ricky. Peony's been asking after you and your Mum.'

'That's great,' Ricky said through his voice aid.

'When will your mum be in?'

'She's away. She'll be back tomorrow evening.' There was silence at the other end. Then Gavin said, 'There's no reason why I shouldn't tell you. The crash. The police don't think it was an accident. They're saying someone tampered with the car. Look, I'd better go, been at the hospital all day, I need to get home to the kids. Ask your mum to ring me when she gets back.'

He hung up.

Ricky and Charlotte were still staring at each other when the doorbell rang.

It took Ricky a moment to register what it was. They rarely had unexpected visitors, and never at night.

It rang again, a prolonged, insistent peal.

'Who is it?' Charlotte said. 'It can't be your dad, can it?'

Ricky shook his head. 'Mum gave him a key.'

The bell rang again.

Charlotte went into the kitchen. Ricky followed her and Piki came along behind.

Charlotte cleared her throat. 'Who is it?' Her voice sounded squeaky, like a little girl's.

'Oh, there *is* someone there. Thank goodness.' It was a woman's voice, high and anxious. 'My name's Mary Thompson, my friend's fallen in the woods and I think she's broken her leg. Our mobiles don't work out here.'

Charlotte and Ricky exchanged glances.

Ricky nodded. Of course they had to let her in.

'OK, hang on,' Charlotte said. 'I'll just find the key. Where is it?' she asked Ricky.

'Isn't it in the door?'

She shook her head. 'Oh hell, where did I put it?'

The work surfaces were covered with things that needed washing up. She started to move glasses and plates.

'Please hurry,' the woman said. 'It's so cold, I'm afraid my friend'll get exposure.'

'I'm coming!' Charlotte said. She lifted up a tea-towel. 'There it is!' She pounced on the key.

Ricky watched her take it over to the door and put it in the lock. Piki growled. He looked down at the dog. She was standing bolt upright, hair bristling. She didn't like this, and suddenly neither did he. What were walkers doing out there when it had been dark for hours? He remembered the anxiety in his mother's voice and her worry about whether the house was locked –

'Wait, Charlotte!'

'What?' She turned the key and looked round. Ricky shook his head. Things were happening too quickly, spinning out of control. 'Just wait a moment.'

'Oh, come on, Ricky.' Charlotte reached for the bolt.

'How do we know she's telling the truth?' he asked, glad for once that his voice was incomprehensible to strangers.

But Charlotte wasn't taking any notice. She was drawing back the bolt – in half a second the door would be open –

Chapter Thirty-two

'Do you remember,' Jay said, 'five, six years ago a woman, Frida Lorenson, she was murdered in Chiswick? It hit the headlines because she was blonde and Swedish, and married to a wealthy man called Lars Lorenson.'

Lisa did remember. 'I read about it.'

'Mia, my wife, she was Swedish, too. That's partly how we knew them. We lived near them in Chiswick in a little house on the mall. Mia was friendly with Frida, the wife.' They had driven out of the city along the same road that Lisa had arrived on only two days ago. They emerged from Stockholm into a snowy landscape that glowed in the light of a full moon.

'When Frida died, the police suspected Lars. They always look at the husband, don't they? And there'd been problems between them. Frida wanted a divorce – she'd told Mia that. She was going to go away and she was going to take their baby daughter with her. The police fixed the time of death pretty accurately because Frida rang her mother at quarter to eleven and the nanny came back from a night out and found the body around midnight. Lars told the police they'd had a row – clever of him to admit to that – but his story was that she had been alive when he had left the house at half-past nine to drive down to their house in Wiltshire. The housekeeper there confirmed his time of arrival. Lars seemed to be in the clear. Jewellery was missing and it looked like a burglary gone wrong.'

Jay was silent. Outside the night and the countryside unscrolled like a film without a soundtrack.

Then he said, 'I was out with the dog and I saw Lars

leave the house at half-past eleven. He didn't see me. I was wearing a dark coat, Benji was black and it was pouring with rain. We were more or less invisible.'

Traffic was sparse. Headlights appeared only sporadically. The road behind them was empty, but Jay's eyes flicked constantly to the rear-view mirror.

'For Lars it was sheer bad luck. For us, too. We'd been happy. We had Sam. We had enough money, a nice little house. Mia was a P.A. and I had a job with a big firm of City accountants.'

'So that bit was true … '

'Yes, I did train as an accountant and, Lisa, I tried not to lie to you. I just didn't tell you very much.' Lisa thought, what is it about travelling in a car at night that makes it easier to talk? It was as though they were the only people in the world.

Jay said, 'That life, our life, in Chiswick ended the moment I picked up the phone to speak to the police. God, how I wish I hadn't –'

'But he'd have got away with it –'

'He got away with it anyway.' Jay's face was pale in the light from the dashboard. 'The police told us things we hadn't known about him. Shady business dealings, maybe worse. They'd been trying to pin something on him for a while, but they met what they called a wall of silence. After I went to the police, funny things started happening, people ringing and then hanging up in the middle of the night. We found a dead cat on the doorstep. Then one day I opened a letter and there was a photo of Sam, taken in his school playground. It had been torn in half. The police took us into Witness Protection. We were gone in a few hours and they took us to a house in the suburbs of Leicester.'

He paused again.

'Are you OK?' Lisa asked.

'Not really. I haven't talked about this for years. There

wasn't anyone I *could* talk to. Do you mind if I pull over?'

There was a layby ahead. He signalled and pulled in. He left the engine running and turned to look at Lisa.

'The house exploded. A gas leak. Killed Mia and Sam outright and would have killed me, too, if I hadn't got up to let the dog out.'

He was facing Lisa but he wasn't seeing her. He was somewhere far away. She reached out a hand and put it on his thigh. He put his hand on hers and squeezed it so hard that she cried out.

'Sorry,' he said.

'What happened next?'

'I woke up in a burns clinic under armed guard. Joe told me what had happened.'

'Wait,' Lisa said. 'Back up a bit – who's Joe?'

'He was the police officer in charge.'

'The explosion ... it wasn't an accident?'

Jay shook his head. 'Lorenson managed to get to someone on the team who were looking after us. Joe thought it was this woman, Sandra, but nothing was proved. She left the police soon after.' Jay felt in the inside pocket of his jacket and brought out his wallet. An articulated lorry rumbled past. 'Joe salvaged some things from the rubble of the house. He shouldn't have done that – disturbing a crime scene – but he was gutted about what had happened. There was a little Dinky Toy, a bread van, that was Sam's. It had been mine when I was a kid. And a photograph of Mia and me and Sam. Here, you can't really see.' He fumbled for the interior light.

Lisa leaned over. With their heads together they looked at the photo. A much younger Jay smiled out at them. His arm was round a woman, pretty, blonde, and there was a little boy leaning against the woman's knees. Behind them, water, a summer's day. The edge of the photo was dark and crinkled.

'And there was this,' Jay said.

213

From an inner compartment of his wallet he eased out a little square velvet envelope of midnight blue. He opened the flap and tipped something out into the palm of his hand. It was a tiny golden horse, standing on its hind legs, wings sprouting from its shoulders.

'Pegasus,' Lisa said, touching it with the tip of her finger.

'It's from a charm bracelet that had belonged to my mother. She gave it to Mia.'

Lisa stroked the charm. The surface was pitted and the link that had attached it to the bracelet was twisted. She looked at the photo with its dark edge, eaten away by fire. That little boy. She swallowed hard. In spite of the heat inside the car, she shivered.

'I must speak to Barry again.'

Chapter Thirty-three

Ricky rammed the joy stick forward and the wheelchair shot across the kitchen floor. Just in time Charlotte saw it coming, and jumped back with a little yelp. The chair slammed into the door, jerking Ricky forward.

'The bolt – push it right back,' Ricky gasped.

'Ric-ky!'

'Just DO it. AND lock the door.'

Charlotte looked appalled, but she did it.

'What's going on?' said the voice outside, plaintive now. 'Come on, kids. Let me in. My friend could die if I don't get help to her.'

'On guard!' Ricky told Piki. The dog flung herself down by the back door.

Ricky turned his wheelchair and headed for the dining room. He gestured to Charlotte to follow him. He turned his wheelchair to speak to her. Her face was stony.

'Ricky – for God's sake –'

'*Kids*,' he hissed. 'She called us kids! How does she know that we're on our own? Why isn't she asking for our parents?'

Charlotte's eyes were wide. 'You mean –'

'She knows it's just us. And another thing – a minute ago her friend only had a broken leg, but now she's *dying*.'

'It *is* weird. Maybe we shouldn't let her in – but Ricky, what if her friend *is* dying?'

'We could just dial 999 and ask for an ambulance. We don't have to open the door.'

'OK.'

'Go and tell her.'

She went back into the kitchen and he heard her say,

'We'll ring the emergency services for you.' When she returned, her face was troubled. 'She's not there anymore. I don't like this.'

Neither did he. He felt queasy. 'Try the phone.'

Charlotte punched in the numbers and frowned. She tried again. She shook her head. 'The line's dead.'

'Jesus.'

They stared at each other.

'Ricky, what's going on?'

'I don't know.'

He looked at the window. It felt safer having the blinds down – a barrier between them and the night and whoever was out there. But it also meant that they couldn't see out.

'Char, go upstairs to Ma's study, and switch on the lights. See if there's anyone outside.'

She hesitated. He could see that she didn't want to leave him.

'Go on!'

'OK.' Her feet clattered up the spiral staircase, sounding loud in the silence. The lights sprung on in his mother's study. A few moments later Charlotte came back, shaking her head.

Ricky sent her across the gallery to Lawrence's room. When she came out, she looked scared. She didn't speak until she had come down the stairs and was close to him.

'I couldn't see anyone. But I could hear someone talking in a low voice. Ricky – she's not on her own.'

The last few words were drowned out by a high, whining noise coming from the direction of the kitchen. For a moment or two Ricky couldn't think what it was. Then he understood. It was the sound of a drill. They hadn't managed to con their way in, so they were resorting to force.

His heart sank. What could he do? He should be protecting Charlotte, but he was just a cripple in a wheelchair and –

Charlotte was speaking, but he could hardly hear her above the noise of the drill.

'Close the living-room door!' he shouted.

She did. When she turned back, she looked as if she was on the verge of tears. 'Who are they?'

'I don't know.' He wanted to cry, too, he was so frightened.

Hold it, a voice said in Ricky's head. *Stop right there, young man.* That was what Lawrence used to say. *We don't do self-pity. When the going gets tough, the tough get going.* Charlotte was off on her own train of thought. 'What would Buffy do?'

'What?'

'Of course Buffy has supernatural powers –' Charlotte was saying.

Lawrence, Ricky thought, Lawrence and his voice.

'So have I,' Ricky said.

'What?' Charlotte stared at him.

'I've got supernatural powers.' He gestured to his voice-aid.

He watched her face as the penny dropped. 'You mean, we could make them think your dad's here –'

'I haven't got Dad's voice, but I've got Lawrence's.'

'Come on. Let's give it a try.'

They went into the kitchen and Ricky manoeuvred his wheelchair to the back door. He ran the fingers of his good hand over the keyboard, selecting, ordering. He looked at Charlotte and nodded: he was ready.

Charlotte put her head close to his. 'Wait until they stop for a moment,' she whispered.

She stood back, her eyes holding his. The drilling stopped abruptly. Charlotte gave a little nod of the head, like a conductor readying an orchestra, and Ricky stabbed a finger at the keyboard.

A voice boomed out at full sergeant-major volume. 'What the blue blazes do you think you're doing! Stop that

217

bloody racket!'

Ricky was expecting it, but he still jumped. Charlotte clapped both hands over her mouth. Piki let off a barrage of barks. But this was nothing, Ricky guessed, to the impact it was having on the other side of the door. There was absolute silence and then he knew, he wasn't sure how, that whoever was outside had moved away. He backed away into the dining room. Charlotte followed him bent double. She extended a foot and kicked the door shut behind her. She straightened up and he saw that her eyes were full of tears. She took her hands away from her mouth and let out a guffaw.

'That was fantastic,' she spluttered. 'Maybe you should have given them Marilyn Monroe. Or Arnie. That would really have put the frighteners on them.' Ricky began to laugh, too, but in a few moments reality kicked in.

'Get a grip, Charlotte. It's not over yet.'

The laughter drained from her face. 'Perhaps they'll just go away?'

He shook his head. 'They'll figure it out. We've got to find a way of getting help.' Piki had followed them through. She went to Ricky and pushed her head against his hand. He fondled her, pulling at the long silky ears.

'There's only one thing for it,' Charlotte said. 'I've got to get out somehow and go for help.'

He shook his head. 'Think about it, Char. How would you get out without them seeing you? And anyway it would take you hours to get up to the main road – and in the dark it's dangerous; you might break an ankle or something. We've got to think. There must be something.'

'OK! Let's brainstorm,' Charlotte put her fingers to her forehead. 'Ways of communicating: radio, Morse code, semaphore –'

'No –'

'There must be something, let me think, let me think.' Charlotte flapped her hands like a desperate contestant on

218

a quiz show. 'What do people do when they're lost on a mountain in the snow? A fire – we could light a fire – and people would see it from out at sea – '

'Brilliant, Char,' Ricky said sarcastically, 'how do we do that without burning the bloody house down –'

'Well, you think of something better,' she snapped, close to tears.

He stared at her. 'Char, Char, you ARE brilliant, you are fucking brilliant – fire, yes, *flares* – I saw them, with the other stuff Frank brought back from the boat!'

'Where are they?'

'In the garage. We can get in through the connecting door in the kitchen.'

'But Ricky – the garage – is it locked to the outside? I mean, could *they* get into the garage?'

Ricky groaned. It was almost certainly not locked. 'Mum might not even have closed the doors,' he said.

Charlotte said, 'I'll have to sneak in. It's our only chance.'

'I'll try to distract them.'

'But how?'

'I'll raise the blinds – the ones at the far end of the sitting room. That should get them to the other end of the house. They'll wonder what's happening.'

'What do they look like – the flares, where will they be?'

'In a big black plastic bin-liner with all Lawrence's things from the boat, jumpers and stuff – just grab the lot.'

'I'll stand at the door and wait until you tell me to go.' Ricky rolled himself over to the far side of the sitting room and positioned himself by the switch that operated the blinds. He could see right through the dining room into the kitchen where Charlotte was standing by the connecting door with her hand on the handle. Her eyes were fixed on him, her face white and set.

He threw the switch and scooted back across the room.

219

Jerkily the blind began to ascend.

There were footsteps on the path outside the window. Yes! He nodded to Charlotte. She slipped back the bolt and opened the door. She disappeared into the garage. He fixed his eyes on the open door. Any moment he expected to see the intruders come through. When at last she appeared, dragging a black plastic bag after her, he wanted to cheer. She slammed the door shut and rammed the bolt home. She stood with her back to the door, breathing heavily, her eyes closed. 'You OK?' Ricky asked.

She nodded and opened her eyes. She took a deep breath, bent forward, seized the bottom of the bag, and tipped out its contents onto the floor. Among the maps, jumpers, magazines and books were two bright yellow-and-red cylinders.

'That's them!' Ricky cried.

'How do they work?' Charlotte picked one up.

'There are instructions printed on them. Char – be careful.'

'Where'll I –'

'The balcony outside Mum's study.'

She was away, sprinting up the spiral staircase. Ricky got into the living room in time to see her disappearing through the study door. There was an agonising pause – maybe the flares were too old – or maybe she couldn't work out how to set them off – and then there was a flash that lit up the night followed by a boom that rocked the world.

Piki yowled and shot under the sofa.

Ricky sent the wheelchair across the floor to the uncovered section of the window. He reached it just as the second flare shot across the pond like a guided missile. It was too low – it must have fallen over as it was going off. A dazzling light blossomed over the garden and there was a second boom that made his ears ring. There was a loud splash.

He squinted out into the night – there was some kind of commotion – and through the ringing in his ears he thought he heard yelling and screaming.

He strained to see what was happening. There was a hand on his shoulder. He jerked so violently that he nearly fell out of his chair. It was only Charlotte.

'There's someone in the lake!' she shouted.

He wanted to leap out of his chair and dance around the room. It had worked better than he could have imagined.

He grabbed Charlotte's arm. 'You've got to go!'

She was looking into his face and frowning. She, too, had been deafened by the boom.

'Go, go, go.'

Then she understood – but for a moment he thought she wasn't going to do it.

'Idiot! Go!' He was in an agony of impatience.

She leaned forward and gave him a fleeting kiss. Then she was on her way through the kitchen. She pulled back the bolt and turned the latch. The door closed behind her and she was gone.

He didn't think there was much hope of her getting help, but at least she could hide in the woods.

Awkwardly he steered his wheelchair so that he could push back the bolt on the door.

Piki was peering out at him from under the sofa.

He clicked his tongue. 'Come on, old girl, it's just you and me now.'

She crept out and slunk to his side.

He guided his chair into his room and through into the bathroom. Piki trailed after him.

'We're not going to make things any easier than we have to,' he told her. He pressed the button for the automatic door lock and the door slid across. Piki rested her chin on his knee.

He settled down to wait for what would happen next.

221

Chapter Thirty-four

The track was just wide enough for the car. A dense forest of pine and birch pressed in on either side. The trees were so tall that Lisa couldn't see their tops.

'Nearly there,' Jay said.

The headlights picked out a narrow entrance between two buildings that looked like lodge houses.

They drove in and a security light came on. The car came to a halt. They were in a semi-circular courtyard. Before them was a long, low house clad in timber, split logs painted iron-oxide red. There were dormer windows and a great tiled roof that swept down to an imposing double door. When Jay said a place in the country, Lisa had imagined a log cabin. This was like something in a fairy tale.

They got out of the car. The air was so cold that Lisa caught her breath. The night was clear and the stars tingled above them. Jay took a flashlight out of the boot and swung the beam around. The snow was pristine except where it merged into the forest. There was a little tangle of animal footprints, foxes, maybe. The silence was intense. Jay took out a key and unlocked the door. They stepped inside. There was a smell of old books and dusty upholstery. It was chilly, but not as cold as Lisa had expected.

Jay said, 'The heating's kept on low to stop the pipes freezing. There's a farmer a mile or so away who keeps an eye on things and clears the track.'

'The phone?' Lisa said.

'In the kitchen.' Lisa dialled the long number and hugged herself against the cold as she waited for a reply.

She watched Jay opening cupboards and taking out jars and bottles. The kitchen looked like a watercolour by Carl Larson: tongue-and-groove boarding on the walls, a white-painted wooden dresser, chairs with blue-and-white striped seat covers.

The phone rang on and on. She felt a trickle of fear.

'No-one's picking up.'

'Try Barry again.'

'There won't be a signal if he's at the house and he must be there by now.'

'Try anyway.' Jay was opening a bottle, setting out glasses.

Barry answered with a terse, 'Yeah?'

'Where are you?'

'I've just gone through Exford.'

'Why aren't you there!'

'Traffic hold-up. An accident. I'll be there in twenty minutes.'

'I've been trying to ring Ricky and there's no reply.'

'I wouldn't worry too much. You know what kids are. Loud music – TV up high – hey, they might even be making out. Woah –' he exclaimed and simultaneously she heard a faint boom. 'Someone's let off a flare.' There was another boom. 'Funny, I didn't see the light from that one. I bet that's why the kids aren't answering, too busy watching whatever's happening in the Channel. I'd better go, give me your number and I'll ring the *instant* I get there, OK?'

When she hung up, Jay put a small glass in her hand and without thinking she took a gulp. There was a burst of heat in her throat and her head swam.

She put her hand to her chest. 'What –?'

'Akvavit,' Jay said. 'I'd better tell you the rest of the story. When I came round in the burns clinic, I couldn't remember much. I was concussed. Joe had to fill in the gaps for me.' There was a bitter twist to his mouth. 'It

224

wasn't just a physical thing. I was dazed with shock and grief. I was in no fit state to testify against Lars. One day I just got up and walked out of the hospital. It wasn't difficult. The police were focused on not letting anyone get to me. It hadn't occurred to them that I might want to get out. I got on a cross-channel ferry and got off as a different person. The police thought I'd committed suicide. I wanted Lars to believe that I was dead.'

'Couldn't we contact Joe? If you can trust him –'

Jay shook his head. 'He's not in the police force any more. Do you want some more of that?' He pointed to her glass.

She shook her head. Her eyes strayed to the phone. 'I'm going to try again,' she said.

There was still no answer at Falling Water. No point in ringing Barry's mobile again, but oh how she wanted to. It took every scrap of willpower to wait.

'Who was that woman in the garden centre?' she asked. 'The one who recognised you?'

'You got onto that, did you? I'm impressed.'

'She left for New Zealand the following week without leaving a forwarding address.'

'She did, did she? I'm not surprised.' There was contempt in his voice. 'Last thing she wanted was to find that I was still alive and there was a chance that after all there might be a trial one day. She was Lars's housekeeper, the one who gave him a false alibi.'

'Was that how they got onto you, Lars and Sandra?'

'I doubt it.' Jay told her how he had spotted Sandra at King's Cross Station. 'I'd have known her anywhere. Do you know, Mia *liked* her, used to tease her about those bloody stupid shoes she used to wear.'

'Shoes?' Lisa said.

'Mia used to think it was funny. Sandra wore these dowdy suits – but always with really sexy and expensive shoes.'

Lisa stared at him. Expensive shoes. Sexy shoes. Black suede shoes with kitten heels?

'What's the matter?'

'That nurse. Karen – but surely –' She sat down on a kitchen stool. She put her hand to her forehead and squeezed her temples. 'There was an accident.' She told him what had happened. 'Do you think –?'

'Accidents are their speciality.'

She shivered. The effect of the alcohol had worn off, leaving her colder than ever.

'You need some food,' Jay said. 'Something to warm you up.' He reached for a jar of fish soup.

'Why, oh why hasn't Barry rung?'

Jay had his hand on the jar. He looked round at her.

'Barry turned up pretty smartly after all this began, didn't he? You *can* trust him, I suppose?'

Barry turned onto the track to Falling Water. It was more familiar now, but still needed his full attention, especially in the dark. Actually he prided himself on never giving less than his full attention to anything.

He concentrated on manoeuvring the BMW down the rutted track, trying to avoid branches that might scratch the paintwork.

His ear caught the sound of a car coming up the track. Probably Charlotte's mother. She must have nipped over to check up on them. But why was she gunning the engine like that?

He glimpsed car lights through the trees. The driver was coming up the track like a bat out of hell. The headlights jerked about as the car was flung from side to side. The car came round the bend and headed straight for him. For Christ's sake – there wasn't room for them both! Barry banged his fist on the horn. He caught a glimpse of someone leaning forward over the steering wheel and a figure slumped in the passenger seat. He wrenched his steering wheel to the left. The car lurched and shuddered over the ruts of the track. The other driver must have pulled to the left too. He broad-sided the BMW. There was the grinding of metal on metal, then the other car was shooting up the hill. Barry slammed the brakes on and the car juddered to a standstill. Almost at the last moment it made contact with something solid. Barry jerked forward and was caught by the seat-belt.

He got out of the car on trembling legs and looked at the damage. The car had hit a sapling and the glass of the left-hand headlight was smashed. He got a flashlight out of the glove compartment and checked the side of the car. There was a long ugly gash. And that, miraculously, was all.

He had time now to wonder why the other driver was so desperate to escape. What he would find at the house? He took a deep slow breath. He must not hurry. That was how mistakes were made. Quicker to drive or to get the flashlight out of the boot and continue on foot? Better to drive. He got back in the car and with infinite care, put the car in reverse, holding his breath as he waited to see if the tires would grip. They did.

He headed down the track.

The house was blazing with light. It took him a moment to work out what was strange about it. In the sitting room one blind was down and the other was up. He ran to the door and hammered on it. He waited to see if anyone was coming, but there was absolute silence. He remembered he had a key. When he turned it in the lock, the door didn't open. He put his shoulder against it, but it held fast. Must be bolted on the inside.

He looked through the sitting-room window. Not a soul to be seen. Where the fuck were they?

He became aware of a strange smell, smoky and acrid, like the aftermath of a firework display. Something was glowing and smouldering out on the other side of the pond. He ran round. The paved edge was covered in water that seemed to have slopped out of the pond and further along there was a trail of something dark and viscous. Was this blood? Oh God.

'Ricky!' he shouted. 'Ricky! It's Dad!'

There was a sound behind him. He spun round. A figure was running towards him out of the wood.

'Barry, Barry!' It was Charlotte.

She hurtled toward him and he received her into his arms. 'Thank God! Thank God!' she was muttering.

He pulled back and looked into her face. Her mascara was smeared in circles round her eyes.

'Where's Ricky? This blood –'

'Not Ricky.'

'He's not answering the door – and it's bolted.'

Even as they spoke, Charlotte was pulling at him, tugging him towards the house.

When they reached the door, she just looked at him. He saw it in her face: he was Ricky's dad, he was a grown-up and he would know what to do. OK then: dollars to doughnuts that the bolt had been there since the house was built. If so, it dated from a less paranoid age and was probably pretty flimsy. A thump or two from his shoulder – hey, they did it all the time on TV cop shows –

'Stand back,' he said, feeling ridiculous.

It didn't yield the first time, or the second, but the third time, there was a ripping and a splintering. The door flew open and he tumbled into the kitchen. Charlotte barrelled in so fast that she slammed into him. They grabbed each other, teetered, regained their balance.

'Ricky!' Barry bellowed. 'It's Dad!'

Piki was barking somewhere at the other end of the house.

They headed towards the sound, ran across the living room to the open door of Ricky's room. The door to the bathroom slid open and Ricky was staring up at them. There was a strange expression on his face, as if he didn't know whether to laugh or cry. Barry understood. He felt the same. As he stood there, looking down at Ricky, a space seemed to open up inside him. It was like the flexing of a muscle he'd never used before. Tears came into his eyes.

There was no time to reflect on this extraordinary sensation. The next moment there was a churning, clattering noise so loud that it was impossible to think of anything else. It was as if a giant lawn-mover were hovering a few feet overhead.

Charlotte put her mouth near his ear.

'Air-sea rescue,' she shouted.

Chapter Thirty-five

There was no hinterland between sleeping and waking. One moment she was entangled in some dream that she couldn't recall and the next her eyes were wide open. The weak bluish light of a winter dawn was filtering through the curtains. Jay's naked body was warm against hers and his head was on her shoulder. Her right arm was numb. She shifted her position as gently as she could and slid her arm out. His head lolled on the pillow, he muttered something, and turned on his side. Memories of the previous night began to assemble themselves. The phone call from Barry to tell her that Ricky was alright and the relief of hearing Ricky's voice: 'First the air-sea rescue people arrived, then the police. It was like that scene in the Marx brothers' film where more and more people try to cram into Groucho's cabin.' He was buzzing with adrenalin. 'And guess what, Dad says we can spend the night at the server farm. There are beds there. Wait till I tell the guys at school. This is way, way cool.'

Later Barry had rung her from the server farm to say that Ricky had gone straight to bed and was fast asleep.

'One of the intruders was injured by that flare,' Barry told her. 'They can't tell how badly. But they've put out an alert to hospitals and doctor's surgeries. The police are assuming that it was a burglary that got out of hand. There's more to it than that, isn't there, Lisa?'

'Tomorrow, when I get back, I'll explain, I promise,' she had said.

More than one glass of akvavit had been drunk last night. She had a raging thirst and a headache. She turned and squinted at her watch. Half-past nine. She crept out of bed and groped around on the floor for her jeans and a sweater. She went into the kitchen and drank down a glass of cold water. There was a coffee percolator, good. She opened cupboard doors until she found coffee and sugar and a carton of long-life milk. While the coffee was percolating, she went back upstairs, had a quick shower, and dressed. When she looked in on Jay, he was still sleeping soundly. They didn't need to leave for the airport until around eleven, so she let him be.

She took her coffee into the sitting room. It had been dark when they arrived. Looking out through the French windows she saw a long, snow-covered slope that ran down to a fringe of frozen rushes, immobile in the ice. A pattern of trees, black against a chilly blue sky, marked the other side of the lake.

She tried the French windows, but they were locked. She looked around for a key and found one handing on a nail. She opened the door and, coffee mug in hand, stepped out into the morning. The cold air seized her, dispelling the last remnants of sleep. She made her way down the slope, lifting her boots high to clear the snow, to a flight of giant stone steps, leading to a jetty.

She brushed the snow away from the top step and perched there, coffee mug in hand. The face the house presented to the lake was elegant: a portico supported by four slender, white, wooden columns, red roof tiles, white paintwork, all a little dilapidated. The furniture in the house, too, mostly dating from the thirties and forties, was comfortable and shabby. This was just the summer home. She saw the outline of a boathouse through the trees and a sunken garden where overgrown rose bushes were muffled in snow.

She sifted through the things that Jay had told her, trying to piece it altogether. She had no doubt that what he had told her was true. There was the drama of the previous night for one thing. And it all fitted too well with her side

232

of the story: the mobile that went missing briefly in Norfolk, Peony's accident. And those other odd things that had happened, the figure that Piki had followed into the woods ... It all seemed to make sense, but she had a feeling that there was a connection that she wasn't making.

They would have to go to the police. Every instinct told her that that was the right thing to do. She was a law-abiding citizen, wasn't she? But first she needed to get back to England and see Ricky. She had the feeling that someone was watching her. She looked at the house, almost expecting to see a figure at one of the windows. The house looked impassively back.

There was the sound of a car engine. She got to her feet. Was this someone arriving? But, no, it was the sound of a car *starting up*. The engine was revving. She dropped her coffee mug, heard it break on the stone step. She ran back to the house, struggling through the snow, falling over more than once, through the French windows, through the sitting room, into the hall. She flung open the front door. She could see straight through the gap between the two guest houses and down the track that ran dead straight between the towering pines. The car was disappearing around the bend at the end.

She stood for over a minute simply staring at the point where the car had vanished, trying to take in the fact that he really had gone.

She went back into the house to look for a note. Perhaps he'd just gone out for milk. She knew she was fooling herself.

The letter was propped up against the coffee percolator and next to it was some money in kronas and the little velvet envelope he had shown her the night before.

The note was written in a scrawl that she could barely decipher.

'I'm sorry. There's something I have to do. The farmer is coming at 11.00 to lock up and take you to the station.

Don't fly back via Skavsta. You'll be able to pick up a standby ticket at Arlanda. Lisa, I can't tell you what you have meant to me. Please accept this with my love.'

She sat down and read the note again, turning over the piece of paper to see if there was anything on the other side – an address, a phone number. There wasn't. It was scarcely credible but, in the rush of events yesterday, she hadn't asked him where he lived. She still had no idea. After everything she has done to track him down, Jay had simply vanished again. She wanted to howl with frustration, she wanted to grab him and shake him and slap him. How could he have done this to her?

With trembling fingers she picked up the velvet envelope and opened it. The tiny gold Pegasus slid out. Leaving her the little gold charm – what did this mean? Something she had forgotten in the rush of events came back to her. She saw Jay straightening up from the grave with a trowel in his hand. What had he been burying there? And then she knew. The Dinky toy. He was clearing the decks. Tying up loose ends.

What was it that he had to do alone? There could only be one thing.

He was going after Lars.

She groped for a chair and sat down. Some words from the analects of Confucius came into her head. 'Before you embark on a journey of revenge, dig two graves.' Jay wasn't likely to emerge unscathed from an encounter with Lars.

Was there really no clue to where he had gone?

She had a feeling that Jay had said something she should have picked up on, that there was a connection she should have made, but what was it?

She went upstairs to pack up the few things she had with her.

It wasn't until she was standing by the kitchen window, and she saw the farmer's truck coming up the track, that

234

the penny dropped and she knew what to do next. It was just a hunch, she could be wildly off the mark, but if she wasn't …

'Junk food saves man's life.' Afterwards she imagined the newspaper headline. Because if it hadn't been for the woman eating a hamburger on the train ...

She'd got on a flight to Heathrow, no problem. The two-hour flight gave her time to reflect and she began to feel more optimistic. OK, so she didn't know where Jay was, but neither did Lars and his henchmen – or woman – but at least Lisa had a plan.

When she got on the tube from Heathrow the smell of the hamburger made her feel queasy. There was time to jump out and get into the next carriage. It was nearly full, but she could see that there were seats free at the other end. The train gave a jerk and began to move. She walked down the carriage, glancing from side to side, passing a business man taking an *Evening Standard* out of his briefcase, a sun-burnt couple surrounded by suitcases and duty-free carrier bags, an elderly woman with her head bent over a magazine – Lisa caught a whiff of expensive perfume. She found two empty seats and took the one nearest the window.

The back of her neck was prickling. Something wasn't right. She took a surreptitious look round the corner of the seat. A ticket inspector was making his way down the carriage. She thought about what she had seen. Young holiday couple – cases on the rack – nothing untoward there. A business man with a newspaper. An old woman with a magazine. So what had it been? Not something she had seen, something she had smelt. Chanel No 19. The elderly woman was only a couple of seats down. Lisa shifted in her seat and tried to catch the woman's reflection in the window. And the woman must have moved as well because for a few moments, her features were clearly etched on the darkness outside.

Lisa drew her breath in and pushed herself back into her seat.

It was the woman who had chatted to her at the bus stop in the Woodland Cemetery.

What was she doing here in London?

Chapter Thirty-six

Lisa took a deep breath. Could that pleasant, civilised woman really be in the pay of Jay's enemies? It had only been a quick glimpse. Perhaps it was just someone who looked like her? But Lisa knew she hadn't made a mistake. Calm down and think things through, she told herself. This meant they hadn't got Jay, because they wouldn't be following Lisa if they had. And at least this time she knew she was being followed – they must have staked out the airports.

The ticket inspector stopped by her seat. She fumbled in her purse. Her tube ticket had got mixed up with other stuff and several cards came out with it – her membership card for the Society of Authors, her National Trust card, her British Library reader's card. After the inspector had passed on, her gaze lingered on that British Library card. It belonged to a different world, a sane world in which most things could be fixed if you were patient and smart and resourceful. Her eyes flicked up to the tube map above her. The Piccadilly line went straight up to King's Cross and St Pancras.

When the tube approached King's Cross she got her things together, taking care not to appear to hurry, and got off. She rode the escalators to the surface and walked out onto the Euston Road. It was bitterly cold and a stiff wind flung stinging drops of rain into her face. She turned right and walked briskly along past St Pancras, schooling herself not to look behind. She crossed at the lights and turned right into the main courtyard of the British Library. Bracing herself against the wind that swept across the open space, she crossed the courtyard and went in through the automatic doors. The light airy space, the warmth and the brightness of the lights: something in her relaxed and her spirits rose. If there was a chance for her anywhere, it was here.

She went down the steps into the basement and into the ladies. She locked herself in a cubicle and took off her coat. She took a fair-isle cardigan out of her backpack – lucky she had the clothes she had worn when she was on look-out duty in the cemetery – she took off her jumper, put the cardigan on, and replaced the jumper. She came out and checked in the mirror. No, she didn't look too bulky. She did her hair, even put on some lipstick. The eyes that looked out at her from the mirror had dark marks under them and she was pale. Otherwise she didn't look too bad. She gave herself a few moments to compose herself.

'OK,' she said under her breath and walked out. She went to the cloakroom and stowed her coat and backpack in a storage locker. Luckily her handbag was small enough to be taken into the reading room. She took a small notebook and a pencil out of her handbag, to suggest that she meant business, and walked back up the steps to the ground floor.

She rode the escalator to the first floor and made her way to Humanities Reading Room I. There were two sets of doors with a lobby between them where there was a desk with a security guard. She produced her reader's card. The man examined it and waved her through. She was gambling that the person following her wouldn't have a reader's ticket and she didn't look round to check. She forced herself to walk at an even pace. As soon as she was out of sight of the door, she broke into a trot. Tucked away on the right was a staircase that led up to a second reading room, Humanities II, which had its own entrance on the floor above. She was up the stairs in seconds and heading for the exit. The security guard took his time checking her bag. She kept a smile on her face, but inside she was cursing his conscientiousness.

At last she was out and walking briskly along the balcony that overhung the vast space of the entrance hall. She prayed that her pursuer was still waiting outside the reading room on the floor below. Then she was at the lifts. One of them was already open and was empty, thank God. She stepped in and pressed the button for the ground floor. The instant the doors had closed, she stripped off her jumper and her cardigan and put them back on in reverse order. She buttoned up the cardigan so that it concealed the jumper. Out of the handbag she took a silk scarf and folded it into a narrow band. The lift was lined with mirrors. She arranged the scarf so that it swept her hair back from her forehead. The face that looked back at her had big frightened eyes.

The lift stopped and she was out, not running, just walking as fast as she dared. As she walked to the main entrance she would be visible to anyone looking down from the balcony. She longed to look up and know for sure that she wasn't being watched, but she kept her head doggedly down and she made an effort not to hurry. There was a metallic taste on her tongue. She had bitten her lip and drawn blood.

Now the automatic doors were sliding back and she was out in the night, cold air against her face and then she did run, veering left towards the side entrance which led out onto Midland Road. She turned left onto Euston Road. A few yards along was the entrance to the Underground. The station was crowded, thank goodness, the tail end of rush hour. She wove her way through the home-going crowd, praying that there would be a taxi waiting outside the other entrance and there was.

She opened the door and hoisted herself on board.

'Where to, love?' the driver asked.

Yes, where to?

'Paddington,' she said without thinking.

He pulled away, only to stop almost immediately at the traffic lights. She turned to look out of the back window. Who was getting in the cab behind? She breathed a sigh of relief when she saw a couple with a small child, busy folding up a push-chair. She scanned the hurrying crowds, looking for the woman who had followed her. It was hard to tell –

The taxi-driver was saying something that she didn't catch.

'Sorry?'

'I said, is it the station you want?'

She was about to say yes, when she realised what a crazy idea that was. They'd be waiting there for her to catch the train to Taunton.

The taxi-driver was looking at her, waiting for a reply.

'Are the shops still open?' she asked.

'Late night opening, Thursday, always has been.'

She had forgotten it was Thursday. He was staring at her as if she had come from another planet. In a way she had: one where the rules of ordinary, civilised behaviour were suspended, one where a police officer could be bought, and a respectable businessman could murder a women and a child with impunity.

'Take me to Oxford Circus,' she said.

The lights changed to green and he pulled away.

She watched carefully as they headed down Euston Road. She didn't think that they were being followed, but she wasn't going to take any chances. She paid off the taxi at Oxford Circus and stood shivering on the pavement while it pulled away and disappeared from sight. She crossed the road into Regent Street. She let a couple of taxis go by before she hailed one and told the driver to take her to Knightsbridge. He dropped her outside Harvey Nichols and drove off. She looked around and saw a shop selling mobile phones. She went in, bought a cheap one and returned to Harvey Nichols.

Inside bright lights and perfumed air enveloped her. She stood for a few moments, getting her bearings. She hadn't been in here for years. She took the escalator up a couple of floors until she saw a brand that she recognised: Nicole Farhi. Expensive, but not impossibly so. She bought a coat of black wool, flecked with grey and trimmed with grey fake fur. It swept down almost to her ankles and wouldn't have looked out of place in a portrait by Holbein. In another department she bought a close-fitting fake fur hat to match. Some underwear, and then for her last purchase she went back to the ground floor, where an elegant young man sold her a chocolate brown leather bag, a cross between a briefcase and an overnight bag.

She got out her new phone and rang Barry.

He answered immediately. 'Lisa!'

'Is Ricky OK?'

'He's having the time of his life. Where are you?'

'I'm, um, I'm in London. Can I speak to him?'

'He's right here. I'll put him on.'

'Hey! Ma!'

'Dad looking after you OK?'

'Course.'

'I need you to stay there a bit longer.'

'Cool!' She was relieved and irritated in equal measure. 'Is Charlotte OK?'

'Dad drove her and her mum to Bristol airport this morning. They'll be in Lanzarote by now.'

'Let me have Barry back.' When he was on the line she asked if he could hang onto Ricky for a while.

'No problem, he'll be fine here for a day or two, but Lisa, what's going on?'

'I can't tell you now – but, Barry, I haven't done anything wrong –'

'Well – I know that –'

'Just look after Ricky – please – keep him there –'

'Wild horses couldn't drag him away. We'll just hole

up here for a while.'

'OK.'

There was a silence.

'Lisa?'

'Yes?'

'Look after yourself.'

'You, too.'

Outside she found a cash point, and took out £500. A taxi came along with its flag up. She let that one go by and the next one, too. The third one, she hailed.

The taxi driver was a comfortable-looking, middle-aged man. The hand on the steering wheel bore a broad wedding ring. She told him that she was in London on business. Her meeting had gone on longer than expected and she needed to stay overnight. She wanted a hotel that was quiet, but central, somewhere she would be able to get room service and would feel comfortable alone.

Quarter of an hour later they were pulling up outside a pleasant Georgian façade in a street just north of Oxford Street. She asked the taxi to wait while she checked if the hotel had a room. As soon as she stepped inside she knew it was the right kind of place. There was an air of discreet opulence. It was more like a private house than a hotel. They only had a double, which they offered her at a reduced rate. She accepted and went back out to pay off the taxi and give the driver a generous tip.

Back in the hotel she registered under her real name, but when the receptionist asked for her credit card, she explained that her purse had been stolen the day before and she was waiting for replacement cards. She was happy to pay cash in advance.

The woman took in the expensive coat and leather overnight bag. 'Not a problem, Madam.'

Lisa asked for a large gin and tonic to be sent up to her room.

She hadn't even unzipped her bag when there was a knock on the door and a waiter arrived with her drink. When he'd gone, she locked the door. The chunk of the bolt going home released something in her. Her legs buckled and she sat down abruptly on the bed.

She poured a little of the tonic into the gin, gulped down a mouthful and received a hit that made her head swim. The tray bore a selection of nibbles: olives, little cheesy biscuits and crisps. She reached for a handful and tossed them into her mouth.

She felt the relief of a hunted animal that has reached its bolt-hole.

Time to plan her next move.

Chapter Thirty-seven

'Ready?'

Robert nodded.

Jay looked him up and down. He was wearing a beige anorak and cords of some nondescript dishwater colour. His mousy hair was slicked back: not his usual style. He looked entirely unremarkable, and that was excellent. Yet Jay had a niggling feeling that they had forgotten something.

'What about your luggage? Is that all you're taking?' Jay asked, pointing to a medium-sized case and a rucksack. They were in the kitchen of Jay's house, where they had so often eaten fish and chips in quiet companionship.

'I can wash things and dry them overnight.'

'OK, then. So: passports, money, tickets. And the envelope. You mustn't forget that.'

They went through the plan one more time and it was fine, Robert knew exactly what to do.

'And don't handle the envelope except with your gloved hand,' Jay said finally. He had still had that nagging feeling that there was something else.

'I won't.'

Now that the moment of departure was at hand, Jay wanted to hug Robert and tell him how much his friendship had meant to him, but any display of emotion would only disturb him. He had to be satisfied with a slap on Robert's arm. Robert smiled. Jay knew that in his bag was a detailed itinerary: not just the hotels and trains and day trips that Jay had booked for him, but a plan for every day, even down to where he would eat his picnic lunches, for the whole month of his stay.

'I should go now,' Robert said.

'The glasses! That's what we've forgotten.'

Robert got them out of his pocket and put them on.
They were dark frames with clear glass. If anyone did
recollect him, that was what they would remember. These
precautions were probably unnecessary, but then again
where Lars was involved it was impossible to be too
careful.

Robert shouldered his rucksack and picked up his case.
Jay opened the door onto the street and Robert stepped
over the threshold. The weather was perfect: cold and
clear, with a frosty sparkle to the air. Robert walked up the
narrow street, treading gingerly. It was icy and the side
streets hadn't been gritted. He looked back at Jay and
raised an arm awkwardly.

It wasn't too late to call it off. The impulse came out of
nowhere. All Jay had to do was run up the street and tell
Robert that he wasn't going through with it after all. He
got a grip on himself. He hadn't gone through all this – the
trip to Hong Kong, the performance at the art gallery – to
back out now. And there was Lisa to think of, too. He
should never have involved her, but he had and now she
could never be safe until Lars had been dealt with.

Jay waved back. Robert passed out of sight.

Jay closed the door and checked that two mobile
phones were laid out on the kitchen table. Two square
cardboard boxes waited there, one of them carefully
wrapped, ready for the courier.

He had spoken to Lars the previous evening from a
public phone at Manchester airport. Lars had been waiting
for the call.

'Tomorrow. The 9.30 train from King's Cross to
Edinburgh. Come alone,' Jay had told him.

Lars had protested as Jay knew he would. 'Impossible
at this notice!'

Jay allowed himself to sound edgy, which wasn't difficult: he *was* edgy. 'It's now or never. If we do this at all, we do it my way.'

There was silence. Lars wasn't used to being spoken to like this.

'I can always dispose of the goods elsewhere,' Jay said.

'Edinburgh, you say?'

'Let me have a mobile number. I'll give you further directions when you get there.'

'Cloak-and-dagger stuff. So tedious – and so unnecessary.'

'Not to me. I'm putting myself on the line with this.' Lars should be boarding the train in London right now. Would he be alone as Jay had stipulated? Jay thought he would be. His henchmen would be in place in Edinburgh to follow at a discreet distance when he got off the train. He might guess that Edinburgh wasn't his final destination, but it was unlikely that he would have men at every station. Even if he did ... Jay went over the plan again. There were things that could go wrong, there always were, but he had covered everything that could be covered. He went upstairs and opened the concealed cupboard, and got out the gun. It was old, but it still worked. He had made sure of that.

The doorbell rang. He took the gun down to the kitchen and put it out of sight behind the toaster. He opened the door to the courier and handed over the square box. He knew they would take good care of it: they specialised in transporting fragile objects and he had used them before. He wished he could be there to see Martin's face when he opened the box and found the Qianlong bowl inside.

He had no sooner closed the door behind the man, than one of the phones rang. Jay answered it. It was Robert to say that he was on the train to York.

So far so good.

By eight-thirty Lisa was waiting on the doorstep of Jonas Miller's office in Newark. She watched him approaching and knew the exact moment he recognised her, though there was no break in his step and not a muscle moved in his face. He was wearing a navy-blue wool overcoat, as well cut as the suit she'd seen him in before.

As he got nearer he adopted an expression of professional friendliness. He opened his mouth to speak.

Lisa raised a hand to stop him. 'I know all about it – well, almost all. I found Jay. I know that he's still alive. I tracked him down to the cemetery in Stockholm where his wife and son are buried.'

'I don't know what –'

'Please, please, I haven't got time for this –'

She thought he was going to go on protesting, but after a moment he shrugged and pulled a set of keys out of his coat pocket.

He gestured to the door. 'You'd better come in.'

He picked up a handful of post from the mat. She followed him in, aware as she hadn't been before, of how solid he was, not tall, but broad.

He led the way to his office. He tossed the letters on his desk. 'We've got half an hour before my secretary arrives.'

He still looked just like her idea of a country solicitor. And of course he was that, but he was also so much more – if she was right and she was more certain than ever that she was.

He gestured to a seat. 'Coffee?' he asked.

He ran a hand over his cropped hair. His pale blue eyes were fixed on hers and she saw what he had been at pains to conceal when she had last met him: just how formidable he really was. She curbed her impatience. She would have to let him set the pace.

'Thanks. That would be good.' She sat down and watched as he fiddled with the coffee-maker on the side board.

'I always make my own,' he said. 'It's too important to leave to other people.' He shot her a sideways glance. 'You must have left home early.'

'I came from London. But, yes, I did leave early.'

He put the cup of coffee down in front of her and took his place behind his desk. He wasn't going to give anything away; he was waiting to hear what she knew. On the train she had gone over and over what she was going to say and now she told him how she had managed to track Jay down, how she had lost him, and how she had realised that she was being followed.

'I've got to find him,' she said. 'I think he's planning some kind of revenge and I think it's going to happen soon.'

'And you've come to see me, because …?'

'Because you are Joe. You're the policeman Jay trusts, the man who helped him to disappear. I don't think he did all that on his own, so I know I can trust you, too. And I think you know where he lives.'

She had managed to surprise him.

He frowned. 'Jay told you –'

'No. I worked that bit out for myself. It wasn't so hard to put two and two together. He referred to you as Joe. That's short for Jonas, isn't it? And he said you'd resigned from the police force. There was time for you to have qualified as a solicitor, particularly if you'd had a degree in the first place. And your hands – those are burns, aren't they? From digging in the rubble of that house.'

'What do you want?' he asked.

'I want to know where Jay lives.'

He thought about that. She watched him fiddle with the letters on the desk, aligning them, tapping the edges to straighten them.

He pursed his lips. 'If he wanted you to know, he'd have told you.'

'He didn't want to get me involved! Don't you see, he's

about to do something dangerous!'

Jonas shook his head.

He got to his feet and waited for her to do the same. He was dismissing her. She couldn't let that happen. She rummaged in her bag, found the zip to the inner compartment, and opened it. She felt about inside – there was a bad moment when she thought that the little velvet envelope had gone – and then her fingers closed on it. She pulled it out.

'There were three things,' she said, 'a photograph, a little toy van, and a little gold horse from a charm bracelet. Jay buried the toy van in Sam's grave.' She tipped the little horse out onto her palm. 'This he gave to me.'

Jonas leaned over the desk and gazed at the charm. He put out a finger, but didn't quite touch it. The horse was smaller than his fingernail.

'It belonged to Jay's mother,' Lisa said. 'Would he have done that if he didn't trust me?'

'I took a risk pocketing that,' Jonas said. He looked at Lisa but he was seeing something else. There was a sadness in his face. 'When I got to the site of the blast there wasn't much left intact. We had to identify Mia and Sam from DNA extracted from fragments of bone.'

'So are you going to tell me?' Jonas frowned. 'What?'

'How I can find Jay.'

He looked at her. She was seething with impatience, but if she rushed him, he would only dig his heels in. At last he said, 'I've got an address in Scarborough.'

She let out a sigh of relief. He took a pen and tore a square of paper from a block on his desk. He scribbled something on it and handed it to her.

She looked at it and nodded. 'Phone number?'

He shook his head. 'I don't have one. We've kept communication to a minimum.'

She got to her feet. 'Are you coming?' she asked.

'Coming where?'

250

'To Scarborough, of course.'

'I'm too busy.'

She shook her head in disbelief.

'I've got meetings all morning and a pile of paperwork: wills, land disputes … '

'Oh, I don't doubt that.'

'There's no guarantee he'll be at home and –'She just looked at him.

'What?' he demanded.

'I'm wondering what happened to the honest cop who burned his hands scrabbling in the rubble of a burning building.' He looked down at his hands and shrugged. 'Guess he turned into a cautious country solicitor. Middle age'll do that to a man.'

She got up and went out without a word. On the way out she passed the secretary coming in. The woman threw her a curious glance.

Outside on the pavement, Lisa stood for a few moments, fighting down her disappointment. She'd have to push on alone. Should she hire a car or go back to the station? Car hire would require her credit card. Too risky. So back to the station. She glanced at the window of Jonas's office. He was opening letters with a paper knife. He had his back to the window and he didn't turn round.

It took her ten minutes to walk to the station.

The time-table told her that she could be in Scarborough by 12.30. She was queuing at the ticket-office, when she heard firm footsteps behind her. She turned and saw Jonas. His face was grim. 'You needn't bother with that,' he said. 'The car's outside. Come on.'

Chapter Thirty-eight

11. 30. The phone rang. Jay took a deep breath and picked it up.

Robert's voice said, 'They've just announced it. His train's five minutes late.'

'Oh, Jesus. What about the other trains?'

'I think they're OK.'

Jay could hear footsteps, voices, all with the hollow echo of the vast engine shed at York station.

'If it's no more than five minutes, we should still be OK. Has everything else gone according to plan? You left the envelope at the information desk?'

'Yep.'

'And you're standing on the bridge where we agreed?'

'Yep.' Robert never wasted words. It made him an ideal assistant.

'OK. Keep the line open.' Jay paced up and down the kitchen. Waiting was a kind of agony. He wished that he smoked or bit his fingernails. At least he'd have something to do. He watched the second hand clicking round on the kitchen clock. In his mind's eye he could see the curving roof of the engine–shed, the big black clock with its hands and numbers painted gold ...

Four minutes passed. Then –

'I can see the train,' Robert said. 'It's coming round the bend and it's slowing down.'

Jay could hear a distant screeching of brakes.

'The train's stopped. The doors are opening now.'

'OK. I'm putting the phone down now.'

He picked up the second phone and pressed the speed-dial.

The person on the other end picked up on the second ring. 'Yes?'

'Get off the train.'

'What –'

'Get off the train. Alone.'

'You said Edinburgh.'

'It's York. If you want the goods, get off the train. Now. Alone. I'll ring again in two minutes.'

He ended the call and picked up the other phone.

'Remember what I said. He'll be wearing a bright red scarf and no hat. He's got hair so blond that it's almost white. And I need to know which carriage.'

'I don't see him yet.'

Jay closed his eyes and prayed. *Please let him get off.*

'I don't think he's – yes, there he is!'

Jay punched the air.

'He's down at the end of the platform. He's just got out of a first-class carriage.'

'Is he alone?'

'I think so.'

'Is he carrying anything?'

'A bag. A black leather one with a long strap – on his left-hand shoulder.'

'OK. Don't look directly at him. Go on holding the phone to your ear as if you're busy talking to someone and I'll get back to you.'

He pressed the speed-dial on the other phone.

Lars answered and Jay said, 'The first thing you need to know is that someone is watching you and I can prove that by telling you that you have just got out of a first-class carriage and that you have a black leather shoulder bag on your left shoulder. When I've finished speaking, you will take the sim card out of your mobile phone. You'll hold it up so that it's in plain view and then you'll flip it onto the railway track. You'll put the phone into the waste-paper basket about fifteen yards to your left. You will go to the information desk where you will pick up an envelope left for Lars. It will contain a train ticket. You'll board the next train to the destination on the ticket. When you arrive a taxi will be waiting for you. Do you understand?'

'Where am I going?'

'You'll see. Someone will be watching you. If you don't do exactly what I say, I'm calling it off. OK?'

For a moment or two there was no sound at the other end.

'Better hurry,' Jay said. 'The train leaves in less than ten minutes.'

'OK. OK.' There was a click and he was gone. Typical of him to retain a tiny bit of the initiative by hanging up first.

Jay picked up the other phone. 'Robert? What's he doing?'

'He's sliding the back off the phone and he's getting the card out. Yes, and now – he's flipped it up into the air, like people flip coins, and it's gone down the side between the train and the platform.'

There was silence, then Robert said, 'He's put the phone in the bin and he's heading towards the Information Desk.'

'OK. Head for the Manchester platform and stand where you can see the Scarborough train.'

'It's already there waiting.'

'Ring me when he's safely on it.'

Jay closed the phone. He let his breath out in a long sigh. He paced the kitchen again. It should be OK, if there wasn't a long queue at the Information Desk, oh hell, why hadn't he allowed more time? But time was exactly what Lars must not have. Time to think or to question might be fatal and –

The phone rang. Jay dived for it.

'We've done it.' Robert said. 'He's on the train. It's pulling out now and I'm watching it go round the bend.'

Jay had never heard him so animated before.

'Was he really alone?'

'He was the last person to get on and he had to run for it.'

'So even if one of his henchman had been following at a discreet distance –'

'No way could they have got onto the train in time.'

'You're a star, Robert.'

'My train's pulling in now.'

'Robert.' Now that it had come to the last moment, Jay didn't know what to say.

'Yes?'

'Say g'day to the Great Barrier Reef from me.'

'I will.' Jay could hear the smile in his voice. There was a click and he was gone.

So that was that. In a few hours Robert would be boarding a flight to Sidney. Jay really was alone now. But it was a relief to know that Robert would soon be safely out of the way. The crocodile had been lured out of deep water, was drifting up through the murky, green water towards the tethered goat.

Soon the hooded eyes and the questing snout would break the surface.

Chapter Thirty-nine

'There was a letter from Jay in this morning's post, well, not really a letter, just an envelope containing a codicil to his will,' Jonas said. 'I think you're right. He's planning something dangerous. And he's tying up loose ends first.'

'Do you know how to get to his house?'

'I've got sat nav.'

'How long will it take?'

'Oh, two and a half hours, tops.' They were on the A1 heading north.

Jonas's car was a dark green sports car, a Triumph. Lisa was surprised: she hadn't pegged him as that kind of bloke. Being so close to the ground was disconcerting, but exhilarating. She stole a glance at the speedometer: they were doing 70, but it felt much faster. She was actually enjoying it. A weight had been lifted off her now that she wasn't alone. It was almost as if they were off on a jaunt, playing hooky.

'I've always wondered if he'd try to bring Lorenson down,' Jonas said. 'It rankles with me, too, that we never managed to nail that bastard. It happened on my watch. And knowing that one of your own's gone bad, that's the worst thing of all.'

'Jay told me about Sandra. But he said there wasn't any evidence?'

'It was her all right.' He thumped the steering wheel. 'She left the force almost straight away. Took a job with a hugely inflated salary at a security firm. I traced it back. The boss had a connection with Lars Lorenson, but it wasn't enough to make a case.' She looked sideways, examining his profile. 'Perhaps you're not so middle-aged after all.'

He smiled.

'I do wonder about this though.' She waved her arm in a gesture that took in the walnut veneer of the dashboard and the fabric of the soft-top. 'Mid-life crisis?'

'What? Oh, the car. Not really. I've got a Saab as well, that's being serviced. Had this one twenty years. Always wanted a Triumph Stag. My first car, saved up to buy it when I was a young copper.' That put a different complexion on things.

'She's a good old girl.' He patted the steering wheel. 'A bit temperamental, maybe, but she's still a goer – at least –' He broke off.

'What?'

'Oh, nothing.'

They lapsed into silence. The throaty sound of the engine lulled Lisa and it was warm in the car. She slipped further down in her seat. She had rung Ricky before they left Newark and he was fine. For now there was nothing to do, nothing to worry about. All she had to do was let herself be borne along. She hadn't had much sleep the night before, or the night before that ... her eyelids closed

'Oh, shit,' Jonas said.

Her eyes snapped open. 'What?'

He gestured to the road ahead. 'The traffic slowed down a while ago. I think there's an accident up ahead.'

'Oh no.' She hauled herself up and peered through the windscreen. They were crawling past the turn-off to Retford.

She looked at Jonas. He was staring at the instrument panel and tapping his fingers on the steering wheel. 'Hell,' he said through gritted teeth. 'She's over-heating. Classic problem with this engine. As a rule I don't take her on trips where I might get stuck in traffic. I'm going to have to pull over on the hard shoulder and put some water in the radiator.' He glanced at Lisa, registered the dismay in her face. 'Oh, we'll get there. In the end.'

Jay forked food into Barrington's dish. Barrington stared moodily at it. He turned away and jumped up onto the window sill so that he could push his head against Jay's hand. It was almost as if he knew that he might not see Jay again.

'Bye, bye, old boy.' Jay rubbed the cat's head, eliciting a reluctant, rusty purr.

Jay shouldered his rucksack and closed the door behind him. He made his way up the alley, treading gingerly on the ice. At the corner he looked back. Barrington was still on the window sill, regarding him gravely.

It was a steep climb up to the castle. The gateway spanned the narrow causeway of rock that was the only approach to the castle plateau. It was the perfect defensible spot and there had been fortifications here since Roman times.

Jay showed his English Heritage pass to the young woman in the shop and went up the long flight of steps. He turned right past the ruined keep into the inner bailey. One more climb, up a wooden scaffold of steps, and he had reached a viewing platform set into the curtain wall. Directly below was a massive double ditch and a view over the tumbled roofs of the town. On one side lay the sweep of the south bay with its harbour and amusements, and on the other the north bay with its beach huts and the white pyramids of the Sea-life Centre. Everything stood out in brilliant preternatural detail: the sun gleamed on wet sand, wheeling seagulls caught the light.

Behind him was a broad expanse of meadow that covered the whole headland and ended in a sheer drop. The castle grounds were deserted, except for a couple in the distance, strolling round the headland. There were only two ways up to the castle, the road he had come up and a

259

footpath that snaked round the northern slope. Both were in plain view. It was impossible for anyone to approach unseen.

He paced up and down, allowing his thoughts to play over the happy years with Mia and Sam in Chiswick and later the good times with Lisa. To have been loved by two such women ... in that respect he had been a lucky man. He had decided to leave his Chinese ceramics to Lisa. Robert would get his chess set and £10,000. Everything else would go to Amnesty International. Jonas would have received the codicil to his will this morning. He hadn't enclosed a letter with it. He hadn't known what to say, but now he felt that he should have said something. Jonas was a good man. The last few years had been hard, but they would have been still harder without him. He opened his backpack and got out his mobile phone. He tapped in a text message – 'thanks for everything' – and called up Jonas's mobile number. He hesitated for a moment, but what harm could it do? He pressed send. The phone took photos, so he held it out at arm's length and with the other hand made a gesture – half a salute and half a wave of farewell. He sent that, too.

There had been a change in the light. It would begin to get dark in an hour or so.

A taxi was coming up the road to the castle. It stopped short of the barbican gatehouse and Lars got out.

Chapter Forty

It was half past twelve by the time Lisa and Jonas reached Scarborough. They had crawled along, making frequent stops to fill the radiator, Lisa's sense of foreboding rising with every mile.

The sat nav directed them onto the seafront.

So this is it, Lisa thought, taking in the ice-cream parlours, the amusement arcades, the people walking dogs on the beach. All these years, this is where Jay has been. They took a left turn past a pub, the Newcastle Packet, and turned left again into a narrow street of modest Georgian houses – with double yellow lines on either side.

'Nowhere to park. The sat nav doesn't tell you that,' Jonas grumbled. The strain was getting to him, too.

'There was a sign to a car park back there.'

They parked the car and made their way to where a narrow alley ran down the hillside and curved out of sight towards the harbour.

'It must be down here,' said Jonas.

The sun hadn't reached this sliver of a street and it lay in shadow. An old-fashioned free-standing street light stood at its entrance. No-one was about and as they set off down the street, they saw that only one house fronted onto it. The others had their entrances elsewhere and turned blank walls or barred windows to the street.

They stopped by the single door. The house was like a child's drawing, two square windows on each floor and a dull red door in the middle. There was something secretive and withheld about it. She looked at Jonas. He looked back at her, then shrugged and looked for a doorbell. There wasn't one. He knocked on the door with his fist.

Nothing happened. He knocked louder. The noise reverberated in the silent alley.

A cat, a stout grey creature, appeared at one of the windows and gave them a baleful stare.

'I didn't know Jay had a cat,' Lisa said.

She felt somehow offended. Surely that was something she should have known.

She looked through the other window and saw that it was all one room downstairs. The kitchen area was spick and span, nothing left lying on the surfaces. Off to the other side she glimpsed a chess set on a table, a basket of logs by a fire place.

'What now?' she said.

'Maybe he'll be back soon?' Jonas looked at his watch. 'How about some lunch? We could come back later.'

They made their way back up the alley.

'Left or right?' Jonas asked when they reached the street.

To the left the road wound back in the direction of the town centre. To the right was a view of the castle, the massive curtain wall outlined along the sky.

'Right, I think, don't you?' Jonas said. 'We could have fish and chips on the sea front.'

Lisa nodded.

They walked down the road in silence. There was a ping and Jonas pulled his phone out of his pocket. 'Someone's sent me a text. Probably my secretary, wondering when the hell I'm going to be back.' He pressed a button and Lisa saw his face change.

'Jesus! It's him. It's Jay. And my God, look at this!' An image of Jay, armed raised in a salute, had appeared on the screen.

'Where is he?' she asked. 'There's something behind him. A tower, a ruin of some kind?'

The same thought struck them both. They looked up in unison and gazed at the castle. A tiny figure was standing on the viewing platform.

'What's he doing up there?' Lisa said. 'You don't think he's going to –'

Jonas was busy with his phone. 'I'll try and ring him back.' He shook his head. 'His phone's switched off. Let's get up there.'

A discussion was going on between Lars and the taxi driver. Jay guessed that Lars was trying to pay him and the taxi driver was explaining that he had been paid in advance. Lars nodded, stood back from the taxi, and looked up at the castle walls. Jay raised a hand and Lars responded. Jay felt a thrill of excitement – and yes, there was surprise there, too – the plan had actually worked. Lars turned towards the gatehouse and a few moments later Jay saw him going into the ticket office. Jay had timed the ascent and estimated that it would take him five minutes.

The taxi was heading back down the hill. Jay turned to look round the headland. The couple he had seen earlier were making their way back, a dark stocky man and a slender fair-haired woman. They looked familiar: probably they lived nearby and he had seen them in the street. They stopped and conferred and for a moment he feared that they were going to come in his direction. But no, they were heading for the steps down to the gatehouse. For some reason Jay thought of Barrington. Would he miss Jay? Cats were such egotists, but Jay thought he would. He looked at his watch. Only a minute had passed.

Lars came out of the ticket office, and now he was visible only intermittently through the gaps in the crenellated wall that ran alongside the steps.

Jay opened his rucksack and got out the box. He took the lid off. The bowl nestled there in its bed of tissue paper and bubble wrap. He put the box down on the floor of the viewing platform and lifted the bowl out. Really, it was a superb piece of craftsmanship, entirely convincing, almost indistinguishable from the real thing. He glanced quickly around. There was still no-one was in sight. He stood up and swung a leg over the metal railings that divided the viewing platform from the castle wall. He stretched out an arm and placed the bowl in a shallow declivity. The next moment he was back on the viewing deck. The bowl looked fantastic, so delicate, so feminine, set against a wall that had its own rough beauty of grey stone and yellow lichen. Jay positioned himself so that he was standing in front of it. He got out the gun and held it behind his back. He made sure that his scarf was covering his lower face and the scars around his mouth.

He was just in time. Lars was making his way round the imposing bulk of the ruined keep. And then he was walking across the grass towards the viewing platform. He looked smaller than Jay remembered, blonder too, his hair virtually white. Over the years he had attained mythic proportions in Jay's mind, but he was just a man after all. Was he armed? Jay didn't think so. With that one exception, the day that he had murdered his wife, Jay guessed that Lars took good care to leave the dirty work to others. Now he was climbing the wooden steps to the platform. He reached the top and was only two or three metres away.

He spoke without preamble. 'Where's the bowl?' Excellent as his English was, he hadn't quite lost that sing-song accent. Strangely it was more evident in real life than on the phone.

Jay didn't speak. He simply stepped to one side. Lars's eyes went to the bowl. He looked to Jay for an explanation. The antique dealer he had come to meet was so well established in his mind as a different person, that he still hadn't recognised Jay.

Jay leaned back against the rail in the corner of the viewing platform. He was roughly equidistant from Lars and the bowl. He brought the gun into view.

Lars raised his eyebrows. 'No need for that.'

'You don't know who I am, do you?' Jay said. He tugged at the scarf and it fell away from his face. Lars stared at him, uncomprehending. Surely Sandra had told him about the scars? Jay saw that she had. Lars was frowning.

'Jonathan?'

'That used to be my name.'

Lars lifted his hands in a placating gesture. 'Are you planning to shoot me?'

His face was impassive, but Jay could guess what he was thinking. There had never been anything he couldn't fix, and why should this be different? Sure it was a tight spot, but, hey, he specialised in tight spots.

'The bowl first,' Jay said. 'Unless you tell me what you did. Confess that you killed my wife and son.'

'You wouldn't do that, the bowl, no! It's so–' Lars fumbled for words.

'So perfect, so priceless, so irreplaceable? Like my wife and child?'

'The child.' A shadow passed over Lars's face. 'That was never my intention. For that I am truly sorry. For that you can thank Sandra. She promised to deal with the problem for me. I had no idea that she intended something so ...' he spread his hands, 'so drastic. I would never hurt a child.'

Jay hesitated. Could this be true? But even if it was ... He shook his head. 'Even if you didn't mean to kill Sam, you did intend to leave him without a father.'

'Maybe so, but still for you a dilemma. If you shoot me, you will not escape unnoticed from a place like this and the woman who killed your son will go unpunished.'

What Jay felt was almost admiration. The capacity to absorb a jarring shock, to consider the options and come to a decision all in an instant: Lars had the qualities of a great

265

chess-player or a general. Or a psychopath.

'Tough call,' Jay said. 'But while I'm thinking about it, I'll start with the bowl.'

He trained the gun on it.

Blood was fizzing in Lisa's ears and the icy air was rasping in her throat. But all those strenuous walks up the coombs of Exmoor had paid off. She was matching Jonas stride for stride, though the grit on the path was slowing them both down.

The steps were steep and led up beside a row of houses so that the castle was for a while lost to view. They emerged below a graveyard and jogged up the path beside it, breathing heavily. They could see the castle again now and the figure of Jay on the ramparts. They reached a road leading up to the castle.

As they turned up it, Lisa groaned.

'A stitch.'

She bent over and rested her hands on her thighs.

'I'll go on,' Jonas gasped.

She nodded.

She remained as she was, taking in grateful gulps of air, listening to Jonas's feet pounding away from her. When she straightened up, Jonas was half way up the hill. She forced herself into a jog. Just one more step she told herself, and another, and another. There was no thought in her head; she was just a running machine, one foot down, the other foot down.

Jonas disappeared into the gatehouse.

Black specks appeared in front of her eyes. She slowed to a walk and looked up at the castle walls. She was close enough now to see that Jay had his back to her. He was speaking to someone she couldn't see.

She pressed on. The path was growing steeper. She was gasping for breath, the icy air raw in her throat.

She looked up at the ramparts. Jay was turning, there

266

was something in his hand, he stretched out his arm, and she saw a gun.

Oh my God! For a moment she felt the terrible of impotence of someone in a dream.

Then she opened her mouth, drew the air down into her lungs and let it out in a sound that surprised even her.

'Jay!'

It rang out like a bell in the clear air.

Jay's head shot round.

That moment's distraction gave Lars the chance he'd been looking for. He sprang forward and his hand came out in a chopping movement.

Jay felt an agonising pain in his wrist. He dropped the gun. It skeetered across the deck and went flying over the edge.

Lars was close enough for Jay to look straight into his pale blue eyes. Jay read his thoughts: should he go for the gun or the bowl? But after all, Lars couldn't leave the bowl unprotected. He swung his leg over the rail and the next moment he was on the curtain wall. He didn't see the slick of ice on its uneven surface. His foot slipped, he flung his arm out and hit the bowl.

It wobbled, teetered. Lars made a desperate lunge, his fingers touched it, his foot slipped again and the bowl spun out into the void.

Lars struggled to regain his balance, his arms flailing, his face all eyes and open mouth, like a cartoon character.

Jay couldn't help it: he stretched out a hand. But it was too late. He closed his eyes. When he opened them again, Lars had gone.

Chapter Forty-one

Sandra was asleep when her mobile phone rang. As she groped her way towards consciousness, she didn't at first know where she was. It hurt when she breathed in and there was some kind of constriction. Her ribs had been strapped. She put up a hand and felt a large dressing on her face. She remembered: she was in the private clinic in Knightsbridge. The story was that she had been injured by a firework and it was almost the truth. She'd managed to throw herself to one side, but still the flare had struck her a glancing blow. She had a burn on her face and was bruised all over. She'd been lucky not to be killed. Wincing with every movement she reached for the phone, expecting it to be Lars. It wasn't, it was Steve, and at first she couldn't make head or tail of what she was hearing. He was hiccupping and he kept saying, 'Mr Lorenson's gone, he's gone.'

'Wait a minute, gone where?'

'The pottery, the new bowl, he went up to Scarborough this morning –'

She pieced it together. Lars had gone off first thing to pick up his new piece of porcelain. Steve had somehow lost track of Lars, but Lars had managed to ring him, and he had got to Scarborough just in time to see – something about a fall.

'He's gone, he's gone,' Steve moaned.

She pulled herself up in bed and a spasm of pain shot up her left side. She spoke through gritted teeth. 'Where is he?'

Steve was still hiccupping – no, he was crying and that was when she understood. 'He's dead?'

269

No reply.

'Steve! When did this happen?'

She spoke sharply and he responded. 'About an hour ago.'

'Where are you now?'

'At the hospital, but it wasn't any good. I don't know what to do. I don't know what to tell the police.'

'I have to think. Stay there. I'll ring you back.'

'OK, OK.' He was reassured. Steve would always need someone to tell him what to do. She put the phone down and dismissed him from her mind. She could do nothing for him and he was a liability now.

Lars gone ... it was huge, it was catastrophic, but she couldn't let herself think about that now. She had to get going. There was no time to lose, but she mustn't hurry, either, mustn't make a mistake. She rang room service and ordered black coffee. Then she levered herself painfully off the bed and looked for her clothes.

An hour later the taxi drew up outside the block of flats in Canary Wharf. She had come via Mayfair where she had cleared out her safe deposit box. Frank, the concierge, came out to open the door for her. He looked concerned when he saw her face. She forced herself to smile and said, 'Nothing important, just a minor operation. I'm fine.' He'd probably think it was plastic surgery. So much the better.

He carried her bag in for her and called the lift. She rode up to the top floor. She let herself into her flat and sat down heavily on the sofa. She could do with a drink, but on top of the painkillers? Not a good idea. She felt groggy enough as it was. She sat for a few minutes, gathering her strength. The pale suede of the sofa was soft under her hand. She eased off her shoes and pushed her toes into the thick pile of the carpet. The flat was huge, all white and beige and slate grey. She had chosen everything from the Smeg oven to the bathroom taps with such care. This place

270

had been the sum of all her hopes and aspirations, everything she had dreamed of during those years growing up on a crappy sink estate. Here she could be herself. Her heart was sore at the thought of leaving it for ever.

She got gingerly to her feet and went to the sliding glass door that led out onto the balcony. It was dark, but nevertheless she stepped outside and let the bitter wind clear some of the dopiness from her head. She gazed down the river towards Greenwich. The reflection of a nearly full moon shimmered on the water. Her face began to throb again and she went back indoors.

She went into the kitchen and pulled a stool over to the stone work top. This was going to hurt like fuck. She clambered up onto the work top and the torn muscles at her waist sent shooting pains right up her neck. She yelped, but kept going. She reached for the kitchen clock and unscrewed the face. There was a small safe behind it. She keyed in the number and the door swung open. She took out a passport, a driving license, a credit card – none of them in her own name – a thick wad of twenty pound notes and another of euros. She was no fool: Lars sailed so close to the wind that something like this had always been on the cards and she had made her preparations long ago.

The phone began to ring. Her heart skipped a beat. The answering machine picked it up. It was Lars's secretary. She wasn't hysterical – she was too well-trained for that – but she sounded close to tears and asked Sandra to get in touch with her as soon as possible.

Moving very slowly and wincing with every movement, Sandra got back to floor level. She went into the bedroom. She got two suitcases out of the wardrobe and stared at the long row of clothes hanging there. She sat down on the bed and took off the jeans she'd been wearing, gritting her teeth as they made contact with the bruises on her legs. She put on her most expensive skirt and a black cashmere cardigan. She got out a long leather coat. Moving like an old woman, she packed her best things. The smaller suitcase she filled with shoes. She hated to leave any of them behind, but she could only take what she could carry.

She looked at her watch. She had been in the flat less than an hour. Good. She rang down and asked Frank to get a taxi for her.

'Where to, Miss Carpenter?'

'Gatwick.'

She looked around to check that there was nothing she had forgotten. She scanned the dressing table. There was a photo of Lars and Brigitta in a leather frame. Brigitta. God. Poor little bugger. What would happen to her? She'd be Ok, Sandra told herself. Frida's parents would take her and be only too glad to. They had never liked Lars.

The bottles of perfume on the dressing table: she could let herself take one and only one, so it had to be *Joy* by Jean Patou. It was the biggest bottle they made and Lars had spent hundreds of pounds on it for her last birthday. She sprayed herself with it and tucked into the case. Time to go. She put her bags in the hall, stood at the threshold and looked at her flat for the last time, saying goodbye. She felt the tears rising and was angry with herself. No time for that now. She stepped out into the hall and closed the door behind her.

As she walked to the lift, the phone began to ring again in the empty flat.

Down in the lobby, Frank hurried to carry her bags for her and to help her into the taxi. She tipped him lavishly. He looked surprised, but he'd understand soon enough. The taxi pulled away from the curb.

'Gatwick, is it?' the driver asked.

'No, St Pancras.'

'Right you are.' She leaned back in her seat and was borne away into the night.

Chapter Forty-two

'It galls me that she got away,' Lisa said. It was two months after Lars had fallen from the castle wall in Scarborough. It was mid-February now and Lisa was strolling with Barry around the garden at Falling Water.

Barry nodded. 'They might still track her down.'

The police had followed Sandra's trail to Paris, where she had got off the Eurostar and caught a plane to Buenos Aires. There they had lost her.

'There are still countries that don't have extradition treaties,' Lisa said. 'She's probably sitting in the sun somewhere, thumbing her nose at us. When I think that I let that woman into my house and left her alone with Ricky ...'

'Her money won't last for ever. And she'll be on the run for the rest of her life.'

'The police are pretty sure now that she fixed the brakes on Peony's car.'

'Is Peony going to make a full recovery?'

'Pretty much.' They stopped at the edge of the garden, where the ground dropped away into the coomb. There had been several days of heavy gales and rain. The stream was the colour of iced coffee laced with white foam. It seemed almost alive, leaping and roaring in its eagerness to get to the sea.

Lisa shivered.

'You OK?' Barry asked.

'Someone walking over my grave.'

'The wind's getting up.'

He was right. The tops of the trees were tossing gently and a breeze was ruffling the surface of the pond.

'About Ricky,' Barry said. 'You're still cool with that?' Inside the house Charlotte was helping Ricky to pack. Barry was taking them both to the company's London flat for half term.

'Of course,' she said, and she was, she really was. In the aftermath of Lars's death, Barry had been a tower of strength. It was early days still with Ricky, but she could see that he relished having Barry in his life. She'd heard the pride in his voice when he talked to Charlotte about 'Dad's software company'. He and Barry were on the same wavelength. She would catch a snatch of conversation and have no idea what they were talking about: it was hard not to feel jealous, but she was doing her best.

'You're sure?' Barry was frowning. 'Don't really like leaving you here on your own. After everything that's happened.'

'I've got Piki. And Stella's coming over later to help me sort out some of Lawrence's clothes. And you know I've got to be here on my own sometimes.'

He didn't speak. She turned to look at him. He was regarding her in a way that was part half puzzled, half speculative.

'What?' she asked.

'You really are ... you know, Lisa, you really are ... alright?'

'Why shouldn't I be?'

'Oh, no reason.' He gave a little shrug, as if dismissing something from his mind. She started to laugh, she couldn't help it. Extraordinary after everything that had passed between them that he still knew when she was keeping something from him. After a moment he laughed, too.

A gust of wind sent down a shower of twigs and dead leaves.

She shivered again. 'Let's go in.'

274

Lisa stood and watched the car until it disappeared round the bend in the track, waving until the last moment. She went back into the house with Piki at her heels.

'Well, old girl, it's just you and me now,' she said.

She listened to the unaccustomed silence, testing her reaction to it. It's OK, she decided.

She went into the living room, up the spiral staircase, and into the room that had been Lawrence's office. Lisa's own papers were set out on the big cherry wood table where Lawrence's correspondence used to be. As she sat at the desk trying to work, she kept smiling to herself. At last she shook her head and pushed back her chair. Today wasn't a day for working. Today was a day for celebrating and for giving herself up to the happiness that was welling up inside her.

She slipped *Elvis is Back!* into the CD player. She turned it up high and danced around the room, singing along and swaying her hips.

Piki poked her head around the door. She looked hopeful. She liked Lisa being in a good mood. There might be something in it for her.

Lisa laughed. 'OK. How about a trip to Lynmouth and fish and chips for lunch?'

Lisa found a bench with a view of the wide sweep of Lynmouth bay and sat there to eat her fish and chips. The salt on her lips, the wind that brushed her cheek and lifted her hair: there was a freshness and intensity to everything. So this was what happiness was like. She had almost forgotten.

She screwed the chip paper into a ball and tossed it into a bin. She set off with Piki along the beach, the pebbles crunching underfoot. She flung Piki's stick as far as she could and watched the dog skittering across the pebbles. As she settled into the rhythm of bending and throwing, she replayed her visit to Jay the day before.

It still surprised Lisa how much the prison looked like, well, a prison, all castellated battlements and it even had a portcullis. When she had first visited Jay she had the sensation of having done something wrong herself and almost feared that she might not be allowed to leave. The visiting room at the prison reminded her of a school dining room, full of noise and movement. She had felt self-conscious, overly aware of other couples whispering, babies crying, bored children fussing. Now she scarcely noticed them.

Lisa and Jay held hands across the table. He had good news for her. The police had decided that there was no case to answer over Lars's death. Jonas had arrived in time to witness what had happened. He'd had even had the presence of mind to photograph it on his phone; Lisa had seen it, too and wished she hadn't. She was still having flashbacks. Out of nowhere it would appear: the body spread-eagled, the hands clutching, though even that wasn't as bad as the dream she kept having that he wasn't really dead, that he was lurking somewhere just out of sight, waiting for her to relax her guard.

Of course there was still the theft of the Qianlong bowl. Though even there, the fact that he had returned it would be offered in mitigation ...

And she had some news, too. That night they had spent together in Sweden ... A test had confirmed what she had suspected for a week or two. She was pregnant.

When she told Jay, his hands tightened on hers, but he didn't say a word. She saw tears in his eyes and realised that he was too moved to speak.

'It's alright then?' she said.

'Alright? It's wonderful. But you – what do you –?

'I think it's wonderful, too. But it's early days. And I'm forty-five –'

'That's not too old.' A shadow passed over his face and

276

she knew what he was thinking.

'No-one will ever replace Sam, I know that,' she said. 'Children ... they're such hostages to fortune, aren't they?'

'I feel that, too. But if we let ourselves think like that'

He nodded and squeezed her hands. 'Then Lars and Sandra and all the other bastards like them have won. We can't let that happen.'

Another child – and Jay, yes, she could hardly believe her luck. She and Piki had walked right to the far side of the bay and the tide was coming in now. Her cheeks were stinging with the cold and she was glowing from the exercise. She glanced at her watch. It would be getting dark soon. Time to get back.

As she drove back over Countisbury Common, she smiled to herself. Fancy Barry guessing ... well, he had been there the first time round.

She turned into the track down to Falling Water.

As she entered the trees she glimpsed something white ahead of her and slowed down. There was a rabbit on the path again, in just the same place that there had been one before. Maybe it was even the same one. She came to a stop and sounded her horn. It didn't move. Oh, hell. She switched off the engine, gave Piki a stern command to stay on the back seat, and got out of the car. The wind stirred the top of the trees, but down here it was still and very dark. The aroma of pine needles hung in the air. She walked towards the rabbit, expecting at any moment to see it dart away. But it didn't. She walked right up to it and squatted down. It wasn't until she put out a hand and felt the rough synthetic fur that she understood. It wasn't a real rabbit.

She jerked her hand back and stood up quickly. Everything beyond the two beams of the car lights lay in darkness. There was a noise somewhere close by in the undergrowth. Lisa froze.

There was a bark and the car door swung open. The next moment Piki was loping towards her. She reached Lisa's side and gave a low, menacing growl. Lisa stood still, listening – another rustling but further off – and then there was silence. She wound her fingers into Piki's collar to keep her close and together they walked back to the car. As soon as they were in, Lisa brought her hand down on the central locking. There was a reassuring clunk. She started the car and drove on.

Chapter Forty-three

By the time she got home, she'd got a grip on herself. Some child out walking with their family must have dropped their toy and even now was no doubt mourning its loss. What a fool she must have looked, standing frozen with fear in the headlights of her own car. An over-active imagination, that was her problem. And maybe some of it was hormonal. She remembered the mood swings of her last pregnancy, though had they started quite so early?

She put on plenty of lights and drew the blinds. She made some camomile tea and set herself to preparing the dinner, taking her time, allowing her nerves to settle as she sliced mushrooms and peppers for a chicken casserole.

It was at quiet times like this that she still felt Laurence close, so close that she almost expected to find him at her elbow. She found herself talking to him – and supplying the other side of the conversation. When should she tell Ricky about the baby, she asked him. Wait until the end of the first trimester, just in case ... Yes, good idea. How would he take it? Would he be jealous, embarrassed, excited? Maybe all of those, but the baby would be a good thing, a new start ... The meal was almost ready when Stella arrived from work, bringing the chill of evening in with her. 'Phew,' she said, rubbing her hands together. 'Getting a bit breezy out there. And talk about hungry. I could eat a horse. What can I do to help?'

'Salad dressing?' Lisa suggested.

Stella nodded and reached for the olive oil.

Lisa put her head on one side, taking in the grey wool trousers and the knee-length, felted wool coat. 'Great outfit, by the way. But those shoes ... how you can walk in them, let alone drive –'

'Practice.'

Lisa frowned.

'What's up?' Stella asked.

'Oh, nothing.' Those shoes reminded her of Karen, or should she say Sandra, but she didn't want to think about that.

Stella poured oil into a measuring jug. 'Got any French mustard?'

'There's a jar in the fridge.' Stella was humming to herself as she walked across the kitchen. Lisa recognised 'Strangers in the Night'.

'Who is he? Lisa asked.

'What?'

'You heard. I know there's someone. You look like the cat that got the cream.' Stella gave a sigh of mock exasperation. 'I suppose you won't give me any peace until I tell you. If you must know, I've got a date with Jonas.'

'Jonas?' Lisa paused with the knife hovering over a cucumber and stared at Stella. 'Well, if you will invite attractive men to dinner … '

A fortnight before Jonas had come down to talk things over. He had stayed the night and Lisa had invited Stella over. Lisa put the knife down and gave Stella her full attention. Could she picture them as a couple? Maybe she could. 'Tell me everything.'

'He rang me up at work last week. We're meeting in London next Saturday. He's taking me for lunch at a little French restaurant he knows.'

'Blimey! I didn't see that coming. Talk about the law of unintended consequences!' She hesitated. Should she tell Stella about the baby? Oh hell, why not? 'And here's something else I didn't see coming. I'm pregnant.'

Stella's arm jerked and she tipped too much vinegar into the dressing.

'Oh shit! I mean, oh good, oh wow!' She came over and enveloped Lisa in a perfumed embrace. 'That is just fabulous.'

Seeing the glow in her face, Lisa wondered. 'Stella, have you ever …'

'Wanted kids? No, but I love other people having them. I've got three godchildren. I'm one of nature's aunties.'

'Consider yourself booked in that capacity. Oh, hell, the rice is boiling over. We'd better eat this meal before it's completely ruined.'

'That's the last one,' Lisa said, folding a heavy tweed jacket.

Stella held open the black plastic bag. 'You're OK about this?' she asked.

'Yep. At least this way someone else gets the chance to wear it.'

'It's good stuff,' Stella agreed.

There was a sound outside. They both looked round.

'The wind's really getting up,' Lisa said. She went to look out of the window.

There was a half-moon and shreds of cloud were streaming across the sky. The treetops were thrashing.

Stella appeared at her side. 'Not looking good. If it's like that here, it'll be worse over the top.'

'You'd better be off,' Lisa said.

'Look, I'll take this stuff with me. You don't want it hanging around now that you've sorted it. I'll pop round to the charity shop in my lunch-hour.'

'If you're sure.'

'Just give me a hand to take it out to the car.'

They lugged the bags down the spiral staircase.

When Lisa opened the back door, the rush of the stream and the wind in the trees blended together into one loud constant noise. Words from *The Tempest* came into Lisa's head. 'The isle is full of noises.'

She helped Stella carry the bags out to the car. Struggling against the wind, they heaved the bags into the boot.

Stella had to raise her voice to be heard. 'Go back in! It's cold.' She gave Lisa a quick hug. 'Sure you're OK on your own? I could stay over.'

'No, no, I'll be fine.' Lisa went back to stand in the door way, hugging herself as she watched Stella drive away. She felt a little pang and wanted to run after Stella and say that she'd changed her mind. She told herself not to be so silly. She closed the door and bolted it.

She went upstairs to get ready for bed.

From her vantage point in the tree-house Sandra watched Stella's tail lights disappear up the track.

She had thought there was no problem that money couldn't solve. She had thought that she could just cut her losses and begin again. She hadn't understood how terribly she would miss Lars. Automatically her fingers sought her face and traced the ragged red scar that ran down her cheek and pulled the skin so that a rim of red showed under her eyeball. And even if she could get over Lars, how could she start over? No man would look at her twice, and that was the literal truth. After their first glimpse, people were careful to avert their eyes. Pacing the floor in the condominium in Costa Rica, she had brooded over the injustice of it all.

Now as she waited in the dark she fed on her anger. Lisa still had everything – this beautiful house, the crippled son, no prize for sure, but *she* didn't see that, and reading between the lines of the newspaper reports, Jay would soon be released and then she'd have him, too. It wasn't fair. Someone had to pay. And it had to be Lisa. That way everyone would be punished.

She fingered the scar again. Stella had been gone long enough. Now there was only the dog to deal with. She wished she'd managed to do that earlier, but she had been afraid that in the dark the brute would get to her before she could shoot it. She had hesitated just long enough for Lisa to get back in the car.

It was blowing a gale and the wind was tugging at the steering as Stella approached the summit of the hill before Lynton. She reached the County Gate car park. On impulse she turned in and pulled up. She sat there for a few moments with engine running. Something had been nagging at her for the last mile or so, ever since she'd turned off the track onto the main road. Something she had seen without taking in the significance, so preoccupied had she been by the weather.

She made up her mind. She turned the car and set off back along the road towards Falling Water. She told herself that she was probably being idiotic, but once you start to wonder about something ...

The sonic boom of two military planes filled her head. She tightened her hands on the wheel. Two black shapes appeared in the night sky and were gone. The worst thing was that you knew they'd be back and you couldn't help waiting for the other shoe to drop.

She turned down the track to Falling Water. Now where was it, the place where she had caught sight of something out of the corner of her eye? She reached the point where a path led off on both sides of the track and there it was: a patch of shiny red metal that could just be glimpsed between the trees. She pulled up, opened the glove compartment, and took out the powerful flashlight she always kept there. She got out of the car. Above her she heard the sighing and groaning of the wind, but down here it was as still and calm as if she were under water. She walked down the path, her heels sinking into the earth. The red metal was part of a car that had been backed as far as possible into the undergrowth. Only a sliver of the bonnet showed. Why had someone been so anxious to conceal it? Illicit love? A couple of adulterers having it off in the back seat? She moved closer, brushing the bracken aside and felt her tights snag. Hell and damnation! Thirteen quid's worth of Wolford's gone west.

She shone the flashlight through the car window. It was empty.

She bit her lip thoughtfully. Maybe she was worrying about nothing, but it couldn't hurt to check on Lisa.

Lisa undressed and pulled her pyjamas on. She laced her fingers across her belly. All she had to do was wait and one day there would be another person in the world. The mystery of it …

There was a sonic boom that rocked the house and rattled the windows. These night flights had become more frequent over the last months. She had a good mind to write to her MP. She was mentally composing a letter when the phone rang.

It was Ricky ringing up to say goodnight – was he checking up on her? She was amused by the thought.

'Give my love to Piki,' he said before he hung up.

Piki ... She'd need to go out for a late-night pee.

Lisa went downstairs, shivering and switching on the lights as she went. The heating had gone off and the house was full of draughts that had leaked in through cracks and crevices, full of funny little noises, too. She wished she had asked Stella to stay after all.

Piki was waiting by the back door. Lisa unlocked the back door and drew back the bolt. Piki slipped out. Lisa closed the door. She drifted round the kitchen tidying up, humming to herself as she waited for Piki to relieve herself. But when she opened the door, Piki wasn't there. She called her name but the wind snatched the words away. Cursing, she took down Lawrence's coat and put it on over her pyjamas. She opened the door and called

284

again. The wind plucked at her, ruffled her hair. She thought she heard something above the sound of the wind. Was that Piki whining? There was one of those strange silences that sometimes falls in a storm. And there it was again, the whimpering of a creature in pain, louder this time.

Lisa had taken a couple of steps outside before it struck her that something was very wrong.

By then it was too late.

Stella stopped short of the house. She grabbed her flashlight and got out of the car. The wind was roaring in the trees. She shone the torch down the path, caught a movement, and heard a dog whine. It was Piki. Stella went to her and squatted down. There was a dark patch on the dog's flank. Stella put her hand out to touch it. It was slick and warm and when she drew her hand back it was covered in blood. She directed the torch to the wound. It had clean edges as if it had been done with a knife. Blood was welling up and it looked deep. Oh, God!

She wiped her hand on the bracken and got to her feet. Her heart thumping, she ran to the corner of the house.

Light was spilling out of the sitting-room window. Inside a woman was standing with her back to Stella and beyond that she saw Lisa, hands to her breast, eyes wide with shock. A step further and Stella could see that the woman was holding a gun. It had to be Sandra.

She crept round to the kitchen door. It was open and she went in. Now she could hear Lisa and Sandra talking, but she couldn't make out the words. She took her shoes off. Holding them in one hand and staying close to the wall, she worked her way round to the sitting-room door. She heard Sandra say, 'It really isn't fair,' and the very reasonableness of the tone made her flesh crawl. She looked round the corner of the door. Sandra had her back half-turned to Stella. Stella measured the distance with her eye. There was no way she could run across that parquet floor and grab the gun before Sandra could shoot Lisa. She slipped round the edge of the doorway and step by step, breathing slowly and evenly, her eyes fixed on Sandra, she moved silently forward in a nightmare game of grandmother's footsteps.

'It really isn't right that you should have all this when I have nothing,' Sandra said. 'You must see that.' She spoke as if this were a self-evident truth. Thank God Ricky isn't here, Lisa thought, but my baby – surely, surely it can't end like this. Her thoughts flew to her father, Daddy –

There was a movement behind Sandra. Stella was standing in the kitchen doorway. Oh, thank God.

Sandra took a step towards Lisa and raised the gun. 'And look what your bastard son did to my face.'

Lisa forced herself to fix her eyes on Sandra, but at the edge of her vision she could see Stella inching closer.

She had to keep Sandra talking. 'I'm sorry,' she said.

But Sandra just shook her head. She took a step towards Lisa and raised the gun. Lisa stepped back and put her hands up to protect herself.

A huge door slammed in the sky. The planes on their return sweep.

The shock registered on Sandra's face. She froze. Lisa's eyes flew to Stella – she couldn't help it – and Sandra saw that. She turned her head.

Stella's arm went back and something flew through the air, spinning as it came, and hit Sandra right between the eyes. She staggered and fell back, her hand shot up, and the gun went off.

The crack of the shot seemed to open a fissure in time. The moment was burned into Lisa's brain. Stella, wide-eyed and open-mouthed; Sandra, sprawled on the floor. A star appeared in the top of the big window and time began again.

Slowly, slowly the cracks spread out, like ice breaking up on a pond. Lisa saw her own reflection shimmer and waver. She backed away. So did Stella. They saw what was coming, but they could only watch as piece by piece the whole vast pane of glass collapsed onto Sandra in a cascade of glittering shards.

Lisa picked up her overnight bag and went out onto the landing. Scene of the crime officers in white suits were busy in the sitting room. Sandra had lost a lot of blood, but the glass hadn't caught an artery. She would recover to stand trial.

Piki had been taken away by the vet and was undergoing emergency surgery.

The wind had died away and it was a clear night. Lisa could see a sprinkling of lights on the Welsh coast. Without glass in the window the house was open to the elements, and she imagined the creatures of the night, foxes, mice, even deer wandering in. The glaziers would be arriving soon to board up the window and of course the glass could be replaced, but her beloved home had been violated. Would she ever feel safe here again? For tonight at any rate she'd be staying with Stella.

She went down the stairs and found her friend on the sofa in the kitchen with her stocking feet curled under her and a glass of brandy in her hand.

'You're going to have to lend me a pair of shoes or wellies,' Stella said.

'Why, what's happened to yours?'

Stella began to laugh. It started as a chortle, and developed into a full-scale guffaw.

'Stella?' She pointed through the open door. Lisa turned and saw a scene of the crime officer holding up an evidence bag and grinning all over his face.

Stella clutched her side. 'Oh, God.'

Hysteria, Lisa decided. Reaction and no wonder: she

felt pretty wobbly herself. 'What's so funny?'

Stella was laughing so hard that tears were pouring down her cheeks. She could only gesture towards the evidence bag. Lisa saw now that it contained one of Stella's shoes. 'No! That was what you threw at Sandra?'

At last Stella managed to get it out.

'Killer heels!'

Epilogue

A YEAR LATER

'Lisa!' Jay was calling up the stairs. 'No hurry, love, but we're ready when you are.'

'I'll be down in a minute.' Lisa lingered by the cot and bent to rearrange a blanket that didn't need rearranging. She drank in the delicious smell of a warm, sleeping baby. Miranda was five months old and looking more like Lisa every day – or so Jay said.

Lisa had never felt so tired in her life – or so happy. True, there were times when she felt a fleeting nostalgia for the days when she and Jay met only once a month, but mostly, looking around at Falling Water she could scarcely believe her luck. The house was cluttered with child paraphernalia and toys. Jay had set up his internet business in Lawrence's office.

The funny thing was that Stella and Jonas had taken over where Lisa and Jay had left off. She and Jonas had been together for over a year and were still going strong – but only every other weekend.

Lisa went down to the kitchen where Jay, Ricky, Charlotte, Barry, and Peony were waiting.

Ricky and Barry were tight these days. Ricky was planning to go to California for his gap year. A toe in the water: he could always come home if it didn't work out, but she had a feeling that it would. She'd miss him, my God how she'd miss him, but she and Jay were hatching a plan to go out for a couple of months with Miranda, and Charlotte would go for part of the time, too.

On the kitchen table was a tray, bearing seven candles

in little paper boats. Charlotte had helped Lisa make them and attach them to wooden floats.

Lisa picked up the tray and led the way into the garden. The others followed. Piki limped along behind. She had made a good recovery, but still ... it was a constant reminder of that terrible evening. It would, thank God, be a very, very long time before Sandra came out of prison. The air was full of birdsong. For the last week or so Lisa had been aware in the mornings of a lift and lightening of the day. Spring was on its way.

'Where are we going to launch them?' Peony asked, gesturing to the candles. There were lines on her face that hadn't been there before the crash, but she had her old air of serenity.

'If we put them on the pond, the current will carry them over to the rim and down the stream,' Lisa said.

'But will they stay lit?'

'I think so. Some of them at any rate, I tried one earlier and it was OK.'

She put the tray down across Rick's lap. Jay counted the candles.

'Seven?' he asked. Lisa smiled. 'Piki needs to say good-bye to Lawrence, too.'

'Of course.'

Charlotte took out a cigarette lighter, and lit the candles. Jay lifted up the tray and set it gently on the rim of the pond. The reeds and the trees were so still that their mirror images were motionless on the water.

They had agreed the order in which they would launch the candles. Jay took his and set it carefully down on the water. He gave it a gentle push and it drifted away. It was caught by a little current and moved faster, turning as it went. It slipped over the rim and disappeared from sight for a moment. Lisa held her breath until she saw the flicker of light reappear and be borne off into the woods.

Not one of the lights went out.

Lisa's was the last.

She watched the candle drift and turn in the current. As it vanished over the rim of the pond, she raised a hand in salute.

She had been afraid that she would forget Lawrence, that her memories of him would fade, but now she knew that he would always be with her.

The others had gone back into the house.

Jay stretched out his arm and pulled Lisa close. She leaned into him. The silence settled round them.

'Mum, Mum!' Ricky was at the door of the house. 'Dad's opened a bottle of wine – and I think Miranda's awake. Come on!' Lisa laughed. 'No peace for the wicked.'

Jay took her hand and they went indoors.

THE END

Other Titles by Accent Press

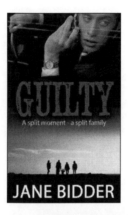

Guilty
Jane Bidder

Simon Mills, a solicitor, isn't the kind of man to go to prison. His new wife Claire, an artist, isn't the kind of woman to have a husband 'Inside'. But one night, after offering to drive their dinner guests home, Simon is involved in an horrific crash down a narrow Devonshire lane and is sent to prison for two years.

GUILTY is written in two parts: the first deals with Simon's life in prison and the second, with his life once he's released. It is told in alternate viewpoints: Claire's and Simon's as well as the ghostly voice of Joanna, who died in the crash. This is a haunting modern-day story that could happen to you.

The Other Half
Dana Edwards

This is a tale of modern family life with all its joshings and jealousies, told with humour and compassion. Catrin is just a normal Cardiff teenager looking forward to going to university when a shocking revelation rocks her world. Before she dies, Granny Lewis reveals that Catrin 'is not blood'. This sets off a chain reaction, causing friction within the family, and forcing them all to re-assess their relationships.

While the story revolves around the Lewis family's home in Victoria Park, a comfortable area of Cardiff, the narrative also moves to Welsh-speaking West Wales and to the Rhondda Valley. Through these trips we glimpse three very different Welsh lifestyles.

The novel, while concentrating on Catrin's quest to find out who she actually is, cannot but touch on very contemporary moral dilemmas – whether it is ever right to conceal truth, nature versus nurture, and boundaries within relationships.

Public Battles, Private Wars
Laura Wilkinson

What lines would you cross for the ones you love?

Yorkshire 1983. Miner's wife Mandy is stuck in a rut. At twenty-three, and trapped by domesticity, her future looks set and she wants more from life. Husband Rob is a good-looking drinker, content to spend his days in the small town where they've always lived – where Mandy can't do anything other than bake cakes and raise her children. When Mandy's childhood friend – beautiful, clever Ruth – and Ruth's Falklands war hero husband, Dan, return to town, their homecoming is shrouded in mystery. Like in their schooldays, Mandy looks to Ruth for inspiration – but Ruth isn't all she appears.

As conflict with the Coal Board turns into war, the men come out on strike. Mandy abandons her dreams of liberation from the kitchen sink and joins a support group. As the strike rumbles on, relationships are pushed to the brink, and Mandy finds out just who she is – and who her true friends are.

For more information about **Christine Poulson** and other **Accent Press** titles

please visit

www.christinepoulson.co.uk

www.accentpress.co.uk

Printed in Great Britain
by Amazon.co.uk, Ltd.,
Marston Gate.